"I don't care what you do to me, do you hear me?"

Connor stood speechless, shocked into silence by his niece's onslaught of emotion. Jaye resembled a cornered, injured animal ready to strike out at anyone who tried to help her.

Abby crouched down beside the nine-year-old, her eyes steady on the girl's face.

"So scared, Abby," Jaye said between hiccuping sobs. "Couldn't figure out how to buy a bus ticket. Walked here to the library. Nobody talked to me. So alone."

"It's okay, honey." Abby smoothed the hair back from his niece's despondent face and made soothing noises. "Connor and I are here now. Everything's going to be all right."

Something thickened in Connor's throat as he watched them—the innocent girl who'd been abandoned by her mother and the woman who refused to desert her guilty-as-sin brother.

But at that moment Abby Reed didn't seem like the half sister of the man who'd murdered his brother.

She seemed like somebody who was on their side.

Dear Reader,

A Time To Forgive represents a departure for me. While many of my previous books were lighthearted, this one involves a ten-year-old murder and its lasting repercussions. It's as much about hate as it is about the amazing power of love.

It's also a book I've wanted to write for years, fueled by the tales of forgiveness I'd sometimes read about in the newspaper. Who hasn't marveled at the people who ask judges and juries to be merciful toward the murderer of one of their loved ones? How, I wondered, could anyone forgive such a terrible crime?

In my book, Connor Smith faces a question that's equally difficult. Can his love for the sister of the man who killed his brother survive the hate eating away at him?

I'm grateful to have been given the chance to write about the flip side of love—and the enduring truth that love is the strongest force of all.

All my best,

Darlene Gardner

P.S. Please visit me on the Web at www.darlenegardner.com.

A TIME TO FORGIVE
Darlene Gardner

HARLEQUIN®

TORONTO • NEW YORK • LONDON
AMSTERDAM • PARIS • SYDNEY • HAMBURG
STOCKHOLM • ATHENS • TOKYO • MILAN • MADRID
PRAGUE • WARSAW • BUDAPEST • AUCKLAND

ISBN-13: 978-0-373-71360-8
ISBN-10:   0-373-71360-6

A TIME TO FORGIVE

This edition published by arrangement with Harlequin Books S.A.

® and TM are trademarks of the publisher. Trademarks indicated with
® are registered in the United States Patent and Trademark Office, the
Canadian Trade Marks Office and in other countries.

www.eHarlequin.com

Printed in U.S.A.

For those who can find it within themselves to forgive.
But even more, for those who can't.

PROLOGUE

THE KILLER WALKED into the courtroom not with the shoulder-rolling swagger Connor Smith had expected, but with his head down, his eyes cast to the floor.

He was maybe five foot nine, not nearly as tall as Connor imagined he would be, and he was handcuffed and dressed in a prison-issue jumpsuit that was a garish orange. An armed guard stood on either side of him.

Connor gripped the armrest of his wooden chair to keep himself from surrendering to the impulse to leap from his seat and attack, reminding himself that the wheels of justice were about to turn.

He'd left the fragrant beauty of a sunny spring afternoon for a preliminary hearing in the austere interior of Laurel County District Court. Very shortly, the Honorable Preston A. Hodgkins would determine whether probable cause existed to believe the defendant had committed murder.

Judge Hodgkins wasn't expected to do anything more than hand over the case to trial, yet the courtroom gallery was nearly full with members of the news media and spectators who had been shocked by the crime.

Connor didn't pay attention to any of them.

He sat between his parents. He was peripherally

aware of his mother clutching his surgically repaired right knee, which would probably give him trouble when he stood, and his father sitting stoically. But Connor's eyes never left the killer as he shuffled to the defense table. Once there, he lowered himself into a seat beside the tired-looking public defender who'd been assigned to his case.

Connor waited, barely breathing, for the killer to lift his head. The newspapers had run his photograph a half-dozen times in the last ten days, but they used a police mug shot slightly blurred around the edges.

Connor wanted to see what evil looked like in the flesh.

The killer shifted in his seat, stared down at the table in front of him and stroked his forehead as though his head hurt. Finally, at long last, he raised his head, then briefly glanced at the gallery behind him.

His eyes were a startling blue, a fact Connor hadn't been able to determine from the black-and-white newspaper photo. His face was pale and unlined, his mouth wide and almost gentle looking, his nose long and straight. His cheeks were apple-red and his dark hair freshly cut.

The killer's name was Drew Galloway. Three weeks ago, he had turned eighteen, the age at which he could legally be charged as an adult.

Eighteen days ago, Galloway had plunged a knife deep into the chest of Connor's seventeen-year-old younger brother and left him to die. A pair of teenagers had found J.D.'s body under the bleachers adjacent to the high-school football field where he regularly covered himself in glory.

The story was that the two boys had scuffled over a

girl the day before and that Galloway had lured J.D. to the field to rid himself of the competition.

The night, Connor was told, had been black. He didn't doubt that Galloway's soul was the same shade.

Dressed in his prison jumpsuit with his cherub's cheeks and sky-blue eyes, Drew Galloway didn't look evil. A middle-aged woman with shadowy circles under her eyes and a teenage girl with long, dark hair and a tear-streaked face sat behind the defense table. Probably Galloway's mother and sister, they furthered the illusion of normalcy.

Connor wasn't fooled.

Galloway had not only robbed his brother of life, he'd stolen the heart from Connor's family. Connor's mother spent her days alternating between grief and rage, and his father walked around in a fog, barely able to function.

Neither parent had the energy to do anything about Connor's sixteen-year-old sister Diana, who stayed out until all hours of the night, not caring that she was flunking out of school. Connor didn't even know where she was right now.

No. His family would never recover from the loss of J.D. He'd been the family favorite, so full of life and athletic talent that he'd been headed to Penn State on a football scholarship. But today, when the judge upheld the charge of first-degree murder, the path toward justice would begin.

A bailiff commanded all rise and announced that court was in session. Judge Hodgkins swept in, his black robes flowing, and took a seat behind the bench. He asked counsel to state their appearances in the case of the state of Maryland versus Drew Galloway.

Connor sat patiently through the introductions. The only lawyer who mattered, in his opinion, was State's Attorney Douglas Benton. A tall man with a head of prematurely gray hair, Benton was a descendant of the town's founding father. Murders weren't common in sleepy Laurel County, nestled in the state's southwest corner less than an hour's drive from the nation's capital, but the state's attorney had a reputation for being as tough as a piece of white Maryland marble.

Judge Hodgkins shuffled some papers, then peered over his reading glasses. "I understand that the parties involved have reached a satisfactory plea agreement. I've reviewed the signed document. I gather you're ready to proceed with a plea hearing and disposition. Is that correct?"

Douglas Benton stood. "That is correct."

The bottom dropped out of Connor's stomach as a murmur of excitement rushed through the crowd. A plea agreement? He turned to his mother and whispered, "How could this happen? Did you know about this?"

She stared at him, her face white, her eyes teary. Before she could answer, Judge Hodgkins pounded the desk with his gavel. "Order. Order."

The murmuring died down and Connor watched with growing horror as Judge Hodgkins proceeded through a series of questions meant to make sure Galloway understood what he had signed. Finally, the judge reached the heart of the plea.

"This agreement specifies that you, Mr. Galloway, are pleading guilty to second-degree murder. It further states that the length of your sentence of incarceration should be twenty years, the first ten without the possibility of parole."

The blood rushing through Connor's body turned icy as the gallery erupted with shouts and angry murmurings. Twenty years, the judge had said. A chance at parole after ten. Galloway could be out on the streets as early as age twenty-eight. He would not rot in prison. But J.D. was already rotting in his grave.

The judge banged the gavel once more. "Order. Or I'll have the bailiff clear the courtroom."

Connor stared at his brother's killer. Something that had been coiled in Connor's gut unfurled, like the body of a snake venturing from the sunlight to the shadows. It reached out to every part of him, thick and sour and filling.

The emotion was so alien that Connor couldn't identify it until it wrapped around his heart and dipped into his very soul.

Then he knew, with sudden and vicious clarity, what had cloaked his world in darkness and blackened his heart.

It was hate.

CHAPTER ONE

Nearly ten years later

CONNOR SMITH HAD SPENT the last decade attempting to outrun the past, but it caught up with him. Again.

The pattern was as familiar as the long, straight rows of gravestones in a cemetery. Just when he thought he'd relegated J.D.'s murder to a terrible memory and started to live in the present, something happened to pull him back into the abyss.

The latest something was his niece, Jaye, an unusually pretty little girl with pale blond hair swept back from the widow's peak on her high forehead and gray-green eyes that were reminiscent of his dead brother's. She'd got her first name from J.D., too.

The girl sat on a stool at the counter-height island in the kitchen nook of his Silver Spring town house picking at the piece of toast and jam he'd fixed her. Her skinny, nine-year-old legs dangled well above the porcelain-tile floor.

He stood between the island and the state-of-the-art black microwave that was built into his golden-maple cabinets, cradling his second cup of black coffee of the morning and waiting for a bagel to defrost.

On an ordinary Saturday morning, he'd already be at the office figuring out how to make one of his clients money. But there was nothing routine about a morning in which his sister chose to abandon her daughter.

"Where's Mom?" Jaye asked.

There it was, the question Connor had been dreading. The microwave beeped, signaling that the bagel had thawed.

He ignored the summons and kneaded the throbbing space between his brows. He'd found his sister Diana's note more than an hour ago but still hadn't figured out how to break the news to Jaye that her mother had taken off for God only knew where.

"She's gone, isn't she?" Jaye asked abruptly in a hard voice that didn't sound as if it belonged to a child.

"Yeah, she's gone," Connor said softly, futilely wishing he could soften the blow. "I think she needed to be by herself for a while."

He expected Jaye to dissolve into tears, the way he imagined any young girl would react upon hearing that her mother had cast her off and left her with an uncle who was essentially a stranger.

Jaye's chin quivered slightly, but her eyes were dry, her petal of a mouth pinched. "What's going to happen to me?"

That was the question that had been swirling around and around in his brain since he'd read Diana's note. She'd claimed she'd be in touch but made no promises about when she'd be back for Jaye. He doubted it would be any time soon.

Diana had nearly jumped out of her skin every time he'd asked her a question last night. He'd recognized that something was wrong, but had unwisely decided to wait until this morning to confront her about it.

He swallowed his anger at his sister and focused on the sad girl with the hard eyes. "Your mother left a note asking me to take care of you."

How, he wondered, had Diana managed to look after Jaye for this long? She'd given birth less than a year after J.D.'s murder, when she was barely seventeen. She'd had sex with so many boys, she said, that she couldn't figure out who the father was. Their parents, still drowning in grief over J.D.'s death, hadn't been able to deal with a new blow.

After arguing bitterly with their mother, Diana had run off. Connor had spent a night and a day looking for her before their great-aunt Aggie had called to say that Diana had turned up at her house outside Roanoke in southwest Virginia.

There Diana had stayed for the next four years until Aunt Aggie's death, when she'd cashed in her meager inheritance and simply taken off with Jaye. She'd called now and then to let the family know she was alive but hadn't resurfaced until last night at ten o'clock when she rang the doorbell at his town house.

And now she was gone—again—but this time she'd left her daughter behind.

"My mom said I have a grandma," Jaye continued, still in that tough, cold voice. "Maybe I should stay with her."

"No," Connor said. His mother could barely take care of herself, let alone a granddaughter. His father, remarried and living in Richmond, was only a slightly better choice. All his energy went to his second wife and their young son.

"Then where am I going to stay?" Jaye asked.

He looked around at the interior of his pricey three-story town house, which a maid cleaned twice a week until it sparkled. It was no place for a child, and he was a poor choice for a guardian.

He worked upwards of sixty hours a week at a high-powered brokerage firm in Washington, D.C., where he was so well regarded he'd recently been fielding offers from Wall Street. The rest of his waking hours, he spent at the gym or on the bar and restaurant scene with his girlfriend, Isabel Pennington, who'd been making noises about moving in with him.

He didn't know anything about raising a child, especially one he wouldn't have recognized as his niece until a few hours ago.

Though, for the moment, there was no other option. He was it.

He swallowed the lump of trepidation in his throat and strived to make himself sound self-assured. "I already told you that I'm going to take care of you. So you'll stay here. With me."

Jaye's mouth flattened in a mutinous line, then she hopped down from the stool and shoved it so hard that it overturned. Without another look at him, she ran out of the kitchen and up the stairs to the guest room where she'd slept the night before.

Connor dragged a hand through the hair on his throbbing head. He made snap decisions involving tens of thousands of dollars every day, but he was lost in how to deal with a nine-year-old child. Should he follow her? Explain that he wanted her with him but had grave doubts about his ability to care for her?

"Diana, how could you do this?" he asked aloud.

The hell of it was that Connor didn't blame Diana for abandoning her daughter. He blamed Drew Galloway.

Galloway hadn't been in direct contact with anyone in the Smith family other than J.D., but the knife he'd thrust into J.D.'s chest had ripped the family apart. It had certainly precipitated Diana's tailspin.

The hate that always simmered beneath the surface of Connor's skin boiled up, nearly singeing him. Even though Galloway had been in prison for almost ten years, the killer was still leaving a trail of victims in his wake. The latest was the discarded little girl who pretended she didn't want to cry.

Connor tamped down the surging hatred. He needed to focus on Jaye, not on Galloway. It was mid-February, more than halfway through the school year. He'd have to figure out which was the nearest elementary school and find out how to get Jaye enrolled. More immediately, he needed to visit the grocery store so the refrigerator contained something healthier than leftover pizza and beer.

Deciding to give Jaye time to get used to being stuck with him, he walked to the table and righted the chair she'd overturned.

He'd have a much tougher time righting the wrong that had been done to Jaye.

He had a fleeting thought of the teenage girl and the sobbing woman who had sat behind Drew Galloway that dark day in the Laurel County Courthouse.

Had Galloway's family suffered even a fraction of the pain and the ramifications as Connor's family?

Somehow, Connor didn't think so.

ABBY REED WAS GOOD at spotting troubled children.

She should be. She'd lived with one for fifteen years until he'd been sent away for murder to the max-imum-security Maryland Correctional Adjustment Center.

She'd had nearly ten years to come to terms with what her only sibling had done, but still couldn't accept that he was a cold-blooded killer. In her gut she knew there was more to what had happened that night than had come to light.

Her heart bled for the boy who'd died and the people who'd loved him, but the Drew who used to read her bedtime stories while their single mother worked two jobs hadn't been evil. He'd been a kid in trouble.

After the murder, hardly anybody in the small Maryland town of Bentonsville had agreed with that assessment.

Her mother had moved their family of three from in-ner-city Baltimore to Bentonsville two years before the boy's death in a failed attempt to get Drew away from the potential to do wrong. After Drew was convicted, sentiment against him had run so high and so hot that Abby and her mother had had to move again.

They'd gone to Wheaton, a suburb of Washington, D.C., that was only fifty miles from Bentonsville but lacking in the acres of unspoiled countryside that had made the little town such a beautiful place to live. The trade-off, though, had been worth it.

Nobody directed hateful looks at them or pointed and whispered behind their backs.

Nobody recognized Abby as the frightened fifteen-year-old half sister of the boy who'd been labeled a murderer.

Nobody maintained that the sister of a convicted killer shouldn't be hired to teach in the Montgomery County public-school system.

Abby had secured the job after graduating from Towson University with a major in music and minor in education. She spent the bulk of her time running the orchestra program at Blue Moon Middle School, but once a week taught a beginning class for fourth- and fifth-graders at the neighboring elementary school.

Montgomery County, with the nation's capital on its southernmost border, was among the nation's richest. The students Abby taught were largely the carefree children of privilege.

The fourth-grader in her strings class at Blue Moon Elementary was not happy-go-lucky. She wasn't in the deep, dark trouble that Abby's brother Drew had found himself immersed in, but trouble nonetheless.

Abby heard a new story about the girl every week. She'd splattered paint on the wall in art class, refused to participate in PE and wrote pithy sayings on classroom blackboards like School Stinks, Down With Learning and Reading Is Wrong. Considering she'd arrived at Blue Moon just four weeks before, it was quite a résumé.

Two weeks ago, she'd noticed the girl standing at the door to Abby's classroom wearing a wistful expression. Abby had impulsively offered to work it out so she could take the class, even though in reality it was much too late to enroll.

After finding all the music stands overturned on

the girl's first day, Abby feared she was in for a long couple of months.

But then the girl had taken her violin from the case and followed Abby's simple directions about how to coax sound from it. The violin had sung, the girl had been enchanted and Abby's problems with the difficult child had been over.

Until today when she'd turned in a forged permission slip to hear an ensemble of National Symphony Orchestra musicians perform at the Kennedy Center.

She stood in front of Abby in the empty classroom, looking adorable in her pink Abercrombie & Fitch T-shirt and designer jeans. Abby handed her the permission slip.

"I know your father didn't sign this so don't bother telling me he did," Abby stated.

The child looked down at her feet, which were encased in brand-name tennis shoes. Her eyes were filled with unshed tears when she gazed back up at Abby. "Am I in trouble?"

Sympathy rose in Abby like the Potomac River after a rainy season. The girl had recently confided that she'd come to live with her father after her mother had died. It wasn't any wonder she wreaked so much havoc at school.

"You're only in trouble if you don't tell me why you forged the signature."

"Because I really want to go on the field trip," she said in a plaintive voice, sniffling not so delicately.

"Did your father say why he wouldn't sign it?"

She nodded. "He says I don't deserve to go because I'm bad."

Abby bit down hard so she wouldn't call the girl's

father-come-lately a cuss word. The nerve of the man. She supposed she should give him some credit for taking in his daughter after her mother's death, but he shouldn't have shirked his responsibilities in the first place.

"You're not bad. You've done some things that are wrong. But you're a good girl with a good heart. Don't let anyone tell you differently."

The girl blinked back tears, not inspiring much hope that Abby's message had gotten through. "He doesn't understand how much I want to hear the symphony, Miss Reed."

Abby understood. Of all the students she'd taught in the four years since she'd worked in Montgomery County schools, this one loved music the most.

The child reminded Abby of her own young self. During the darkest times of her childhood, Abby had turned to the violin and let the music lift her soul. The music could fill a similar void in this child if only her hardheaded jerk of a father would let it.

Abby vowed in that instant to do whatever possible to gain permission for the girl to attend the field trip, even if she disliked what it would entail. "Would you like me to talk to your father, Jaye?"

Jaye Smith smiled, the misery on her face turning to hope. "Oh, yes, Miss Reed. I'd like that very much."

CONNOR SMITH WAS NOT HAVING a good day.

It had started off on a sour note when Jaye had "accidentally" dumped his potted amaryllis onto the cream-colored carpet in his living room, throwing their uneasy morning routine so out of whack that she'd missed the bus.

He'd gotten snarled in traffic on the way to Blue Moon Elementary, causing him to deposit the silent-as-a-stone Jaye to school after the bell had rung. Then somebody had rear-ended his Porsche on the way to the office. And now one of his clients was talking nonsense.

"I think we should dump it, Connor." The panicked, masculine voice belonged to a bank president who had trusted Connor with his investments for the past three years. "I checked the paper this morning and the price of a share is down eight cents."

Connor leaned his head on the backrest of his office chair and stared at the white ceiling. He usually had more patience with Daniel Mann, who called every time the market fluctuated. This time he was panicking about an emerging pharmaceutical company in which he'd invested.

"Remember how I told you that checking the markets is my job, Daniel? The fluctuations can drive you crazy if you let them. But trust me on this. If the FDA approves the drug the company's developed, the stock will go way up. Sit tight and wait to see what happens."

By the time Connor ended the connection ten minutes later, Daniel Mann had heeded his advice. But then most of his clients did, as well they should. Connor had made impressive amounts of money for himself and his clients since he'd passed the stockbroker exams and joined the Capital Company six years ago.

Connor glanced up at the flat-screen television in his office that was tuned to the financial news network, satisfied himself on the status quo and reached for another client portfolio. If he was going to get off work by six so he could spend time with Jaye, he needed to cram as much into the day as possible.

Before he could open the folder and dial the number listed inside, his secretary's smooth, professional voice came over the intercom.

"Ms. Abby Reed is here to see you, Mr. Smith."

The name was naggingly familiar, but Connor couldn't place it. He glanced down at the list of appointments scheduled for that day, but didn't find an Abby Reed. Had his usually efficient secretary added an appointment she hadn't told him about?

He pressed down on the intercom button. "Does she have an appointment, Mary Beth?"

"She says she's here about Jaye."

Connor grimaced, although he wasn't surprised. In the five rocky weeks Jaye had lived with him, every day brought a new problem. He depressed the intercom button. "What was her name again?"

"My name's Abby Reed." The voice that traveled over the intercom and filled his office had a low, sultry quality even though it was heavily laced with annoyance. "I'm Jaye's strings teacher. And I'm not leaving until you see me."

Of course. Abby Reed was the Ms. Reed who had been leaving messages at his office and home, trying to get him to reconsider his refusal to allow Jaye to attend a field trip. He'd neither the time nor inclination to call her back because he had no intention of changing his mind.

But what was she doing here? The Silver Spring office of the Capital Company was only a mile from

Blue Moon Elementary, but he'd never known a teacher to make office calls.

Jaye's reign of terror on the fourth grade must have taken a turn for the worse.

"I can vouch that she's serious when she says she's not leaving until you see her," his secretary added.

Connor pinched the bridge of his nose. He really did not have time for this, but he couldn't send the child's teacher packing.

"Send her in," he said and took off his headset.

The door flew open, and a slender, dark-haired woman marched to his desk with a determined stride. Her hair was cut so short it fell shy of her collar, giving her face a gamine quality and making her resemble the young Audrey Hepburn in the old movies he liked to watch. Her lips were unpainted, her makeup minimal and brown eyes angry.

He wasn't a stupid man. Recognizing the signs of an imminent verbal eruption, he took the offensive. "I don't intend to make excuses for Jaye, Ms. Reed. So just tell me what she's done now."

She recoiled. "Excuse me?"

He rubbed the back of his neck. "What's Jaye done? Gone on musical strike? Bashed in an instrument? Bloodied a classmate's nose?"

"What makes you think she's done any of those things?"

"She's no angel," Connor said, wondering at the narrowing of her eyes. "And you wouldn't be here if she hadn't done something wrong."

She placed her palms flat on his desk and leaned forward. She couldn't have been much older than twenty-four or twenty-five, but projected an air of authority a senior statesman would envy. "The reason I'm here, Mr. Smith, is that you haven't returned my calls."

He quickly rationalized away his flash of guilt. She'd clearly stated the unsigned permission slip as her reason for calling.

"If you had phoned me about a problem with Jaye instead of about a field trip, I would have called back," he said.

Her lips thinned and her low voice grew even lower. "The problem I'm having isn't with Jaye. It's with you."

"Excuse me?"

She removed a sheet of paper from her handbag, unfolded it and slapped it down on his desk. He picked it up, recognizing it as the permission form he'd refused to sign. Somebody had forged his signature with a childish scrawl.

"Son of a bitch," he said, then raised his eyes to where Abby Reed leaned over his desk. "So how much trouble is Jaye in?"

"You haven't been listening, Mr. Smith," she all but hissed. "You're the one I'm having trouble with."

"I didn't forge a signature."

"Jaye wouldn't have felt the need to forge one either if you'd signed the form in the first place."

"So you're not here about the forgery?"

"I'm here to make you understand how badly Jaye wants to go on the field trip. She's the only student in the class who doesn't have permission."

Connor blinked. Was Abby Reed for real? Had she actually stormed his office because he had the sense to realize his niece didn't deserve to go on a field trip?

"You must know how disruptive Jaye has been since she started school this year," he said slowly. "Who knows how she'd act on a field trip. She's not what you'd call well-behaved."

She straightened from the desk and placed her hands on her hips. She was dressed the way a teacher should dress, in a modest-length dark skirt and nondescript blouse, but he still noticed her gentle curves. Her voice wasn't gentle. "Then you chaperone the trip and make sure she acts the way she's supposed to."

Connor blew out a breath. "Why would I reward her with a field trip? She's flunking almost all her classes."

"It's hard to move to a new school in the middle of the year. And she's not flunking strings." Abby Reed seemed to stand up even straighter. Still, she wasn't very tall. Five foot four tops, he guessed. "She's one of the best students in the class."

Connor wasn't nearly as surprised as he'd been when Jaye had asked if he'd rent her a violin so she could take the strings class. He knew his niece practiced because he'd heard muffled musical sounds from behind the closed door in her bedroom. So far, she refused to play for him.

"I'm pleased to hear she's doing well, but I still won't sign the permission slip."

She released a short, harsh breath. She seemed to be making an effort to hold on to her temper. She failed. "You are a piece of work."

"Excuse me?"

"We're talking about a child who's confused."

"I know that she's—"

"This is a child who needs to feel passionate about something. The field trip is to hear an ensemble of

National Symphony Orchestra musicians. Do you know how inspiring that could be?" She didn't give him a chance to answer. "Jaye's only started to learn and she already loves playing the violin. You'd recognize how much music could come to mean to her if you paid her any attention at all."

He felt his blood pressure rise and his head pound, the dangerous signs of his own temper about to erupt. "You don't know what you're talking about."

"I know that Jaye goes to after-school care, which she hates, and that you don't pick her up until it closes at six o'clock. And that half the time your girlfriend picks her up for you. A girlfriend who told her, incidentally, not to get too comfortable because she wouldn't be staying with you for long."

He breathed sharply through his nose. "I can't believe Isabel said that."

"How do you know what anybody says to Jaye when you're never around her?"

"I'm a busy man, Ms. Reed," he said, holding on, just barely, to his temper.

"Too busy to go on a field trip, obviously."

"I have a demanding job," Connor said in his defense.

"Your most important job is to take care of Jaye," she said and his head spun. His job wasn't the reason he'd refused to sign the slip.

"I am taking care of her."

"Not well enough. You should understand that she needs extra attention after losing her mother."

Connor might have asked how much she knew about Jaye's situation if her insult hadn't registered. "I'm doing the best I can," he said tightly.

"Then help to nurture her interest in music. Jaye's heading toward trouble. She needs something to care about. That something could be music."

"I don't disagree," he said.

"Then sign the permission slip and chaperone the trip," she challenged.

The concert was three days from now. That was a Friday, which was no less busy than any other weekday. He'd have to reschedule a business lunch and no fewer than three appointments.

"What's the matter, Mr. Smith?" she asked. "Are you too busy for Jaye?"

The dare was in her stance as well as her eyes. Somehow he'd failed to convey that he was a well-meaning uncle doing the best he could for a child he loved but hardly knew. He didn't know why Abby Reed's opinion mattered so much, but he hated that she thought so badly of him.

He picked up a pen, scribbled his name and handed her the permission slip. "Satisfied?"

She took it without the smile of triumph he'd expected.

"If I let myself become satisfied so easily, Mr. Smith, I hardly would have come to your office. The bus leaves Friday at nine-thirty sharp. Chaperones should arrive at nine-fifteen."

Without another word, she swept out of the room. The quiet was absolute when she was gone, as though she'd taken all the life and energy of the day with her.

He sat stock still behind his desk, thinking about his jam-packed workweek.

Why, then, had he signed up to chaperone a field trip he hadn't wanted Jaye to go on in the first place?

ISABEL PENNINGTON WAS a striking woman. Tall, dark and willowy with high cheekbones, an exotic slant to her eyes and a flawless complexion, she'd modeled extensively in her teens and early twenties before opening a boutique in Georgetown.

Connor had started dating her after she'd hired him to build her stock portfolio. In the nine months since then, he'd never seen her look anything but her best.

That included tonight. Despite the pout she wore, along with her beaded, curve-hugging designer dress, she still managed to look beautiful. "What do you mean you can't go? We've been planning this for weeks."

By this, she meant a two-hundred-dollar-a-plate dinner supporting the D.C. Professional Women's Association at a venerable downtown hotel. She'd offered to swing by and pick Connor up since his place was en route to the hotel, and she now stood in the foyer of his town house.

She'd arrived at a bad time.

Thirty minutes after he'd told Jaye to pick up her dirty clothes, he'd found his niece lying on her bed listening to her CD player with the clothes still on the floor. She was testing him, he knew. The school guidance counselor had told him to choose his battles. He'd been considering whether this one was worth fighting when the doorbell rang.

"I'm sorry, Isabel." Connor brought his focus back to her lovely pouting face. "My neighbor just called a few minutes ago to say she can't babysit."

"Can't you call somebody else?" Her voice was persuasive, her smile coaxing. "I was really looking forward to tonight."

He ran a hand over his smooth-shaven chin. He'd been getting ready for the benefit when he'd gotten the call from Mrs. Piper, a widow in her sixties who lived next door. "I don't know anybody else to call. I'm lucky to have the one babysitter."

"So what am I supposed to do?" Her lower lip thrust forward a fraction more. "Go to the dinner by myself?"

"Not if you don't want to. I already paid for the dinners so we're covered there. I was going to order out for Chinese for Jaye and me. You could join us."

She ran a hand down the cloth of her expensive dress. "In this? I don't think so. I'll go to the benefit myself and take my chances that someone will want to have dinner with me."

She knew very well she wouldn't be dining alone and wanted Connor to know it, too. Wherever Isabel went, men followed. It was a fact of life he couldn't get worked up about.

"Have a good time, then," he said, without a touch of the jealousy he suspected she'd tried to arouse.

"Oh, believe me, I will. But before I go, there's something I've been meaning to ask you." She carefully and unnecessarily brushed her hair back from her face with long, slender fingers. He noticed that her nails were tipped with white in what looked like a fresh manicure. Abby Reed's nails, he remembered, had been unpainted. "How much longer will you be taking care of Jaye?"

He shrugged. "Like I've told you before, I don't know. It depends upon how long it takes Diana to get her act together."

"What if she never gets it together?"

The question was one Connor hadn't considered

but supposed he should have thought about before now. Diana wasn't a kid anymore. She was twenty-seven, past the age when he could chalk up her actions to immaturity.

"Then I'll keep on taking care of Jaye. I'll become her legal guardian or adopt her if I have to."

"Are you serious?" Her voice turned disbelieving. "You'd raise somebody else's child?"

"I'd raise my *niece*."

"But why is she your responsibility? You have parents, Connor. Why can't your mother take her? Or your father?"

He'd explained his family situation to Isabel before. He wasn't about to do it again. "The best place for Jaye right now is with me."

"I understand that, and I'm trying to be patient. But can't you see what a strain this is putting on our relationship? We talked about living together, getting to know each other better, but how can we do that with your niece around?"

"I'm getting to know you better than I want to," he said in a low voice.

"What's that supposed to mean?"

He thought of Abby Reed standing in front of his desk, censure on her face. "Did you tell Jaye she wouldn't be staying with me for much longer?"

"I thought I was doing her a favor," she said, pasting on a look of innocence. "I never dreamed her stay here didn't have an end date."

Connor shook his head, wondering why he hadn't picked up on this aspect of Isabel's character before.

Probably because he'd been so blown away by her good looks.

"Jaye can stay here as long as she needs to." Connor crossed his arms over his chest, wondering what he'd ever seen in her. "You're the one who should go."

Her lovely eyes widened. "Are you breaking up with me?"

He didn't need to think about his answer. "Yeah. That's exactly what I'm doing."

Isabel even looked beautiful when her mouth thinned. "This is unbelievable. One day you'll realize that you just threw away the best thing that ever happened to you."

He let her have the last word. It was the least of his concerns. The angry click of her high heels on the hardwood of the foyer followed by the slam of the door echoed in his ears as he trekked upstairs to deal with Jaye and the pile of dirty clothes.

Isabel was wrong.

He'd never come to believe that a woman who couldn't open her heart to an unhappy, displaced child was the best thing that had ever happened to him.

He was more likely to think of her as one of his many mistakes.

CHAPTER TWO

ABBY STOOD IN FRONT of the school bus, her arms crossed over her chest, the sole of her right shoe tapping on the pavement. All of her students and two of her three chaperones were on the bus, not so patiently waiting for her signal that they could leave.

She checked her watch, the face of which showed one minute before she'd told her third chaperone the bus was leaving. It was well past the time she'd instructed him to arrive.

Damn it. Where was that arrogant Connor Smith?

She had half a mind to hop on the bus and tell the driver to head out, but the other half warned her of the consequences.

The principal had made it crystal clear that Jaye Smith couldn't attend the symphony unless Connor Smith chaperoned. If Connor didn't show and she allowed Jaye to come along anyway, Abby would be in a world of trouble.

She had no intention of denying the child an opportunity to hear the symphony, but she'd prefer accomplishing that without jeopardizing her job.

She leafed through a folder, searching for the emergency care form on file for Jaye. Hopefully it would list a cell-phone number for Connor Smith.

Abby was pulling the form from the stack when a sleek silver sports car slid into the parking lot. She didn't need to see the driver to know who was behind the wheel.

Blue Moon Elementary School was in Silver Spring, one of the priciest communities in prosperous Montgomery County. A fair number of well-to-do families sent their children through the excellent public-school system, but almost all of them drove sensible vehicles.

A Porsche 911 Turbo was not sensible, but then in her estimation neither was its driver.

She waited impatiently while he unfolded his long length from the car and walked unhurriedly to the bus with a limp so slight she wondered if she imagined it. Probably. He was so perfectly put together, he could have been plucked straight from an ad in a magazine aimed at the young, affluent professional.

She couldn't recognize brand names but his dove-gray suit was expertly cut to flatter his tall, leanly muscular frame. His burgundy tie—silk, of course—perfectly complemented his dark gray shirt. His leather shoes were a tasteful cordovan.

The wind gently gusted through the parking lot, rustling his coffee-brown hair. It was skillfully cut, not too long, not too short. It looked just right, like the rest of him.

His handsome face—with the requisite square jaw, dark eyes spaced the perfect distance apart and sculpted cheekbones—split into a smile when he spotted her. As he got closer, it surprised her that his grin was slightly crooked and that his nose wasn't entirely straight. She wasn't about to give him points for his physical imperfections, though. Especially when they only served to make him more attractive.

"You're late," she said.

His smile disappeared, and a crease appeared between his brows. He looked down at his watch, which was probably a Rolex.

"It's exactly nine-thirty," he said as he reached her. She expected him to reek of expensive cologne but she smelled soap and warm male skin. "That's right on time."

"I told you the bus was leaving at nine-thirty," she said. "Chaperones were supposed to arrive fifteen minutes ago."

He shrugged. "As long as I'm not holding anybody up, I don't see the problem."

"Are we ready now, Miss Reed?" the bus driver called, his white teeth flashing against his dark skin. His name was Mr. Greeley, and he was a retiree who'd been married for thirty-five years. During the wait, he'd confided that his wife had urged him to apply to drive a bus three months into his retirement because she was tired of him following her around the house.

Abby swallowed the urge to argue with Connor Smith. Although she had a fiery temper, she could usually keep it under control, but this man had gotten under her skin and burrowed.

"We're ready, Mr. Greeley," she said.

Connor indicated the school-bus stairs with a sweep of his hand. "After you."

She trudged up the stairs before he could do some other faux-gallant thing, like offer her a boost. The murmuring on the bus died down and the children, all of them fourth- and fifth-graders, gazed at her expectantly. She smiled at the sight of their eager young faces, her mood instantly brightening.

"Are you ready for some symphony?" she shouted, and at least half of them cheered. "Then let's go."

The bus driver chuckled as she settled into the seat behind him. "That was priceless, Miss Reed. You make going to the symphony sound as much fun as a football game."

"That's because it is," she told him, then became aware of Connor hovering over her.

"Mind if I sit down? Jaye's back there, but she didn't save a place for me, and I don't see any other spots."

Before she could answer, he slid into the seat beside her. She scooted over, the side of her body slamming uncomfortably against the wall of the bus.

"I don't know about the symphony beating out a good football game," Mr. Greeley said conversationally, "especially if you drink a couple of beers while you're watching."

The bus pulled out of the parking lot onto the highway, and the children resumed their happy chatter. Abby preferred to believe they were in high spirits because they looked forward to the symphony, but realistically knew they'd celebrate any reason to get out of school.

The soft strains of Bach's Fifth Sonata filled the bus. She'd asked Mr. Greeley to tune the radio to a classical music station before they left, but Bach didn't have his usual calming effect on Abby. Not with Connor Smith sitting so close that their shoulders almost touched.

"I'm a football-and-beer guy myself," he announced in a voice loud enough for both her and Mr. Greeley to hear.

She gazed at him, thinking she'd never seen a man who looked less like a beer drinker in her life. "Oh, yeah. Which brand?"

"I usually drink whatever's on tap," he said.

"Really? And here I would have guessed you drank a specialty brand from some microbrewery."

"I'd guess that you drink milk."

She frowned at him, and he smiled as though he'd gifted her with a compliment. She had a sneaking suspicion, though, that it had been backhanded.

She straightened her spine, annoyed at herself for letting Connor Smith get to her. Normally she'd be eagerly anticipating the performance. She'd attended the symphony countless times, but every time was a treat.

Music had been a major part of her life since her childhood when she'd found her grandmother's violin and fallen in love hard and fast. Her cash-strapped mother, who was too sentimental to hock the instrument, couldn't afford to get her private lessons.

So Abby had taught herself to play, filling the hours with music while her mother had worked two jobs and Drew had been off getting into mischief.

Abby's love of music had turned out to be a godsend, getting her through her darkest days. There'd been a lot of them, none darker than when Drew had been accused of murder and subsequently convicted.

Abby supposed she should take the milk-drinker comment as a compliment, after all. Connor might not have issued it if he knew about her family.

"I like milk," she said, hating the defensiveness that crept into her voice.

"And chaperones who arrive early."

"Arriving fifteen minutes before the bus is scheduled to leave is not early. It's on time."

"You ever heard the one about time being money? Those fifteen minutes, which I spent getting a floor broker on the New York Stock Exchange to dump some shares, made my client a lot of it."

"And yourself a healthy commission, I'm sure."

He shrugged. "Nothing wrong with that. It's how I make my living."

"Hey, you a stockbroker?" Mr. Greeley asked without taking his attention from the road.

"Sure am."

"You any good?"

"Yes, I am," he said.

She was prepared to erect another black mark against him for boasting but he didn't sound like he was bragging. He sounded confident. Since she tried to instill that quality in her students every day, she couldn't fault him for that.

"Maybe I can hire you to give me some financial advice," Mr. Greeley said.

Abby waited for Connor to dissuade the bus driver of that notion. She'd seen his pricey office and doubted he catered to the common man.

"Be happy to," he said instead. "Remind me to give you my business card later."

He leaned back against the bus seat, looking completely relaxed. Abby felt herself vibrating with suppressed energy.

He tilted his head and gave her a lazy look. His eyes were hazel with little flecks of gold in the irises. He was clean shaven but she could tell he wouldn't be for long, another hint of imperfection.

"I'm hoping you're right about letting Jaye go on this field trip," he said in a soft voice. "Because I'm still not sure it's a good idea."

"It is a good idea," Abby said with the same confidence she'd displayed earlier.

She swiveled her head and located Jaye in the back of the bus. Because of her blond hair, the child was easy to spot. She sat perfectly still, giving the impression that she was all alone even though she was surrounded by classmates. They laughed and sang and talked, but Jaye didn't seem to be part of any group.

Abby turned back around. "She'll be just fine. You'll see."

She'd barely finished her sentence when a shrill, childish voice rang out. "Row, row, row your bus, gently down the stream. Throw your driver overboard and listen to him scream."

Abby whipped her head around to locate the culprit but already knew who she'd find. Jaye Smith's mouth formed a perfect O as she sang at the top of her pretty little head.

CONNOR NEVER TOOK PLEASURE in saying "I told you so," so he kept quiet.

It was hardly Abby Reed's fault that he'd caved in to her pressure to sign that permission slip, not when Connor had suspected his niece would create some sort of scene.

He could have stood his ground. He damn well should have. But he hadn't, so now the bus was pulling up in front of the Kennedy Center at barely ten minutes before the performance was to begin.

It had taken a good fifteen minutes to deal with Jaye's outburst. When Jaye wouldn't stop singing, Mr. Greeley had pulled the bus over to the side of the road. She'd quieted quickly then, but had resisted Abby Reed's order to trade seats with a student at the front of the bus. Jaye had only complied when Connor had insisted, but then it was Connor who'd ended up in the other student's seat with Jaye sitting next to Abby.

Now it was up to Connor to see that Jaye suffered the consequences of her actions. When the bus stopped, he'd call a taxi and instruct the driver to drive them home. A girl who erupted into spontaneous song on the bus couldn't be trusted not to do so at the symphony.

He made sure he got off the bus before Jaye, then put a restraining hand on the girl's arm so she couldn't lose herself among the crowd headed for the Kennedy Center.

"You're not going anywhere, young lady," he said.

She directed a mutinous glare at him but held her ground while her classmates disembarked. Abby was at the back of the group, organizing the students into a cohesive pack and issuing orders about walking in an orderly manner.

"Miss Reed," he called, "can I have a word?"

Her eyes widened. "Now? We don't have much time. The performance is starting soon."

"This won't take long," Connor said.

She hesitated, casting a glance over her shoulder at the impatient group. But then she nodded to a stern-faced chaperone Connor had overheard say she was retired military.

"Mrs. Bradford, would you see to it that the group

gets to the Concert Hall?" Abby asked. "I'll catch up in a minute."

"I've got it," Mrs. Bradford said before assuming her position at the front of the class and issuing orders for one of the other chaperones to bring up the rear.

The group hurried off. Abby Reed, her foot tapping and her body coiled for flight, obviously longed to join them. She gazed at him expectantly. "What is it?"

"I'm calling a cab and heading home with Jaye."

Abby's expression fell, but Jaye was the one who exclaimed. "No!"

He directed a hard look at the child. "After that outburst on the bus, Jaye, you don't deserve to see the performance."

Jaye's chin lifted, and her expression turned mutinous. "See if I care. It's just a stupid concert."

"Then you won't mind missing it."

"Why would I? Who cares about the stupid violin anyway?"

"Then it's settled." Connor switched his gaze to Abby. Her brows and the corners of her mouth were turned downward in a classic expression of disapproval. But what else was new? She'd disapproved of him from the first.

"Excuse us for a minute, Jaye," she said.

She took Connor's upper arm in a surprisingly firm grip and led him away from the defiant child. It was the first time she'd touched him, causing his awareness of her to heighten. She looked lovely in a simple slim-fitting navy skirt topped with a dark pink sweater that complemented her dark hair and creamy complexion. But her eyes were flinty.

"Let me guess," he said on a sigh. "You don't agree with me."

"Normally I would agree that you shouldn't award that kind of behavior," she whispered, meeting his gaze head on, "but I'm afraid Jaye will never pick up her violin again if you take her home."

"She'll learn a lesson."

"At what cost? You already know she's not headed in the right direction. Weren't you listening to me in your office? The violin could save her." Her voice grew impassioned, her eyes shone, her hand on his arm tightened. "Kids like Jaye need to care about something. When their troubles get too big, they need something to bring them out of the darkness into the light. Music can do that. It lifts the spirit with its beauty. It makes the world seem like a better place."

He stared at her, this attractive, accomplished young woman who seemed so very sure of herself. When she'd made a similar speech in his office, he'd thought she was talking only about Jaye. But now he was certain there was more to what she was saying. She had layers, and one of them had peeled away as she made a case for Jaye.

"Is that what music did for you?" he whispered. "Gave you a refuge from your troubles?"

A shutter closed over her face. "We're not talking about me. We're talking about Jaye." She nodded toward his niece. "Punish her some other way," she said in an urgent tone, "but don't take the violin away from her."

He glanced at Jaye. The girl's small chin was still raised stubbornly, but she was blinking rapidly, as though fighting tears.

"If we don't hurry, we'll miss the start of the performance." Abby leveled him with another of her challenging looks. "Are you and Jaye coming?"

She expected him to say no. He could see the resignation in her eyes, as though she believed he couldn't possibly understand that nurturing Jaye's love of music could benefit her.

"Yeah, we're coming," he said, enjoying her look of surprise. In a louder voice, he called to Jaye, "C'mon, Jaye. We don't want to miss the beginning of the concert."

The child's defiant expression lifted, replaced by hope. "Do you mean I can go?"

"As long as you understand this is the last place you'll be going all week. You're grounded, young lady. You also have to sit next to me and promise to behave yourself."

She seemed about to protest, but then nodded. Walking past Connor, Jaye told her teacher, "Thanks, Miss Reed."

Abby smiled, transforming her face from merely attractive to beautiful. Connor wondered if she'd ever smile at him that way.

"You're welcome," she said and took the girl's hand. "But now we have to dash if we're going to make it on time."

Connor followed them into the Kennedy Center as they hurried down the red carpet of the Hall of Nations past the walls draped with the colorful flags of foreign countries en route to the Concert Hall.

Before Abby had pleaded for Jaye outside the Kennedy Center, he'd thought of the teacher mainly as a nuisance to bear. But something had changed in that instant when she'd pleaded his niece's case and he'd gotten an inadvertent glimpse into her soul.

This was a complicated woman, with hidden depths that made her the most interesting person he'd met in a very long time. The passion she could interject into a simple sentence got his juices flowing the way no woman had for as long as he could remember.

Somewhere along the line, the annoyance she'd inspired had turned to attraction. Abby Reed was somebody he'd very much like to know better. A hell of a lot better.

"THAT WAS TOTALLY AWESOME. Wasn't that totally awesome, Miss Reed?"

Jaye Smith didn't try to contain her excitement as the bus barreled away from the Kennedy Center north on New Hampshire Avenue toward Silver Spring.

"Totally awesome," Abby agreed. The only thing that had prevented Abby from completely sharing in her enthusiasm had been the feel of Connor Smith's eyes on her throughout the performance.

She'd ensured he didn't sit next to her by positioning him at the flank of the group of students. But every time she'd turned her head, she'd caught him looking at her.

She wasn't sure why she noticed. He was exactly the kind of man who didn't interest her. Even though she gravitated toward the world of music, she wasn't drawn to the sophisticated, moneyed sort of male who inhabited that world. The men she'd dated in the past had been simpler, the sort who took her to a pizza place for dinner and ordered beer.

Despite his earlier attempt on the bus to portray himself to Mr. Greeley as the common man, Connor Smith seemed like he'd order champagne. Probably at a five-star restaurant. He'd given in and allowed Jaye to come to the concert, but she had a dozen other reasons to dislike him. The way he put his work before his daughter, for one. He'd left the performance at one point to take a call. The phone hadn't rung, but she'd seen him remove the slim device from the pocket of his suit jacket and check a number.

She turned her head. Connor was sitting two rows behind the seat she shared with Jaye on the opposite side of the aisle. Their eyes locked, and she quickly broke the contact.

"I'll never be able to play like that."

She transferred her full attention to the girl, dismayed at how quickly the excitement had leeched from her voice. "Why would you say that, Jaye?"

"Didn't you hear them? They were totally awesome."

"If you want it bad enough, you could be awesome, too."

The eyes that raised to hers looked hopeful. "You really think so?"

"I really think so. But you'd have to put your mind to it and practice hard."

The hope disappeared from Jaye's face in another lightning-quick change of moods. "I'm not allowed to practice."

"Oh, I can't believe that," Abby said. "I've never heard of a parent who didn't encourage their child to practice."

"Mine doesn't." Jaye's mouth set in an obstinate line. "And he was really mad about me singing on the bus. He says he's going to punish me. He'll probably take away my violin."

"He won't do that, Jaye."

"How do you know?"

Abby hesitated. "I've talked to him. He seems like a reasonable man."

"He locks me in my room without supper," she announced. "And he makes me go to sleep at seven o'clock."

Jaye's pronouncements reeked of exaggeration, however tempted Abby was to believe the worst of Connor Smith. By the same token, Abby could tell that father and daughter were not as close as they should be. That was evident in the rebellious slant of Jaye's mouth.

She tried to put herself in Jaye's position. After all, she'd grown up without a parent, too. But in Abby's case, that parent had been her father and he'd been absent by choice. It was far worse to be forced to deal with the death of a mother. Especially at Jaye's young age.

She was no guidance counselor, but she longed to help the girl. She couldn't do that without more information. All Jaye had told her so far was that her mother had succumbed to cancer. "How long has your mother been gone?"

Jaye sniffed. "About a month."

Abby bit her lip. She'd known the loss had been recent but hadn't realized how recent. "How long had it been before then that you'd seen your father?"

"A long time," Jaye said. "Years."

"One or two years?" Abby pressed.

"More." Jaye turned her face away and stared out the bus window. They were passing through a particularly lovely section of northwest D.C. Rock Creek Park was immediately to the west, and large colonial and Tudor-style houses lined the street, their lawns losing the dullness of winter and starting to turn a richer shade of green. Abby doubted Jaye saw any of it. "Mom and I lived in Tennessee."

Physical distance, in Abby's opinion, was no reason to keep emotionally distant from a child. Especially when it was your own. But she was jumping to conclusions without all the facts. She didn't know for certain that Connor Smith hadn't kept in touch with his daughter.

"It must have been tough living so far away from your father," she said, leading into her question as tactfully as she could. "It's a good thing for telephones."

"He never called me," Jaye muttered, her face still turned to the window.

Abby's estimation of Connor plummeted, but then she reminded herself that he was trying to do right by Jaye now. Whatever his sins of the past, he had an opportunity to atone for them.

"He's here now, Jaye." She tried to dredge up something encouraging to say. "He probably wants to make up for lost time."

Jaye's head shook violently back and forth. Her shoulders trembled, as though she were fighting tears.

Abby laid a hand on her arm, unsure of what she'd said wrong. "What is it, honey?"

Jaye looked at her then, her eyes wet with unshed tears. "My dad doesn't want to make up for lost time. He doesn't want me at all."

Emotion clogged Abby's throat, making it tough to speak. She'd run out of words anyway, not that anything she'd said so far had made Jaye feel the slightest bit better.

The cheerful chatter of the children behind them contrasted vividly with the despair on Jaye's face. Abby stroked the girl's arm as resentment built inside her toward Connor Smith.

She knew his type all too well.

Her father hadn't wanted her, either.

CHAPTER THREE

WHEN CONNOR SMITH MADE UP his mind to do something, he followed through. The practice had served him well both in business and in his personal life.

As he'd listened to the symphony perform in the gilded Concert Hall, somewhere between the bullfighter theme from Bizet's *Carmen* and the finale from Rossini's *William Tell Overture,* he'd set his mind on getting to know Abby Reed better.

His venue of choice would have been a quiet dinner for two at his town house, but with the addition of a nine-year-old, his home was no longer so private.

When he'd caught Abby peeking looks at him during the concert, he thought that accomplishing his mission wouldn't be difficult. But something imperceptible had changed since the concert's end, because the looks she'd stolen on the bus seemed more like glares.

The bus had arrived at Blue Moon Elementary five minutes ago. An hour remained in the school day, so Abby had already sent the protesting students back to their classes. Connor had called a goodbye to Jaye, but she'd given him her back. Neither of them, it seemed, looked forward to the punishment he'd mete out tonight.

He waited for the ex-military chaperone to finish telling Abby how much she'd enjoyed the field trip before he approached Abby, who was heading for the brightly colored main hall of the school. "Miss Reed, can I talk to you for a minute?"

He thought she might ignore him and keep on walking, but then she turned. It was a windy day, and her short dark hair had gotten slightly tousled in the brief walk from the bus to the school. The appealing disarray should have made her seem more approachable, but he read reluctance in her stance. "What is it, Mr. Smith?"

It had been a long time since he'd been so nervous at the prospect of asking out a woman. He cleared his throat, thinking it best if he eased into the subject. "You were right about letting Jaye stay to hear the concert. I could tell she was enraptured."

He sensed some of the tension leaving her body and imagined she looked a fraction more relaxed.

"She was. You should look into getting her private lessons." Her gaze sharpened. "You do let her practice, don't you?"

"Why wouldn't I?"

She hesitated, then said, "No reason. As I was saying, extra lessons would help her. There's only so much I can teach her when she's part of a group. If you're interested, I have a sheet with names and phone numbers of private teachers that I'll send home with her."

"That'd be great."

"Fine." She seemed to think the conversation was over and started to turn away.

"But that wasn't what I wanted to talk to you about."

She regarded him so coolly, it felt as if the temperature in the elementary school had dropped. Now was probably not the optimum time for what he had in mind, but he wasn't sure when he'd get another chance.

Nothing ventured, nothing gained.

One of the inspirational quotes J.D. used to spout during football season sprang to mind. The kid had a ton of them, all meant to motivate himself to become the best athlete he could be. They'd worked, too. J. D. Smith had been well on the road to athletic glory before that son of a bitch had robbed him of his life. Biting back the familiar rush of anger, Connor thrust his brother from his mind and concentrated on the saying.

"I'll get straight to the point. Would you have dinner with me this weekend?"

If he'd asked if she'd cut off her right arm and give it to him, she couldn't have looked more appalled. "No."

He rocked back on his heels, surprised at the firmness of her response. He'd been refused before, but never so baldly. But maybe he'd made a mistake. Once again he checked her left ring finger. Yes, it was still bare.

"Are you involved with someone else?" he asked.

"No. Now, if you'll excuse me, I need to get back to my classroom."

She took two steps before Connor recovered enough to find his voice. "Wait."

Reluctance written plainly on her face, she turned back to him. "What's the matter, Mr. Smith, aren't you used to being turned down?"

"It's not that. It's the way you did it." He scratched

his chin. "You could have softened the blow, said something about how it's against your policy to date relatives of students."

"I don't have a dating policy," she said. "But if it bothers you that much, let me rephrase my answer. Thank you for the invitation, but no thank you."

He frowned. "If I've done something to offend you, I'd sure like to know what it was."

"You mean besides not signing the permission slip until I came to your office and then showing up late for the bus?"

He was about to point out that technically he hadn't been late, but they'd already covered that ground. "Besides that."

Her chest rose, then fell. Clearly she wanted to be rid of him. "Jaye's told me some things."

"What things?" he pressed.

"I know you hadn't seen her in years until recently."

"That's right," he said slowly, wondering where she was going with this.

"And I know you felt like you had to take her in."

"That's right, too," he said. "The alternative was foster care, and I couldn't let that happen."

"Am I supposed to give you points for that?"

He cocked his head. "What do you mean?"

"It was your responsibility to take her in after her mother died. You—"

"Hold on a minute," he interrupted, trying to make sense of her tirade. "Jaye's mother isn't dead."

"But Jaye said…" Abby's voice trailed off, and her brow knotted before understanding dawned on her face. "I take it her mother never had cancer, either?"

"No cancer, as far as I know. But then I don't know a lot about the situation. She and Jaye showed up at my place one night a month or so ago. The next morning, Diana was gone."

"She just left Jaye without a word?"

"Without a word to Jaye. She left a note for me, saying she needed time to work things out and get her head on straight."

Abby shook her own head. She clearly didn't understand what would drive a mother to abandon her child, but neither did Connor. "No wonder Jaye's having such a tough time."

"Yeah, tell me about it. I'm doing the best I can, but it doesn't seem to be enough."

"Am I supposed to be impressed that you're now doing what you should have been doing all along?" Her voice held an edge.

"I'm not trying to impress anybody." He felt as though he were defending himself, but he wasn't sure for what. "Jaye's family. It's my responsibility to help her out."

"It was your responsibility to work harder at keeping in contact with her," she snapped.

He cocked his head, wondering at the cause of the unfriendly glint in her eyes. "Do you have a problem with me?"

"Yes, I do," she retorted. "Don't you think Jaye knows that you don't really want her? That's a hard thing for any daughter to swallow about her father."

Connor gaped at her as her resentment toward him finally made sense.

"Jaye's not my daughter," he said. "She's my niece."

ABBY WAS SURE SHE'D BEEN struck speechless before, but couldn't remember when.

She stared at Connor, suddenly viewing him in a brand-new light. He wasn't a deadbeat dad. He was a bachelor uncle who'd taken in a young girl who had nowhere else to go.

"If you're not her father," she said slowly, "where is he?"

"Diana—that's my sister—doesn't know who Jaye's father is. She had Jaye when she was seventeen. Rumor was that most of the boys in town had Diana before that."

He related his sister's history in a flat voice Abby suspected hid a wealth of emotion.

"After she got pregnant, Diana went to stay with our great-aunt near Roanoke. She lived there until Aunt Aggie died about five years ago. Then she just took off with Jaye. She'd call from time to time to say she was okay but we didn't know where they were until last month."

"When they showed up on your doorstep," Abby finished.

He nodded mutely.

"But why leave Jaye with you? Why not leave her with your mother?" Something occurred to her. "Your mother is alive, isn't she?"

"Very much alive," Connor assured her, "but she and Diana, they clash. I guess Diana thought I was the best choice."

The next time Abby was alone with Jaye, she'd take her to task for the outrageous lies she'd told about her uncle and mother. But tattling on the girl now would be like heaping kindling onto a fire. Jaye was already in enough trouble with Connor for her behavior on the bus.

Abby bit down on her lower lip. She'd been so off the mark that she was tempted to find the nearest desk so she could crawl under it. But that wasn't the way she lived her life. She owned up to her mistakes.

"I owe you an apology," she said and gulped. "I'm sorry. I shouldn't have said those things to you."

He nodded, keeping his eyes on her face. "I know of a way you can make it up to me."

She felt her heart slamming against her chest wall. He couldn't possibly mean to renew his dinner invitation, could he? Not after she'd unfairly accused him of neglecting a daughter he didn't even have?

"You can give Jaye private lessons," he said. "You are one of the teachers on the list, right?"

Disappointment shot through her that he hadn't asked her out again, followed by annoyance at herself. High-powered stockbrokers who worked long hours weren't her type, even if they did take responsibility for their nieces.

"Yes," she said. "I'm on the list."

"Great," he said. "How does Saturday morning sound?"

"Just in case my neighbors want to sleep in on weekends, I don't teach on Saturday mornings. I don't take students late on weeknights, either. I live in a duplex converted into apartments. I've managed to schedule all my students Monday through Thursday before six o'clock."

He grimaced. "I couldn't get Jaye to you until six at the earliest."

She did some quick mental calculations. Most of her

neighbors didn't arrive home from work until after seven. In the two years she'd taught private lessons and practiced her own music, they'd yet to complain that they could hear her through their shared walls. "I can work with that."

"Then we have a deal. When you send home that list, write down whatever night fits into your schedule."

"Okay," she said.

He nodded in agreement. It appeared as though he might say something else, but then he turned and walked away. She stared after him, rationalizing away the lingering disappointment.

She'd treated him unfairly so it was only logical for her to make amends. She'd done that by agreeing to adjust her teaching schedule in order to give Jaye private lessons.

Wishing he'd given her a second chance to accept a dinner date that would probably have turned out badly did absolutely no good. No good at all.

ABBY WATCHED THE MINUTE HAND on the clock in her living room tick by until it reached six-thirty, a half hour past when Connor was supposed to have arrived with Jaye for her first private lesson.

She picked up her own violin and played a few notes before becoming distracted. Had Jaye and her uncle forgotten? That seemed unlikely considering the talk Abby had with Jaye after strings class that afternoon. Abby had made it clear that she wouldn't stand being lied to, nor would she keep any future misbehavior from Connor. Jaye had nodded mutely, then asked Abby not to change her mind about giving the private lessons. So then where were they?

Abby's duplex apartment in Wheaton, a less attractive but more affordable area than Silver Spring, was about five miles and fifteen minutes north of the elementary school on a good day. Had Connor and Jaye gotten caught in unexpectedly heavy rush-hour traffic? If so, why hadn't they called? And why was she so anxious at the prospect of seeing Connor again that she kept checking the front window every five minutes?

She parted the mini blinds, spotted the silver Porsche in front of her duplex and jumped back so they wouldn't see her peering out at them. When the doorbell rang, she made herself wait a good ten seconds before pulling open the door.

Jaye stood on the stoop in front of Connor, her lower lip trembling and her face streaked with tears. Forgetting her anxiety at seeing Connor, Abby quickly ushered the nine-year-old inside. "Jaye, honey, what's wrong?"

Jaye dipped her blond head, her thin shoulders shaking. Abby's eyes raised to Connor. He was dressed in an expensive tailored suit, the same way he'd been the other times she'd seen him, but the similarities ended there.

His hair was disheveled, as though he'd been running his fingers through it. Smudges appeared under his eyes, and he seemed at a loss.

"She's been like this since I picked her up at the school," he explained. "Granted I was a little late—"

"Fifteen minutes late," Jaye interjected.

Connor finished the sentence at the same time. "But it was only fifteen minutes."

"I was the last one there," Jaye said unhappily.

Abby rubbed the girl's shoulder, silently conveying that she understood. She had experience dealing with children of this age. Promptness might not seem like that big of a deal, but every minute counted when a child was waiting to be picked up.

Especially a child whose mother had left her and hadn't come back. Couldn't Connor see that?

"I'm sure your uncle didn't mean to be late, Jaye," Abby told the girl in a soothing voice.

"He's late all the time," Jaye said.

"Some of the time," Connor clarified.

"And now we're late for the lesson." Jaye glanced at the clock, which showed the time at twenty-five minutes before seven. "There's only ten minutes left."

"I don't usually do this." Abby never did this. "But you're my last lesson of the day. How about we go until seven-twenty. That way, you won't miss a minute."

Jaye's tears stopped flowing. "Really? You'd do that?"

"I most certainly will. Go over to the sofa and take your instrument out of the case. Will you do that, Jaye?"

"Sure," she said and headed away from them.

"Thanks," Connor said. "You're saving my life."

He looked so relieved that she nearly let him off the hook but realized she couldn't. For Jaye's sake. "This is a one-time thing," she said quietly. "From now on, you need to get her here on time."

He swiped a hand over his brow and lowered his own voice. "I don't have the kind of job where it's that easy to leave at a prearranged time. Clients call. They're paying me for my time. I can't just hang up on them."

"You're going to have to figure something out," she said.

"I know that. I just don't know what it's going to be."

His vulnerability touched a chord deep inside her.

"Maybe we can talk about it later. But for now, Jaye's waiting for her lesson. You can pick her up at about twenty after seven."

"Would it be okay if I stuck around?" He lifted his portable computer. "I have a couple things I need to check online. Any flat surface will do. Your kitchen table would be great."

She glanced at the still-sniffling Jaye. She sensed that something more serious than Connor showing up late was bothering her. Jaye would never reveal what it was if she thought her uncle could overhear.

"I find that my students do better without their parents—or in this case, their uncle—in the room." She nodded toward the door. "Seven-twenty."

She expected him to argue, but instead he asked, "Any suggestions on a place I could go for forty-five minutes?"

"There's a public library a half mile down the road. It has lots of cubicles, all with flat surfaces."

He tipped a nonexistent hat to her, said goodbye to a nonresponsive Jaye and left. Pasting a smile on her face, Abby turned to the girl. "Are you ready for your lesson?"

Jaye nodded, but made no move to pick up her violin from the open case. Abby lifted the delicate instrument, turning it over while she examined it. It was a rental from a popular music store, adequate for a beginner but not of the caliber Abby suggested for her more serious students. For now, though, it would do.

She handed the violin to Jaye. The girl took it but didn't lift the instrument onto her shoulder the way Abby had taught her in class.

"What's wrong, Jaye?"

"I already told you. Connor was late picking me

up." Jaye's lower lip thrust forward, but the way it trembled betrayed that something more serious than her uncle's tardiness distressed her.

"Okay," Abby said, sensing that Jaye would clam up if she tried to force a confidence. "If that's all it is, then let's start the lesson."

Jaye nodded, but her violin remained at her side. Staring at a point on the carpet, she said, "Remember when I told you my mother was dead? Well, I said that because I wish she was dead."

Abby swallowed a cry of dismay and forced herself to speak in gentle, even tones. "You don't mean that, honey. Whatever your mother's done, she's still your mother."

"I hate her." Jaye sniffed but didn't cry. "She left me with Uncle Connor."

"Your uncle seems okay to me."

She shrugged. "He is okay. But he doesn't have time for me. He doesn't pick me up from school till six o'clock and half the time he's late."

"He has to work, Jaye." Since Abby had taken Connor to task for putting in too much time at the office, she found it surreal that she was sticking up for him. "I imagine he's doing the best he can. He didn't plan on you coming to live with him."

"He doesn't want me any more than my mom does."

Although Connor's life would obviously be easier if his niece hadn't come to live with him. Abby couldn't let the girl paint him with such a negative brush stroke. "He's your uncle, Jaye. I'm sure he loves you."

"Then why can't I come home after school and be with him?"

"I told you, Jaye. He has to work. And you're not old enough to stay home alone."

"I'm too old to hang out with the babies at day care."

"Surely there are other children your age there."

"They don't want me there. They're all boys. They barely talk to me. And they won't let me play with them."

Abby swallowed a sigh because she well understood how it felt not to be wanted. Jaye's situation was doubly difficult. Not only had her mother left her, she was meeting with rejection in every direction she turned. "Have you talked to your uncle about how much you dislike the school-based day care?"

She nodded. "He says it's the best he can do and that I need to stick it out."

Abby had a sense that she'd regret her next question, but couldn't keep from asking it. "I can't promise anything but would you like me to talk to him for you?"

Jaye nodded eagerly, making Abby feel marginally less apprehensive about the offer. "Oh, yes, please, Miss Reed."

Abby smiled at her. "When we're not at school, you can call me Abby."

Jaye smiled back. "Okay, Abby."

"Now are you ready for the lesson?"

Jaye nodded.

"Settle the instrument into playing position and let's do a D scale. Remember to keep your fingers curved and the bow flat on the strings."

Her lower lip thrust forward in concentration, Jaye did exactly as she was told.

For the next forty-five minutes, Abby tried to focus on the techniques involved in giving a student her first lesson. But every time Jaye played a scale, Abby's mind wandered to Connor and the conversation she'd promised to have with him.

She wasn't sure why, but she had the strong impression it wouldn't go her way.

CONNOR STOOD OUTSIDE THE DOOR of Abby's duplex a few minutes before he was due to pick up Jaye, listening to the sounds of his niece playing the violin.

She wasn't anywhere close to a performer's level of proficiency, but he recognized that she was playing a song.

He felt an odd pride that Jaye could coax any sound at all from the instrument, let alone identifiable notes. Maybe Abby was right. Maybe she did have a talent for the thing.

Not wanting to interrupt the lesson, he tried the door and found it unlocked. He slipped inside, making a mental note to tell Abby that she really should use her dead bolt. Jaye stood in front of a music stand, her concentration fully engaged. Abby was off to one side, looking over her shoulder.

Her eyes met his and held. The air between them seemed to charge with awareness, but then she put a finger to her lips. Maybe he'd only imagined the connection because he wanted it to be there. By adamantly refusing his dinner invitation, she certainly hadn't given him any reason for hope. But hope he did.

Jaye finished the song, a small smile of triumph on her lips. It faded when she caught sight of Connor.

"That was good, Jaye," Connor said, but the girl didn't respond. He stifled a groan. What was it going to take for him to build a relationship with her?

"Your uncle's right. It was good," Abby told the girl. "You'll be graduating to more difficult songs before you know it. Just remember to practice at least twenty minutes every day so you don't forget what we went over."

"I always practice more than that."

"That's great. You know what they say. Practice makes…"

"Perfect," the two of them said in unison, then laughed.

When Jaye started to pack up, Abby came directly toward him. His pulse sped up until he realized she only meant to hand him a sheet of paper.

"I wrote down the name of a beginning violin book I'd like you to buy before the next lesson. Any of the area music stores should have it in stock."

"I'll do it," he promised, even as he wondered when he'd have the time.

She'd started to retreat when Jaye stopped her with a loud whisper. "Aren't you going to ask him?"

"Ask me what?" he said.

"Can I use the bathroom, Abby?" Jaye said before she could answer. It didn't escape Connor's notice that she used her teacher's first name, which Abby must have authorized. Good. The child needed a female role model in her life, and Abby fit the bill. The more comfortable Jaye felt around her, the better.

"Sure. It's upstairs, first door on the right." Abby waited until the girl was halfway up the stairs before turning to him. "Jaye wants me to talk to you about her after-school care."

He rubbed the back of his neck. "Why can't she talk to me about it herself?"

Abby shrugged. "I get the impression she thinks you'll pay more attention if it comes from me."

He frowned, troubled by the notion that Jaye thought he wasn't paying enough attention to her. He knew firsthand how that could undermine a child's confidence. Connor had grown up in the shadow of a younger brother so athletically gifted he'd stolen the spotlight whenever he'd taken a field or a court.

Their parents had dwelled so heavily on J.D.'s accomplishments that it often seemed as though they had little time left for him and Diana. After J.D. had died, they'd become even more hyper-focused on him. Not that Connor had resented his brother for any of that. He'd loved J.D., too. Everybody had.

"What about Jaye's after-school care?" he asked Abby.

"She hates it."

He sighed because he'd expected the answer. "I'm not completely oblivious to what's going on with her. One of the teachers there told me she wasn't mixing well with the other students."

"Then you won't be surprised that she wants you to make other arrangements for her."

"I'm ahead of you on that. I already got the names of the day-care centers in the area that can pick her up after school."

"That's great."

"No, it's not. All of them were full. Since I can't get off work at three o'clock every day, she's stuck. I don't have anywhere else for her to go."

"Maybe the mother of one of her friends will take her."

"As far as I know, she hasn't made any real friends."

He thought of the way Jaye had smiled at Abby and called her by her first name. "Except you."

"Unfortunately that also doesn't help you," she said, "because I can't take her."

"Why not?" Now that the solution had occurred to him, it seemed perfect. "I'd pay you."

"It's not a matter of money. I give private lessons after school four days a week. A child would be bored to tears."

"Not a child who loves music," he argued.

"I don't know if it's a good idea," Abby said slowly.

"You don't want me, either, do you, Abby?" The small voice came from the staircase. Jaye sat frozen in place on one of the middle steps, looking small and vulnerable. And very, very sad.

"It's not that, honey," Abby tried to reassure her. "I'm just afraid you wouldn't like being here while I was giving lessons."

The misery in Jaye's expression ebbed, but only slightly. "I wouldn't be bored. I could watch TV or play games on your computer."

"Or, better yet, read and do homework," Connor added. To Abby, he said, "What do you say? Are you willing to give it a shot?"

A part of him knew he was being unfair to Abby by putting her on the spot, but a bigger part wanted her to agree. Because then not only would Jaye get to see Abby more often, he would, too.

Jaye held her body tautly, with her shoulders hunched, as though expecting a blow. It couldn't be more clear that she expected to be rejected.

Abby realized it, too. Connor could tell by the way her mouth softened while she regarded the child.

"Okay," she said. "Let's give it a try."

"Do you mean it?" Jaye's voice held a mixture of hope and suspicion.

"I mean it," Abby said. "I'm only at your school one day a week, but the rest of the time I'm across the street at the middle school. I'll collect you at three and bring you here. Your uncle can pick you up when he gets off work."

Jaye's face creased into a rare smile. She jumped to her feet and scampered the rest of the way down the stairs, not stopping until she flung her arms around Abby's waist.

Abby stroked the girl's hair, exchanging a look with Connor above Jaye's head.

He smiled at her, more sure than ever that she was a woman he wanted in both of their lives.

CHAPTER FOUR

JAYE HELD THE EMPTY BOX of brownie mix, little lines of concentration appearing on her forehead as she read the directions on the back. "It says we should add two eggs."

Abby opened the refrigerator door, retrieved the eggs from the tray and put them down on the counter next to the mixing bowl. "You know how to crack them, right?"

The girl's eyes rounded. "Of course. I added the right amount of oil and water, didn't I?"

"Yes, you did. In fact, you're a natural in the kitchen. Want to tell me how you got to be that way?"

"My mom taught me some stuff," Jaye mumbled.

Abby would have liked to pursue the subject, but the girl picked up an egg and kept talking.

"You tap gently on the edge of the bowl," Jaye said, explaining to Abby the fine points of cracking an egg. The girl's tongue stuck out slightly as she focused on the task. "Then you let the egg guts slide inside it."

"Egg guts," Abby repeated. "You do have a way with words as well as brownies."

Jaye giggled, something that had been happening more as the first week of their new arrangement wore on. It was Friday, the fifth day they'd been together but the only one in which Abby hadn't taught lessons.

So far, the arrangement had worked far better than Abby had expected. Because of Jaye's penchant for attracting attention, she'd feared that the girl would disrupt her lessons.

But Jaye proved adept at entertaining herself. She usually chose to stay in the room where Abby gave lessons, but even that caused no problems.

Connor Smith was the one causing a problem.

He was just so…sexy.

Abby wasn't sure when she'd started to associate that description with him, but now that she had she couldn't get it out of her mind.

She noticed small things about him, such as the way he gave her his undivided attention, as though nothing were more important than what she had to say.

She found herself appreciating the simple act of breathing because of the clean, male way he smelled.

And his mouth… His mouth was sheer masculine perfection. More than once, she'd daydreamed about how it would feel to kiss him.

Not that kissing him would be smart, considering how she felt about his work-centered lifestyle.

Besides, despite his invitation to take her to dinner, which he hadn't repeated, she was relatively certain he had a girlfriend. Relatively certain, but not positive.

"Should I pour the batter into the pan now?" Jaye asked. "I already sprayed it with cooking spray."

Abby brought her attention back to the girl. "Go ahead."

Jaye poured, assigning the task the same attention

she'd given everything else. When she finished scraping the batter from the mixing bowl into the pan, she carefully set the pan into the preheated oven.

"One more hour," Jaye announced.

Abby tilted her head quizzically. "Are you sure? I thought the brownies only took forty minutes to bake."

"I meant one more hour until Uncle Connor comes to get me." Jaye thrust out her lower lip. "I wish I could stay here with you tonight."

"Your uncle hasn't seen you much this week. I'm sure he wants to spend some time with you."

Jaye made a face. "He'd probably rather go on a date."

There couldn't have been a more perfect opening to find out if Connor was involved with anyone. "Is your uncle still seeing that woman who used to pick you up from after-school care?"

Jaye made a face. "I didn't like her. She was mean to me. She wanted me to move out so she could move in. But she's gone."

It was news to Abby that Connor had been dating someone seriously enough to contemplate living with her. It was probably also none of her business. Except now that she was spending so much time with Jaye, anything involving the girl was sort of her business. Or so she told herself.

"Is he dating anyone new?"

"I don't think so." Jaye pointed to the clock, which showed that it was nearly five o'clock. "Would it be okay if I watched Nickelodeon? There's a funny show on at five o'clock that I like."

"Go ahead," Abby said.

Jaye was still watching television forty minutes later

when the oven timer beeped, signaling that it was time to take the brownies out of the oven. Fifteen minutes after that, when they'd cooled enough for Abby to cut them, the television was still on.

The telephone rang. Half expecting it to be Connor saying he'd be late, Abby picked it up, ignoring the sudden racing of her heart.

"Hello." Her voice sounded slightly breathless.

"Hey, girlfriend. What's happening?"

Abby's heartbeat returned to normal at the sound of her friend's voice. Some years ago she'd met Rae Ann at a pottery-making class. In spite of the fun they'd had, making pottery hadn't caught on with either of them, but their friendship had blossomed. "I'm baking brownies."

"For a man?" Rae Ann asked.

Abby laughed. Rae Ann had a one-track mind. "For one of my students. What's up?"

Abby cradled the phone between her shoulder and her ear as she cut the brownies.

"I called about tomorrow night. Did you line up a date yet?"

"I already told you, Rae Ann, I'll come but I'm not bringing a man with me."

"Oh, come on, Abby. We're all bringing dates. That's the entire point of getting together on a night we don't usually meet. It's supposed to be something different, something fun."

Abby used a spatula to start transferring the brownies from the baking pan to a Tupperware container. "I can have plenty of fun without a man."

Rae Ann sighed dramatically, and Abby imagined

her rolling her eyes. "Listen to yourself, Abs. You might as well become a nun with an attitude like that."

"You know I like men as much as any of you."

"Then what's your problem?"

Abby paused. "I don't have anybody to ask."

"Nonsense. Open your eyes and smell the testosterone. There are men everywhere. You can't tell me that one of them doesn't ring your bell."

"Well," Abby said slowly and licked her lips. She could hardly believe she was going to bare her soul to Rae Ann, not when she'd hardly admitted as much to herself. She could hear the television playing in the next room and figured it was safe to talk. "There is somebody."

"Who?" Rae Ann demanded. "And when can I meet him?"

Abby smiled. "I didn't say we were going out, Rae. I said I'm attracted to him."

"You mean he gets you hot?"

"Okay. Yes. He gets me hot."

"What does he look like?"

"Tall, dark and luscious. He has the most beautiful mouth God put on a man. I can't look at it without fantasizing about kissing him."

"How about his body?"

Abby put down the spatula, the brownies remaining in the pan forgotten. "I can't say for sure because he's always wearing too many damned clothes, but I'm betting there's some prime beef under there."

Rae erupted into laughter. "So who is this mystery man?"

"The uncle of one of my students. He'll be by any minute to pick her up." She lowered her voice. "I swear,

Rae, lately when I see him, my heart races so fast my head can hardly keep up."

"So why don't you bring him?"

"Oh, I couldn't. He's the sophisticated type. He wouldn't come with me to something like this."

"Wanna bet?" asked a low-throated, masculine voice.

Abby's eyes flew to the entrance of the kitchen, where Connor leaned negligently against the door frame.

She closed her eyes in mortification. What was he doing here on time? His usual modus operandi was to show up anywhere from ten to twenty minutes late, although he usually called to let her know when he wouldn't be on time.

Something clanked, and it took her a moment to realize she'd dropped the phone. She heard Rae Ann's panicked voice coming over the line. "Abs, what happened? Are you all right?"

Connor's gorgeous mouth curved into a smile. Her heart raced, exactly the way she'd described to Rae Ann.

She bent to pick the phone off the floor. "Rae, I gotta go. I'll call you back later."

"But—"

Abby hung up, cutting off her friend. She wet her suddenly dry lips.

"Jaye let me in," he explained.

"I figured that. Um, exactly how long ago was that? I mean, how long have you been standing there?"

"Long enough to hear that you want to see what's under my clothes."

She felt her face flame. "I wasn't talking about you. I

was talking about the uncle of one of my other students," she said with as much haughtiness as she could muster.

"Okay. But in case you were talking about me, in the spirit of fairness, I'm going on record as saying I'd like to see what's under your clothes, too."

Her face grew warmer. "Now you're teasing me."

He walked purposefully toward her. Her heart sped up, but he only reached over and took a brownie. He kept his eyes on her as he took a bite. "Mmm. Delicious."

"Be serious," she chastised him.

"I am being serious. The brownies are delicious, and I would like to see what's under your clothes." His eyes danced. "I'd also like to go with you."

"You don't even know where I'm going."

"Doesn't matter. I'll go wherever."

She arched an eyebrow. "Really?"

"Really."

Why not? If nothing else, the date would drive home to her how incompatible she and Connor Smith were. Maybe then she'd stop fantasizing about him. "Pick me up at eight tomorrow night and you're on."

"I'm looking forward to it." No sooner had he said the words than his expression clouded. "Except I might not be able to go."

"You're chickening out already?"

"It's not that. It's Jaye. I'm new at this guardian business or I would have thought of it before. But I can't go unless I have a babysitter."

"Let me guess. You don't know any babysitters."

"My next-door neighbor will babysit but she's out of town a lot," he said. "I left Jaye with another babysitter a couple times early on. Let's just say, it didn't go well."

"Then how about if I supply the babysitter? One of my neighbors has a sixteen-year-old daughter who's not only responsible but a lot of fun. If she's free Saturday, I can drive her over to your house and bring her home."

"So you'll pick me up?"

She raised her eyebrows. "Do you have a problem with that?"

His grin started slowly and grew, making that word spring to mind. The one she could no longer stop associating with him: *sexy.* She hadn't always thought of him that way. That first day in his office, he'd seemed too plastic, too perfect. But now she knew that he started to get a five o'clock shadow at the end of the workday, that his hair curled slightly at the ends when it wasn't freshly cut and that he was an all-around good guy.

"No problem at all." He reached out and touched the short strands of her hair. "I like the idea of a woman whose hair smells like chocolate picking me up."

She couldn't have come up with a witty retort right then if a lottery jackpot had been at stake.

Because she was starting to like the idea of picking him up, too.

A lot.

"How much longer do we have to be here?"

At the sound of Jaye's question, Connor looked up from the file on his desk. His niece squirmed on the sofa in the corner of his office, whereas a few minutes ago she'd looked completely comfortable.

He should have known the peace and quiet wouldn't last.

"Not much longer," he replied.

"That's what you said a half hour ago." Her pretty petal of a mouth flattened, the look reminding him sharply of his sister. "I don't know why you had to come into the office on Saturday, anyway."

"I told you, Jaye. It's not a nine-to-five job. And I'm not working as many hours as I used to."

"Because of me," she said, her expression petulant.

He thought about denying it, but figured he owed it to her to be honest. She'd see through any attempt to sugarcoat things, anyway. "Yes, I'm working fewer hours because of you. But it's because I want to."

"It's because you have to," she retorted.

As recently as a week ago, she would have stormed off. Or thrown whatever was within reach. But all she did now was bury her nose in her book. At least he'd had the foresight to take her to the library before coming to the office.

Her choice of reading material had taken him aback. She'd checked out the latest installment in the *Series of Unfortunate Events* books, about orphans trying to make their way in the world. A circumstance that was a little too close to home.

He brought his concentration back to his work, determined to get through it as quickly as possible. But a few minutes later, his cell phone rang. He'd barely had enough time to speak a greeting when the question came, "Connor, have you been passing out the flyers I mailed you?"

"Hello, Mother," Connor said. "How are you?"

"Have you?" His mother's voice was deceptive, soft and with a singsong quality that belied her single-minded nature.

Because when Elaine Smith decided upon a course of action, she seldom deviated from it. Ten years ago, when her younger son had been murdered, she'd vowed that his killer would never be a free man. Now that the parole hearing was approaching, her mission seemed more like an obsession.

"Most of the people I see every day are either my co-workers or my clients," Connor said. "Handing them flyers isn't appropriate."

"Why not? The more people we can get to write to the parole board, the less chance Galloway has of getting out of prison."

He glanced at Jaye. She'd put on the headphones of her CD player, which allowed him to speak freely. "I don't want him to get out of prison either. You know that, Mother. But I'm not sure handing out flyers is the way to keep him there."

"If only one person writes a letter, it's worth it. And remember, I have the petition, too."

He rubbed his brow, resigned to talking about the subject that consumed her. It could consume him, too. If he'd let it. "How many signatures do you have?"

"I'm up to two hundred twenty-five, but the parole hearing's still almost three months away. My goal is at least a thousand signatures by then."

Jaye shifted her position on the sofa, leaning her head back against the armrest and tucking her legs up under her. He had another flashback of Diana, who used to strike the same pose when she read.

"When are you going to visit Jaye?" he asked quietly even though his niece couldn't hear.

"Jaye?" His mother repeated the name as if she'd never heard it before. There was a significant pause. "Why don't you and the girl come to Bentonsville to visit me?"

"The last time we did, you weren't home."

"I already explained that, Connor. I needed to check on my newspaper ad," she said, referring to one of the many Keep the Killer in Prison ads she'd placed in the local newspaper. "I didn't know it would take that long."

"You didn't remember we were coming," he stated.

"Why are you being this way, Connor? You know how important these next months are."

Connor thought the important part was showing up at Drew Galloway's parole hearing. The protests they aired in person to releasing the bastard would hold the most weight. But how could he blame his mother for wanting to do everything possible to protect the memory of her dead son?

"I have some things going on this weekend, Mother. But I'll see if I can work something out for next weekend."

"Next weekend I'm having lunch with Dex Tucker." Before he could ask why she was getting together with J.D.'s old high-school football coach, she continued, "I want to see if he knows anyone else who might be able to help us with this."

She chattered on for another ten minutes in the same vein. It was only after she'd hung up that it occurred to him that she hadn't asked a single question about Jaye.

ABBY WALKED WITH HER MOTHER on the sidewalk that would eventually take them to Dee Dee's high-rise apartment building on Connecticut Avenue in northwest Washington, D.C., sipping on one of the caramel frappaccinos they'd picked up at the neighborhood Starbucks.

The sidewalk was busy, as it usually was on Saturday afternoons when the weather had started to warm up. Abby knew this because going out for coffee had become a staple of her weekly visits to her mother. People ducked in and out of small specialty shops, ate late lunches at outdoor tables at a sidewalk café or merely walked along enjoying the unusually warm late March day.

Abby smiled at a young mother pushing a stroller, then swerved to make way for a thin man with a dog who was traveling in the opposite direction, but he stopped in his tracks.

"I know you," he said, focusing on her mother. "You're Dee Dee Galloway."

Her mother's posture stiffened, her unease transferring to Abby. They never got stopped on the street anymore, especially not here in Washington, D.C., where what Drew had done wasn't an enduring topic of conversation.

"You don't recognize me, do you? I used to have a lot more of this." The man ruffled what little hair he had. "And a lot more of this." He patted his stomach. "You were the one who told me I needed to lose weight if I wanted to stick around."

"Keith Broyles?" Her mother visibly relaxed, her face creasing into a smile. "Is that you?"

"Fifty percent less of me, partly due to one of the best darn nurses I ever had."

The two of them embraced while Abby's relief that

the man wasn't a Bentonsville resident gave way to pride. Considering the tough times they'd gone through, her mother's transformation was remarkable.

She'd emerged from a string of dead-end jobs to fulfill her lifelong dream of becoming a nurse. Abby had tried to persuade her to enroll in nursing school earlier, but she'd insisted on waiting until Abby finished college.

She now worked on the surgical floor at George Washington University Hospital, a short Metro ride from her apartment in the desirable northwest sector of the city. She also found time for small pleasures like frappaccinos and evenings at the theater.

Abby squeezed her mother's hand when they were once more walking down the city sidewalk. "I'm so proud of you."

"For what?" she asked. She looked so pretty with her dark eyes sparkling and the sun shining on brown hair that hadn't yet begun to gray, but then she was only forty-five.

"For following your dream. For making a difference in that man's life. For being my mother."

Her expression clouded. "I wasn't that great of a mother."

"Don't say that."

"I wasn't. Look what happened to Drew."

"Drew made his own decisions. What happened wasn't your fault."

They walked the next half block in silence. The shops had thinned, giving way to apartment high rises, office buildings and the occasional single-family home.

"Drew might have made different decisions if I was home more." The flatness of her mother's voice was at odds with the lively sounds around them: the bark of a dog, the honk of a horn, the sweet music of the wind.

"You were working two jobs to support us." Abby took her mother's hand and squeezed it. "You did the best you could."

"My best wasn't good enough. If it had been, your brother wouldn't have dropped out of high school or spent a third of his life in prison."

"Drew's not even thirty years old. He has a lot of life ahead of him. His parole hearing's coming up soon. If he gets out, he can prove he's a good man."

Her mother didn't say anything for long moments. When she did reply, it was to change the subject. "Want to tell me why you keep looking at your watch?"

Abby made a face. "Sorry. I hadn't realized I was doing that. I'm going bowling tonight with Rae Ann and the gang."

"You're worried about being on time for bowling with your girlfriends?" Her mother looked disappointed. "I was hoping you had a date."

Anticipation fluttered through Abby. She hadn't intended to tell her mother about Connor. Not yet. Talking about what she was starting to feel for him seemed premature. But she could hardly keep it from her mother now that she'd asked.

"Actually, I do have a date. I must be a little nervous about it."

Her mother's face came alive with interest. "I can't ever remember you being nervous about going out with someone."

Abby could have shrugged off her mother's observation. She could have denied that a first date with

Connor Smith meant anything more than a first date with a dozen other men. But quite suddenly, she wanted to voice what had been rattling around in her head since Connor had invited himself on their bowling outing.

"I think this one's special."

If her mother had asked a follow-up question, Abby might have clammed up. But she didn't, and Abby's thoughts coalesced.

"I didn't think he was, not at first. He's a stockbroker and I assumed he was all about making money. But his sister took off and left her daughter—she's one of my students—with him. He's doing the right thing, Mom, even if he's not entirely sure how to go about raising a child."

Her mother smiled. "He sounds special."

Abby chewed her bottom lip, thinking about that. "I believe he just might be the real thing."

"Maybe he's The One."

Abby laughed, even though her mind didn't totally reject the idea. "You say that like there's only one person for everyone. Do you really believe that?"

"I used to, back when I was married to Drew's father. But I'm too practical to believe that now. Especially because I've had friends who have had happy marriages after their husbands died or they've divorced."

"Then why did you say it?"

"We weren't talking about everyone else. We were talking about you. When was the last time you had a date?"

Abby had to think about it before responding. "Four or five months ago. I doubled with Rae Ann when her cousin visited."

"That's my point. You've never put a high priority

on dating, yet you can hardly wait for tonight." She paused before continuing. "I've always wondered if you're so cautious about dating because of my history with men."

Abby mentally considered the possibility. Her mother had been married twice—once to a good man she'd adored and another time to someone who'd disappointed her completely— and neither relationship had ended well. "I've never thought about it too hard, but you could be right."

"Then hopefully you've learned from my mistakes. For somebody as wary as you, maybe there is only one person. Because you're so excited about this date, maybe this man is it."

Chuckling, Abby said, "I wouldn't go that far. I told you he was a stockbroker, right? He's kind of stuffy, and I can't see myself with somebody who doesn't know how to have fun."

Her mother linked her arm with Abby's. "With my track record, you probably shouldn't listen to me. But I think you should give him a chance. It's the quiet ones who'll surprise you."

CHAPTER FIVE

THE STROBE LIGHTS FLICKERED red, then blue, then yellow, casting Abby in a kaleidoscope of color that Connor thought brought her even more alive.

She was at the line, lifting a pink bowling ball to her chest before drawing back her arm and letting the ball fly. She was grace in motion, her form perfect, her body beautiful in her form-fitting blue jeans reflecting the shifting colors.

Only when she clapped did his gaze shoot to the end of the lane. Nine of the bowling pins were already down. The final one tottered, staying relatively upright for a sheer second, before toppling over.

Abby pivoted, a smile of delight wreathing her face as she did the tiniest of victory jumps on the way back to the group.

"Way to go, partner." Connor greeted her with a high five and a smile. "That'll inspire fear in our opponents."

Her friend Rae Ann, an overblown redhead who didn't do subtle, laughed. "It might scare us if you could bowl at all."

"Hey, I'm doing great." He indicated the electronic scoreboard overhead. "I have seventy-five."

"We're on the last frame, dude. Seventy-five stinks,"

Rae Ann's date, Rob, pointed out. He had long blond hair tied back from a strong, angular face and a habit of calling everyone—even the women—*dude*.

"Not when combined with Abby's one-hundred fifty three, it doesn't," he said. "Isn't that right, Abby?"

She touched his arm, her pretty face animated. "The next time we do this, I'm bringing you here to practice first."

The next time. Connor liked the sound of that. After the way things had gone with Isabel, he hadn't thought he'd be ready for another relationship for a long while.

Isabel had been high maintenance, exhausting him with her wishes to attend this benefit dinner or that socially correct party. Abby was her polar opposite. For proof, all he had to do was look around him at the flickering lights.

Cosmic bowling. Who would have thought it could be so enjoyable? Or that he could have so much fun with her and her friends? Connor had a few friends of his own at work, but none of them were close. The group Abby hung out with made him realize he'd devoted too much time to his job and too little to cultivating the friendships that could enrich a life.

"Practice?" He pretended outrage. "I don't need no stinkin' practice."

Abby's grimace was comical. "I hate to break it to you, Connor, but Rae's right. You're a terrible bowler."

She looked so sincere that he had to laugh, something he realized he hadn't done much of lately. Hell, he hadn't laughed much in the ten years since J.D. had been murdered.

There'd been too much time for responsibility, too little time for fun and no time to search for what would make him truly happy. Abby, he realized, made him happy.

"It's okay if we don't make a habit of bowling together, you know," she said, still with that earnest expression. "Mostly I like to bowl with the girls anyway."

Rae Ann sidled up next to her. "Abs, if you can't think of something to do with a hot guy like Connor besides bowl, it's time you and I had a little talk."

"Any chance I can tell you what to say before that talk?" Connor wiggled an eyebrow and everybody laughed. Including Abby.

She sat down next to him in the semicircular seating area. He put an arm around her, drawing her against his side. Their bodies fit, as though separate parts of a whole. She seemed as content to be there as he was to have her there.

Later, in the bar adjacent to the lanes, he, Abby and three other couples sat around a large table hoisting lagers. In addition to Rae Ann and Rob, there were Patty and Billy, both blond and talkative, and Deirdre and Stan. Deirdre and Stan were the most interesting couple. Stan, large and muscular, had shaved his head and pierced his ears. Deirdre was tiny, with short hair as red as a tomato.

"What do you do, Connor?" Stan asked him after they'd ordered another round of beers and Connor told the waitress to put it on his tab.

"I'm in personal finance," Connor answered.

"Connor's a stockbroker," Abby chimed in.

"Ah, then you make people money. I like money." Stan leaned toward Connor. "You'll be my friend, won't you?"

"Hey, weren't you the one who ragged Connor about his bowling?" Rae Ann asked.

"That was you and Rob, Rae," Stan protested. "I never said a word about how bad he stunk."

"I dated a stockbroker once." Patty talked with her hands. "But I didn't go out with him long enough to find out if he could bowl."

"You seldom date anyone long enough to find out squat about him, Patty," Deirdre said.

"Billy's sitting right here." Patty rolled her eyes. "Is there anything else you want to tell my date about me while we're at it?"

"Okay," Deirdre said, a wicked grin on her face. "How about the way you won't swallow cold liquid until it has time to warm up in your mouth first?"

"Patty and Deirdre are sisters," Abby told Connor in an aside as the two women got into a spirited back and forth about their respective faults that somehow managed to be both funny and good-natured. "Giving each other a hard time is what they do."

Connor looked from Patty, with her blond hair and pale skin, to the wild, red-haired Deirdre. "Really?" he said in a quiet voice. "You look more like Patty's sister than Deirdre does."

She whispered in his ear, her breath sending a shivery sensation down his spine. "That's because Deirdre's hair color isn't natural."

He shouted with laughter, but the bar was so noisy the sound blended in.

"I don't even know if you have a sister," he remarked. Although he had a good handle on what sort of person Abby was, he realized he knew very little about her past.

"No sister," she said.

"Brothers?"

"I've got one of those," she said, then hardly took a breath before asking, "How about you?"

He got the impression she didn't want to talk about her brother and would have pressed the issue if they hadn't been inside a noisy, crowded bar. More and more, he wanted to know what had formed the person she was. But, truth be told, he didn't want to talk about his brother, either. Not yet.

"One sister, one brother." It was the same reply he always gave when someone asked. He never offered that J.D. had been killed. His brother might be dead, but in some ways the memory of what had been done to him kept him shockingly alive.

"I didn't know you had a brother," she said.

"There's a lot you don't know about me, sweetheart." He lowered his voice. "So you'll just have to spend more time with me and find out."

"Is that so?" She looked at him flirtatiously from under her lashes, and awareness hit him hard. "How will you get me to do that?"

"You babysit my niece, and I pick her up. Every day." He leaned close so that only three or four inches separated them, heartened when she didn't move away. "I'll have lots of opportunity to get you to see things my way."

"Maybe I already do," she whispered, her breath feathering over his lips.

"Earth to Abby and Connor," Rae Ann said in a loud voice. Connor reluctantly broke eye contact with Abby and brought his attention back to the group. "Settle an argument for us. Is Vin Diesel the action star related to the man who invented the diesel engine?"

Abby laughed, the sound traveling over him like a caress. "What do you think, Connor?"

He thought he was having a wonderful time with an amazing woman and a group of people with whom he might never have socialized otherwise.

"Let's see. Vin Diesel. The diesel engine." He paused, deliberately tapped his chin, then asked, "Are you guys drunk?"

CONNOR SMITH WAS A LOT of fun.

Abby was still trying to wrap her mind around that fact as they walked together from the town-house garage where he'd parked his Porsche for the night to his front door. A full moon glowed softly, providing the appropriate atmosphere for what had been a magical night.

"I liked your friends," he said. "Especially Rae Ann. I thought I'd bust a gut when she told that story about calling the cops when she was at the tanning salon."

The kicker to the story was that she'd thought the guy in the next booth was having a heart attack when in reality he was having sex with the woman in the booth with him.

Abby laughed. "Things like that only happen to Rae Ann, which is why it's fun to be around her. But she's in the throes of a new relationship, so I don't see her much. Now, if she breaks up with Rob, I'll see her all the time."

"Does that bother you?"

"Not in the slightest. I know she's there for me if I really need her."

"I don't have a friend like that," he said.

"That's because you work too much. If you got out

and played a little, you'd have plenty of friends. You're a lot of fun, too."

"Yeah?" he asked.

"Yeah," she agreed. "So start asking around your office for names of teenage girls so you can provide the babysitter next time."

His hand was under her elbow, warm and firm. "I'm taking it as a good sign that this is the second time you've said 'next time.'"

"It's a very good sign." She smiled at him, wondering why she'd ever thought him stuffy. In khakis, a short-sleeved polo shirt and boat shoes, he was more casually dressed than she'd ever seen him. The moonlight showed a hint of a beard on his lower face, further distancing him from the image of the uppity stockbroker.

But it wasn't only his appearance that made him seem different. She'd seen another facet of him tonight, a side that was lighthearted and fun. Quite suddenly she wanted to know everything about him. Where he'd grown up. Whether he was the oldest, youngest or middle child. What kind of people his parents were. What made him who he was today.

She wasn't only attracted to him, she liked him—a combination that could grow into something deeper once they got better acquainted. At the knowledge that he wanted that to happen as much as she did, her heart beat harder.

"So if I asked you out again, you'd say yes?" he asked.

"What do you mean again?" she teased. "You didn't ask me out this time."

"That's right." He stroked his chin and looked

thoughtful. A smirk touched the side of his mouth. "You wanted me along because you like my body."

She felt her cheeks heat, as they'd already done a few times in his presence. She couldn't remember another man who had the power to make her blush like a school-girl. "I didn't actually say that."

"You said you suspected there was some prime beef under my clothes."

Her cheeks grew hotter. "You can't believe every-thing you overhear."

They'd reached his front porch. Jaye's babysitter hadn't turned on the porch light, but it didn't matter. The moon already provided enough of a glow that Abby could see him clearly. She focused on his mouth, re-membering that she'd called it the most beautiful mouth God gave a man. She'd said she couldn't look at it without fantasizing about kissing him.

"I remember what you said about my mouth, too," he whispered.

The air between them crackled with energy—and promise. "Then what are you waiting for?" she asked softly.

Even though his eyes had darkened, his mouth twitched in amusement. "A sign?"

She put a hand on his shoulder to anchor herself. Without taking her eyes from his, she slowly lifted her chin and offered her lips. He took over from there, closing his mouth over hers, the feel of it so electric that she could have sworn a warm surge of energy flowed through her veins.

He kissed her gently, leisurely, as though they had all the time in the world. One of his hands gently cupped the back of her head, his fingers playing with the hair at her nape and heightening the sensations swirling through her.

She'd barely had a taste of him and already knew he was the best kisser of any man she'd ever dated. Or maybe he was simply the man whose kiss she responded to the most.

Wanting to get closer, she pressed her body against his, closed her eyes and let the warmth spread through her. She smiled against his lips.

He drew back, but only slightly. "What's funny?"

"It's embarrassing."

He trailed a hand down her back and over the swell of her hips. "We're beyond embarrassment, sweetheart."

"It's just that…" She paused, then whispered into the swell of his neck. "I was right. You do get me hot."

He gave a low growl. "That's not something you should say to a man who has his arms around you unless you want to face the consequences."

"Oh," she said in a breathy voice, "but I do."

He captured her mouth again, deepening the kiss so the heat seared through her. Her tongue dueled with his, her heart pounded against his and two words reverberated in her head.

The One.

It was too soon to know that, of course. Especially since his kiss had scrambled her brains so that she wasn't sure she could recite her own name. She only knew that she wanted the kiss to go on and on, that whenever he stopped kissing her would be too soon.

The light seemed suddenly brighter. She might have believed it was from the effect of being close to him if she hadn't heard the sound of the door opening. Connor must have heard it, too. He drew back, but still held her in his arms, almost as though he couldn't bring himself to let go.

"You're back. I—" Jaye stood in the doorway, her mouth open, her eyes wide. She was dressed in a Dora the Explorer T-shirt that covered her to mid-thigh and made her look years younger than her actual age. Her brow creased. "Were you two kissing?"

"Jaye, what are you doing out of bed?" The teenage babysitter appeared behind her, her hair and clothes rumpled as though she'd just been awakened. "Sorry, Mr. Smith. She went to sleep like two hours ago, just like you told me."

"That's okay, Erin." Sounding far more composed than Abby felt, Connor withdrew his arm from Abby but kept a hand at the small of her back.

"You were kissing, weren't you?" Jaye asked again, and Abby's stomach sank. She hadn't considered how Jaye would react to the developing relationship between her teacher and her uncle. But when Abby looked more closely at Jaye, she saw that the girl didn't seem annoyed. She seemed…pleased.

"Yes, we were kissing." Connor stepped back, the gentle pressure of his hand letting Abby know she should precede him into the house. "And you, Jaye, should be in bed."

"We should be going," Abby told Erin. "I told your parents I'd have you home by twelve-thirty and it's nearly that now. As soon as you get your stuff, we can leave."

"Sure. I'll be just a minute." Erin padded into Connor's living room, which was immediately to the right of the foyer and was decorated in golds and greens and oranges. When Abby had dropped off the teenager earlier tonight, she'd thought the warm tones didn't suit him. But now she knew she'd been wrong.

"What are you doing out of bed anyway?" Connor asked Jaye, his affectionate rustling of her hair at odds with the stern tone he tried to interject into his voice. "I thought you promised to stick to the bedtime we agreed on."

"I did. But I woke up when I heard you and Abby talking, and I wanted to remind her about the zoo tomorrow."

"I didn't forget," Abby said. "Eleven o'clock, right?"

"The zoo?" Connor's eyebrows shot up. "I didn't realize that was tomorrow."

"I told you about it days ago," Jaye said, her gaze imploring. "Remember? You said I could go."

"You can, but on one condition." He focused on Abby instead of Jaye, concentrating on her with the same intensity he had before he kissed her. "You can go if I can come, too."

With great difficulty, Abby broke the gaze and addressed Jaye. "Is it okay with you if your uncle comes, Jaye?"

"As long as I get to go, sure. Good night, then." She ran up the stairs as though somebody was chasing her.

"Something makes me think she's afraid you'll change your mind about going to the zoo," Abby said, chuckling.

"Not on your life," Connor said.

"In that case, I'll see you in about eleven hours," she

said. "But, for the record, this doesn't count as you asking me out, either."

He grinned at her, and she smiled back, looking forward to the day ahead of them. She imagined it was as bright with promise as the glow of the silvery moon.

CHAPTER SIX

ELAINE SMITH'S FEET HURT. She'd stood outside the grocery store this morning for three hours, gathering more signatures for her petition.

Just about everybody in Bentonsville who was going to sign it already had, so she'd traveled to a neighboring town, equipped with old newspaper clippings to show to anyone unfamiliar with the crime.

Her throat didn't feel any better than her feet. She was coming down with a cold but had spent the better part of the last week on the phone, trying to talk her way into meetings with her congressman and senators.

When that hadn't worked, she'd shown up at their offices and waited until the politician in question had agreed to see her. Then she'd done her level best to extract promises that a letter would be sent off to the parole board.

All the activity was taking a toll on her but she couldn't stop now. She'd never stop. Not as long as the bastard who'd taken her precious son from her had a chance in hell of getting out of prison.

She was so preoccupied that she nearly missed the turn leading to Connor's town house. At least she thought it was the right turn. She hadn't visited often enough for the route to become commonplace. She spied a corner drugstore similar to one in Bentonsville and remembered stopping there the last time she'd been in Silver Spring. Yes, this was the right way.

Just yesterday she'd told Connor she didn't have time to visit but circumstances had changed. Yesterday she hadn't known how much it cost to place an ad in the *Washington Post*. It was money she didn't have. Connor did.

She wasn't worried that he wouldn't give her the money, but a visit was better than a phone call. This way, he could write her a check. She'd deposit it first thing Monday morning, then she'd personally visit the newspaper's advertising department. She'd insist on waiting while the ad was designed. Something like that was too important to leave to chance.

The route to Connor's seemed more familiar now. The professional landscaping in front of pricey single-family homes. The row of oaks that formed a canopy over the street. The oh-so-classy three-story town houses with the brick facades where Connor lived.

She pulled to the curb in front of his town house and got out of the car. The sun shone in such a way that she could see into his garage, which was empty. She frowned. She hadn't considered that he might not be home at eleven o'clock on a Sunday morning, but perhaps he'd gone to church. She wasn't sure whether he and the girl attended services or not.

But no. This wasn't the right town house. His had a bay window over the single-car garage and showy red flowers hanging from a basket on the porch. There it was, another half block down.

A slender, pretty young woman dressed in blue jeans and a red jacket was walking up the short stack of steps to his front door. Was she Connor's girlfriend? Elaine wasn't sure if her son was involved with anyone or not.

No matter. If Connor and the woman had plans, they'd have to wait until she was through with her business.

She walked determinedly down the block toward the town house. The door was open, the young woman already inside, when Connor spotted her. He stepped onto the porch. The sunlight glinted off his brown hair, turning it golden, bathing him in a glow that made him look even more handsome than usual.

Her heart constricted, the spasm almost painful. J.D. would have looked very much like Connor had he lived. She squared her shoulders. J.D. was dead. So it was up to her to see that the cretin who'd murdered him had no life.

"Mother? It's good to see you, but did we get our signals crossed? I didn't know you were coming today," Connor said when she was within hearing range.

"I have something I need to discuss with you," Elaine stated, hoping the young woman, whoever she was, wouldn't get in the way.

"Come in." He stood aside so she could precede him into the town house.

The woman was in the foyer, a polite smile on a face that looked vaguely familiar, probably because Elaine knew someone who resembled her. Jaye stood at her elbow, unsmiling. She had J.D.'s green eyes, but otherwise looked little like a Smith with her blond hair and fair skin.

"Hello, Jaye."

The girl mumbled a greeting, then said something

about getting a sweatshirt and ran up the steps. Not only had she not inherited the dark good looks that ran in the Smith family, Elaine thought, she had bad manners to boot.

She switched her attention to the vibrant young woman, who had short hair framing a heart-shaped face. The hair didn't look familiar, but the face did.

Connor stood next to her, closer than he would have if she'd been merely an acquaintance. "Mother, let me introduce you to Abby Reed. Abby, this is my mother Elaine Smith."

Disbelief washed over Elaine as the sense of familiarity clicked into place. She stared at her, remembering how she'd looked as a girl. The long, dark hair. The coltish body. The teary eyes, as though her family had been the one that had been so grievously wronged.

The blood in Elaine's veins rushed through her like icy water in a raging river.

"You have a hell of a nerve coming here," she roared. She pointed to the door with a finger that shook with fury. "Get out. Get out this instant."

The woman had the audacity to look confused, but Elaine didn't buy her act. Abby Reed should have understood that Elaine would never welcome her kind.

"I said get out." Elaine stepped toward the motionless woman, prepared to drag her out on the street if she had to, but Connor suddenly blocked her way.

"Stop it, Mother. Abby's a guest here. You can't speak to her this way."

She stared at him agape. Why on earth would he protect such a woman? Unless…she'd wormed her way into his life without telling him who she was.

"I have every right," Elaine bit out. "Don't you know who she is?"

"She's Jaye's violin teacher," he said.

"She's more than that," she retorted, hardly able to hear herself speak above the roar of blood in her head. "She's the sister of that monster who killed your brother!"

ABBY SHOOK HER HEAD. It wasn't possible. Connor couldn't be related to the poor teenage boy who had scuffled with her brother and died. But even as her mind tried to reject the connection, stray facts shot to the surface of her brain.

The fact that the dead boy and Connor shared a resemblance. A hazy memory of a young, dark-haired man sitting between his grieving parents at the sentencing. The way Connor changed the subject whenever she brought up the past, as though something lurked there that was too painful to talk about.

Their family of three hadn't moved to Bentonsville until she was a freshman in high school, at which point Connor would have already graduated. But still she might have put the clues together sooner if Smith wasn't such a common surname.

"Stop it, Mother." Connor sounded like the voice of reason. "You're wrong. Abby's last name is Reed. She's not related to Drew Galloway."

"Ask her." Elaine Smith's command sounded like a shriek. "Ask her and see if she denies it."

Still keeping his body protectively positioned between his mother and Abby, Connor turned to her. "Tell her, Abby. Tell her she's mistaken."

His gaze was level, his eyes clear. He obviously had no doubt that she would deny the connection.

She hesitated, wishing she never had to tell him, not wanting to risk anything changing between them. On the heels of her hesitation came annoyance that she would be slow to claim her brother. He'd made a terrible mistake, yes, but that didn't change the way she felt about him.

"Your mother's not mistaken, Connor. Drew Galloway is my brother. We have different last names because we have different fathers."

He couldn't have looked more shocked. He shook his head.

"I don't understand." His voice cracked. "Why didn't you tell me?"

"Because she's trying to get in good with you before the parole hearing, that's why," Elaine Smith shouted.

"That's not true," Abby retorted, addressing Connor rather than his mother, silently pleading for him to understand. "I didn't know who you were any more than you knew who I was."

"Don't listen to her." Elaine Smith's voice, thick with anger, rose. "She probably thinks you can make me stop campaigning to keep her evil brother in prison."

Elaine Smith's commitment to keeping Drew in prison came as no surprise. One of the few friends Abby's mother had left in Bentonsville kept them abreast about the petitions and local newspaper ads.

Abby had toyed with contacting Mrs. Smith to attempt to get her to understand that Drew had been just a boy who'd made a horrendous mistake, but her mother had talked her out of it. She'd claimed it wouldn't make a difference, that Mrs. Smith had lost a son but held fast to the bitterness in her heart.

Abby's impulse was to jump to Drew's defense, but she reminded herself that this woman had lost her son because of a poor choice that Drew had made.

"I'm sorry about what happened, Mrs. Smith. I truly am. But you're wrong about me. I didn't know who Connor was until just now, when you told me."

"You're not wanted here!" Elaine Smith's face was red, her chest heaving, the veins in her temples bulging. Negative energy shot off her like bullets, causing Abby to take a step backward. "You stay away from my family and never come back."

A muffled gasp drew Abby's gaze to the stairway. Jaye stood on one of the steps, a small girl with huge eyes dressed in a sweatshirt depicting a giraffe.

"What's going on?" Jaye asked.

"Go back upstairs." Elaine Smith motioned up the stairs with a slash of her hand. "Go upstairs this instant."

Jaye didn't budge. Her face contorted with confusion. Abby longed to go to her, but couldn't risk making matters worse. "But Uncle Connor and me are going to the zoo with Abby."

"You're not going anywhere with her. Do you hear me, young lady? Now go upstairs like you were told."

"You're scaring her, Mother." Connor seemed to find his voice. *Finally,* Abby thought. Finally he'd somehow manage to defuse the situation and make things right.

"I'll scare her if I need to. I'll do anything to keep her away from that woman and her family." She directed her gaze at Jaye. "Now get upstairs, Jaye."

"No," Jaye yelled. She ran down the steps over to Abby, hugging her tight around the waist. Feeling the child's pain as acutely as her own, a lump formed in Abby's throat. Jaye choked out, "We're going to the zoo."

"Get away from my granddaughter," Elaine Smith yelled.

Tears streamed down Jaye's face. Abby stood frozen in the foyer, not sure what to do. Her eyes flew to Connor, looking for direction. Surely he didn't feel the same as his mother.

It seemed an eternity before he spoke, but it could only have been a few seconds. "I think it would be best if you left, Abby," he said in a soft, sad voice.

"Nooo," Jaye yelled.

Abby's eyes locked with Connor's. She sensed he was trying to neutralize the situation, but couldn't help feeling betrayed.

She smoothed Jaye's hair back from her anguished face. "Your uncle's right, Jaye. I should leave."

"No," the girl protested, tears streaming down her face. "We're going to the zoo."

"Today's not a good day for that." Abby gently pried the girl from her and set her away. In a softer voice that only Jaye could hear, she told her, "Maybe another time."

Feeling like she was walking the plank, she headed for the door. But not before Elaine Smith approached her.

"Stay away from my family." Her voice was low and hateful. "I'm going to see to it that your brother rots in prison."

"Stop that, Mother," Connor said, again putting his body between the two women.

Abby looked at him, hoping for something—a word

of support, an encouraging nod—but he was stone-faced. It felt as though she and his mother were on two sides of a battle and he'd already sworn his allegiance.

It wasn't to her.

She blinked back tears she wouldn't let fall. Even though her brother had been the one who'd wielded the knife, she couldn't help but feel that Connor had stabbed her in the back.

CONNOR SAT IN HIS PORSCHE in front of Abby's duplex, kneading his temples in a failed attempt to ease his headache.

It had been that kind of a day.

It had taken him hours to calm his mother, who had worked herself into such a state that she wouldn't listen to reason. She'd repeated the same assertion until it sounded like a mantra: The sister of the devil was tainted with his blood. Period.

Jaye had locked herself in her room, refusing to come out until dinner, when she'd silently picked at her food before disappearing upstairs once again.

And Abby wasn't answering his calls. He didn't blame her. He'd been so shocked when he'd discovered her connection to his brother's killer that he hadn't defended her the way he should have. Abby hadn't chosen to be Drew Galloway's sister. The family association was entirely out of her control.

He hadn't known Abby long but recognized her for a good, kind person. She was probably as disgusted by what her brother had done as he was.

He got out of the car, noticing the contrast between the previous moonlit night. Tonight's darkness had a murky gray cast and no stars twinkled from above. The time was nearly ten, too late to come calling, but he'd thought it best to wait until his mother had finally returned to Bentonsville and Jaye was in bed before leaving his town house.

His next-door neighbor Mrs. Piper, who was in town for once, had agreed to stay with the sleeping Jaye until he returned.

Tomorrow would be too late to settle this, not when he could think of nothing else.

Abby's small green Honda Civic was parked in front of the duplex, confirming his suspicion that she'd been dodging his calls. Lights shone in her bedroom, a further clue that she was home.

Drawing a deep breath, he pressed the doorbell. Long moments passed. He imagined her on the other side of the door, peering through the peephole, trying to decide whether to let him in. He wouldn't fault her if she didn't.

"Abby, please open up," he said in his most persuasive voice. "I need to talk to you."

More time went by, the seconds so long they seemed like minutes. He knocked again, louder this time. "Abby, please. I want to apologize."

The door swung open. She hadn't switched on the light inside the door, and her face was a pale oval in the darkness. She was unsmiling, her arms crossed over her chest. The grinning cartoon duck on her nightshirt contrasted sharply with the solemn lines of her face.

"I'm sorry to show up like this," he began. "I know it's late, but you wouldn't answer the phone."

Silence.

"Okay. I understand why you didn't answer. But I

need to talk to you. To tell you how terrible I feel about what happened today."

A car door slammed and one of her neighbors hopped out of the car, singing along to a song he must have heard on the radio. The young man openly watched Connor as he crossed to his apartment.

The lights were on in the unit next to hers. He could hear the faint sound of the television but imagined the occupant peeking through the blinds, the drama taking place outside the door more entertaining than the program she was watching.

"Can I come in?" he asked. When Abby didn't move from the doorway, he continued, "Not for long. Just until I say what I have to say."

In answer, she stepped aside. He hesitated, then crossed the threshold, pulling the door shut behind him, plunging them into darkness.

It lasted only a moment before she turned on the light, but Connor thought the darkness was symbolic. He needed to bring her into the light about what had happened today, make her see that it wasn't her he blamed.

"I'm sorry, Abby. I was wrong."

More silence.

He saw each one of her features clearly now. The corners of her mouth turned down. The light that came into her eyes when she smiled was dimmed. Even her complexion looked sallow.

"Jeez, Abby, aren't you going to say anything?"

Her sigh was the first sound she'd made. "What do you want me to say, Connor? Thanks for letting your mother throw me out of your house and warn me away from Jaye?"

He ran a hand over his brow. "That's what I'm trying to apologize for. I didn't handle things well. She was so upset, so unreasonable, that I didn't see another solution."

"For today?" Abby asked. "Or for always?"

He peered at her as her meaning became clear. "You can't believe that I don't want you around Jaye."

"What am I supposed to think? You didn't exactly stick up for me."

He rubbed the back of his neck, mentally reviewing the incident. The edges of it blurred like a bad dream, making it difficult for him to see it clearly. "It came as a shock. I'm sure I didn't handle things well."

"You didn't," she confirmed. "You let your mother traumatize Jaye and treat me like I was…contaminating her."

"I know. I was wrong. But you don't know the situation. My mother doesn't only blame…" He couldn't bring himself to refer to the killer as her brother. "…Galloway for what happened to J.D. She blames him for what happened to my sister, too."

It would be so much easier to have this conversation sitting down. They were steps inside the living room, but Abby showed no signs of inviting him deeper into the apartment.

"What do you mean?"

"Diana changed after J.D. died. It was like she didn't care about anything. She started skipping school and staying out until all hours of the night. And then she got pregnant with Jaye."

"So your mother blamed my brother for the pregnancy instead of herself for not keeping a closer eye on her daughter?"

Connor's spine stiffened. "My parents should have kept better track of Diana but they were devastated over losing J.D."

Her chest heaved up and down under the thin fabric of her nightshirt. He'd come to know Abby as a sensible woman. Surely she could understand the role Galloway had played in his sister's descent. The role he was still playing.

"It's not fair of your mother to treat Jaye like she's a mistake," Abby said. "It's not good for Jaye."

"I know that. And I'll talk to her about how good you are for Jaye. About what a difference I've seen in her since you brought music into her life."

He watched some of the tension seep from Abby's shoulders. "Your mother won't like that," she said. "She made it clear that she wanted me to stay away from you and Jaye."

"Jaye doesn't want that. And neither do I." He reached out and touched her cheek, softly tracing the contours of her face. "I thought we made a connection the other night. Was I wrong?"

She moistened her lips, shook her head. "No," she whispered, "you weren't wrong."

"Then let me worry about my mother. I'll explain that it's not your fault you're related to a cold-blooded killer."

"A cold-blooded killer?" she repeated, her voice strangely quiet. "Is that how you think of my brother?"

"Hell, yeah." He instantly regretted the heartfelt retort. She'd been a kid when Galloway had murdered J.D. An innocent. But he doubted he could keep the hatred from lacing his voice no matter how hard he tried.

"That's because you don't know him," she said.

For a moment, he didn't want to acknowledge he'd heard her. Because what he'd heard was a statement of support. Support? For a murderer?

"I know he was convicted for plunging a knife into my brother's chest." Again, he acknowledged the edge in his voice.

"I know that, too," she said, and he started to relax. "But I can't help thinking there were extenuating circumstances."

"A girl who preferred my brother," Connor retorted. That was the story. That Galloway had been jealous because he was sweet on a girl who'd had her head turned by J.D.

"Drew wouldn't kill anybody over a girl. He's not like that. Yes, he'd made a mess of things before your brother died. But he has a good heart, a kind soul. Something else must have happened."

Connor couldn't believe what he was hearing. "If something else happened, it would have come out. Galloway lured my brother under those bleachers, pulled out a knife and stabbed him. How many kind-hearted young men do something like that?"

She shook her head. "There had to be more to it. Drew still won't talk about it, but—"

"You're in touch with him?" Connor interrupted, hearing the incredulity in his voice. The possibility hadn't occurred to him that sweet, kind Abby would have anything more to do with him.

"Of course I am. He's my brother."

"He's a murderer." Bile rose in Connor's throat. "He's the reason my brother is dead."

"I'm sorry for your family's loss. I wish to God that it had never happened and that your brother was alive today. But Drew isn't dead. He's a boy who made a mistake."

"A mistake?" Her use of the word was so unbelievable that he couldn't stop his voice from rising. "A mistake is when you fill in the wrong answer on a test. Or when you dial a wrong number. Murder is not a mistake."

"I think it was," she said stubbornly. "I know my brother, and he wouldn't deliberately take somebody's life."

"That's exactly what he did!"

"You weren't there that night your brother died. You don't know what happened."

"Your brother pled guilty."

"He didn't want to take a chance on a trial with the town so set against him."

"I can't believe I'm hearing this. Galloway killed my brother, Abby. He tore my family apart. My parents are divorced. My sister's God only knows where. And Jaye's troubled. You've seen that for yourself."

"Drew's paying for what he did. What more do you want from him?"

"I'll tell you what I don't want. I don't want some bleeding heart to make excuses for what he did. I don't want my niece to hear anything that puts the idea in her head that J.D. might have asked for it."

"I never said that," Abby denied. "You're—"

He didn't let her finish. He felt the blood rushing to his head, the words pouring from his mouth. "She's named after him, did you know that? Jaye. For the *J* in J.D. She would have loved him, too. But because of Galloway, she never got that chance. And you say that it wasn't his fault."

"You're twisting my words. I said I thought there was more to the story than we know."

"It's the same thing. What are you going to say if Jaye asks you why Galloway killed her uncle? Will you make excuses for him then, too?"

She inclined her head. "I'm not going to turn away from my brother. I told you before. I know him. You don't. I know what he's capable of."

The crime-scene photo that Connor had insisted on viewing flashed in his mind. His brother lying in a pool of blood, his head thrown back, his eyes open, his face waxy in death. That was what Drew Galloway was capable of.

He shook his head, dragged a hand over his face. "I thought my mother was overreacting, but maybe she was on the right track. Our two families, maybe we shouldn't be around each other."

"Jaye's in my class," Abby said, her voice thick, her eyes wet with unshed tears. "I'm her teacher. I have to see her."

"You have to see her in class, not out of it. It would be best if she didn't come home with you after school anymore. I'll find another private violin teacher for her, too."

She winced as though his words had struck her, but he couldn't relieve her pain, not when he felt so much of it himself.

He met her eyes for a long moment, and in them he saw what might have been. Then he turned and left her apartment, mourning not only his brother but the end of something beautiful that had hardly had a chance to begin.

CHAPTER SEVEN

NO MATTER HOW MANY TIMES she visited the Central Correctional Institution, Abby experienced the same reactions.

A sense of panic when the gates closed behind her. An invasiveness when she walked through a metal detector, then when her belongings were searched. Sadness at the sight of the small children and teary-eyed women in the visitors' room.

An utter disbelief that the big brother who had taught her to tie her shoes had ended up here.

Here was better than the Maryland Correctional Adjustment Center in Baltimore, the maximum-security prison where the judge had originally sentenced him. That prison was reserved for the worst of the worst, the hardened criminals, most of whom should never be allowed to taste freedom again.

Drew hadn't belonged there, a belief made fact five years into his sentence when he'd been transferred to the medium-security prison located roughly midway between Frederick and Baltimore.

Abby didn't think her brother belonged here at CCI, either. A little more than a month from now, when he went before the parole board for the first time, she prayed the people in power would agree with her.

The Drew who sat across from her now was a lifetime removed from the boy who had awakened her in the mornings and made sure she breakfasted and brushed her hair and teeth before school.

That Drew had been a skinny kid with long, stringy hair and slumped shoulders, perhaps because of the weight of responsibility their mother had thrust upon him.

This Drew had hair cropped close to his head, a body sculpted from years of doing pull-ups in his cell and a face more closed than a book whose pages had been glued together.

But sometimes, like now, when he dropped into the seat across from her at a table in the spacious visiting area, a smile crept onto his face and she glimpsed the boy inside the man. The boy in whom she'd never stopped believing.

"Didn't expect to see you for another couple of weeks, sis." His voice was deeper than it used to be, raspier, as though conversation wasn't one of his prison pastimes. "You never showed on a Monday before."

She'd never before visited twice in a month, either. The trips sapped her emotionally, but she forced herself to continue them because she and her mother were Drew's only visitors. She wrote him regularly and accepted the charges on his infrequent phone calls to make up for the lack of face-to-face time.

"I didn't decide to come until this morning." She'd made up her mind in the wee hours to cancel her after-school lessons and visit Drew. Her cheeks had been damp with tears as she had lain in bed unable to sleep, thinking about the ugly things Connor had said to her.

She wished Connor were here with her now, so he could see for himself that Drew had been a boy without malice. Except her brother was a man now, the years he'd spent in prison bleeding into each other until they formed a decade. A decade lost to him forever.

"Did you smuggle me in any smokes?"

It was a question he asked every so often, as though he actually suspected she might help him defy the smoking ban that Maryland prisons had in effect.

"You know I wouldn't do something like that. You shouldn't try to get around the system, either."

He laughed as though she'd said something funny. "It's too late to turn me into a saint, little sis."

"You can't risk doing anything that will jeopardize your chance at parole. You need to think about your future and what you'll do when you get out."

"So you think I'll get parole, do you?"

"Why wouldn't you?" She didn't wait for him to answer. "You have most everything in place. A good institutional conduct record. Your GED. And didn't you say you'd found a placc to live?"

"Yeah," he said shortly. "With a friend of a friend."

"All that's left is for us to get you a job, and I have an idea about that. I'd say you're in great shape to get out of here soon."

At the slight curl of his lower lip, her body tensed. "There's something you're not telling me. I can see it on your face."

"It's nothing." He paused and shrugged, as though he could fool her into believing that this "nothing" wasn't bothering him. "Mom was here yesterday. She said there's opposition to me getting out. Letter writing. Petitions. That kind of thing."

Abby pressed her lips together. She knew of course that Elaine Smith would stop short at nothing to keep Drew in prison, but now wondered if Connor was helping in her efforts. After the unreasonable way he'd acted last night, Abby wouldn't be surprised.

"You haven't been in trouble since you've been here," she said in a rush. "They'll take that into account. They'll see that you're a good person."

Drew slouched back in his seat, his eyes hooded, his expression unreadable once more. "I killed a man, Abby. They don't call that good behavior 'round here."

"You're paying for it. You've been paying every day for the last ten years." She clenched, then unclenched her fingers. "Maybe it would help your case if you told the parole board what really happened that night."

He made a harsh noise. "Don't start this again."

"Why not? Why do you always say that? Why won't you talk about it?"

"What's done is done. I was convicted and sentenced. Talking about it won't do anybody any good."

"It would do me good to know the whole truth." She swallowed. "I know there's more to it than you've told. You're not a killer, Drew."

He leaned forward, his muscled forearms resting on the table. A dragon, its mouth breathing fire, decorated his right arm. He'd gotten it stenciled into his skin a few months before J.D. Smith had died. Abby remembered how upset her mother had been when she'd seen the tattoo for the first time. Nice boys his age didn't get tattoos, she'd said.

"Where's this coming from? Why are you bringing this up now?"

She supposed she might as well tell him. Maybe that's why she'd come. Maybe her subconscious had driven her here. "I've been spending time with J.D. Smith's brother and his niece. Yesterday, I met his mother."

He swore, a particularly nasty word. She winced, but he didn't seem to notice. "What the hell are you doing hanging around those people?"

"I met J.D.'s brother through his niece, who's one of my violin students. Smith's such a common surname that I didn't know who they were until yesterday."

"Do they know who you are?"

"They do now."

He exhaled a harsh breath. "I bet that didn't go well."

"They said some hurtful things," she acknowledged, "but that's because they don't know you like I do."

"So that's why you're here asking these questions." He shook his head. "Nothing good can come of this."

"Maybe it can." She covered his roughened hand with hers and felt his unleashed strength. "Maybe if you tell me everything that happened that night and I tell them, they'll drop their opposition."

"No." The word was harsh. He slipped his hand out from under hers and crossed his arms over his chest. "Don't make more trouble for me, Abby. Just stay away from those people."

Staying away from Connor wouldn't have been difficult a few weeks ago, but that had been before she'd discovered how he'd taken responsibility for a niece with nowhere else to go. And before they'd talked and laughed and kissed. If the opportunity had arisen, she had no doubt she would have slept with him.

And now Drew was asking her to stay away.

Something in the smile she attempted must have seemed false because he uncrossed his arms and leaned forward, his eyes boring into hers.

"Just so you know," he said gruffly. "I'm glad you're on my side."

At the realization of how few people supported him, she blinked back sudden tears. "You're my brother. I love you. Of course I'm on your side."

"So you'll stay away from those Smiths?"

"That won't be hard, Drew. It's not like they want to be around me."

Her heart clutched, but it couldn't be helped. She couldn't abandon her brother. She wouldn't. And she feared that's what it would take for her to be with Connor.

CHAPTER EIGHT

THE SILENCE WAS GIVING CONNOR a headache.

Jaye sat next to him in the passenger seat of his Porsche, her head turned away from him as he maneuvered through the early morning traffic.

"You'll have to talk to me eventually, Jaye," he said.

Silence, uncomfortably reminding him of the way Abby had treated him when he'd come to her apartment to apologize. He hoped the outcome with Jaye would be better, but so far she hadn't provided much encouragement.

When he'd informed her that Abby would no longer either give her private lessons nor babysit her after school, she'd knocked over a lamp, shattering the bulb.

Then she'd dashed up to her room and locked the door, refusing to come out until she'd gotten so hungry he'd caught her sneaking food from the refrigerator.

He'd tried to talk to her, but she hadn't responded with anything more than angry glares.

She'd been so uncooperative this morning getting ready for school that she'd missed the bus. Even with Connor driving, she'd arrive after the late bell.

He stopped at a red light. In the car next to them was a girl about Jaye's age who was chattering nonstop to the man in the driver's seat.

As far as Connor could see, they didn't have the specter of a murdered relative between them.

"I'll call the after-school program when I get to work and let them know you'll be staying with them today." He kept his voice matter-of-fact, as though they'd mutually agreed on this plan of action. "I won't be able to leave work much before six, but I don't want you to worry. I'll be there in time to pick you up."

She didn't respond, her silence communicating what she thought of his plan. He sighed.

"I know you don't agree with my decision, but some day when you're older you'll understand that grown-ups have to do what they think is best."

She whirled to face him, her face pinched and unhappy. "I'll never understand. Never!"

Her broken silence took him by such surprise that he didn't notice the light had turned green until the driver behind him honked his horn. He transferred his foot to the gas pedal. "That's because you don't understand the circumstances."

"Yes, I do. I heard Grandma. I know what Abby's brother did."

He phrased his next words carefully. "Then you should appreciate what an awkward position that puts us in. Drew Galloway caused our family a lot of heart-ache."

"He did. Abby didn't."

Abby had, however, stood squarely in the corner of the man who had murdered Jaye's uncle.

"Why can't I go to Abby's place after school?" Now that Jaye had started to speak to him again, the words spilled out of her, like water pouring from a broken dam.

"Abby didn't do anything wrong. It isn't fair. It's like you're punishing her just like you're punishing me."

"It's more complicated than that," Connor said and attempted to explain. "Abby's still in touch with her brother."

"So?"

"So he killed J.D."

"I don't care about her stupid brother. I don't care about stupid J.D., either."

"You shouldn't talk that way, Jaye. J.D. was your uncle. You were named after him."

"Abby's my friend. She's who I care about. She's nice to me. I didn't ask to be named after some dead guy."

He pulled up to the circular drive in front of the school and put the car in Park. The child's furious words reverberated in his head.

"That's not fair," he said. "J.D. would have loved you."

"Well, I hate him. He's the reason Grandma's so mean and Mom's not here. I would have stabbed him myself."

"Jaye…" he began to admonish her, but she'd al-ready opened the door and jumped out, slamming it behind her.

She ran up the sidewalk that led to the front of the school, her backpack banging against her hip, her thin legs furiously eating up the ground.

A feeling of inadequacy spread through him. He'd spoken to Jaye of being grown-up, of doing what was right. But he'd proved yet again that he didn't know the first thing about parenting a child. He hadn't even been able to adequately explain why she shouldn't spend copious amounts of time with the sister of the man who'd murdered her uncle.

Jaye stopped before she reached the glass double doors and looked back at him. He had a moment's fear that she wouldn't go through the door but take off in another direction. But then she opened it and disappeared inside the building, rescuing him from having to figure out how he'd deal with her truancy.

He sat outside the school for another five minutes until he was relatively certain she'd checked in at the office.

Just in case she was hiding out somewhere waiting for him to leave so she could bolt, he called the school to make sure she'd reported in.

Then he drove slowly away from the curb, one of the accusations Jaye had made crowding his mind. She'd claimed he was punishing Abby for her half brother's crime. Was he?

He thought of how she'd stuck up for Galloway when he'd given her a chance to condemn what he'd done.

No. He wasn't punishing Abby. By taking the position she had, she was the one hurting him.

JAYE BENT OVER HER VIOLIN, trying to force music from it, but the bow kept squeaking against the strings. She glanced up at the music on the stand and saw that the next note was a D.

She and Abby had gone over the basic fingering for all the whole notes during their private lessons, but she couldn't remember where to position her fingers. She took a guess and almost clamped her hands over her ears when the violin emitted another terrible squeak.

Abby—Miss Reed—was suddenly behind her, her

voice encouraging and nonjudgmental. "Keep the bow level, Jaye. That way you'll get better sound from the instrument."

Jaye leveled her bow and looked back at the music. This time the next note was C. The fingering eluded her so she took another guess. The note she struck was obviously wrong, the sound out of sync with the rest of the class.

This wouldn't be happening if she'd been allowed to continue going to Abby's after school.

It had been five days since her grandma yelled at Abby, but it seemed a lot longer. Jaye had only missed one private lesson so far but she hated practicing by herself. When she practiced at Abby's, the teacher gave her pointers. But now she couldn't even play the violin until she got home from after-school care. And nobody was there to help her.

She tried playing another note, but this time the instrument wailed a most pitiful cry.

Frustration boiled up in her and she flung the bow. It hit the boy sitting in front of her on the back of the head before bouncing off a music stand and clattering to the linoleum floor.

The music abruptly halted, and the students in the room gaped at her.

She was busted, and she didn't even care.

"Are you okay, Timmy?" Abby rushed over to Timmy Lapata, who rubbed his head even though she hadn't thrown the bow hard.

"Yeah," he answered, casting an unhappy glance over his shoulder at Jaye. She had a moment's remorse, because she liked Timmy okay. Once at lunch, he'd given her his barbecue potato chips. Yeah, he didn't like the flavor. But he'd still given them to her.

"Jaye Smith, apologize to Timmy this instant. Then pick up that bow," Abby ordered.

She thought about refusing but it wasn't Abby's fault her Uncle Connor was a jerk. She mumbled an apology to Timmy, wishing she could take back what she'd done. She slowly got out of her chair, bent down and picked up the bow. Then she gazed at the floor.

She knew the drill. She'd be sent to the principal's office. Mr. Turturro, who was overweight and bald and wore so much cologne he made her sneeze, would give her detention.

As though that was any worse than the school's stupid after-school program.

The principal might even suspend her. He'd threatened as much the last time she'd been in his office.

"Now put your instrument in its case, move your chair to the corner of the room and sit quietly until class is over."

Jaye's head jerked up. Had she heard wrong? Abby hadn't said anything about visiting Principal Turturro. And she hadn't sounded all that mad. She sounded... disappointed.

Jaye bit her lip. She could stand lecturing. But she hated it when adults let you know they were disappointed in you. That made her feel like more of a loser.

She trudged to the corner and sat there for the rest of the class period while the other students worked on the song that had frustrated her. If Abby would work with her again, she knew she could learn how to play it.

Her eyes watered. She dashed the back of her hand against them. Crying never did her any good, and she wasn't going to start now. What she needed was a plan. By the time the bell rang, she'd come up with a wonderful one.

"Remember to practice at least twenty minutes a day. That's the only way you'll improve," Abby told Jaye's classmates. To Jaye, she said. "Wait right there, young lady. I need to have a word with you."

Jaye wasn't going anywhere. She needed to talk to Abby, too. When the room had cleared, Abby pulled up a chair beside her and sat down. She didn't smile. Neither did she raise her voice. "What was that about, Jaye? Why did you throw your bow?"

She sucked her lower lip into her mouth so it wouldn't tremble. "I kept squeaking," she said. "And I couldn't remember how to play the notes."

"You could have raised your hand and asked for help. Letting your temper get the best of you was not the right way to handle it."

"I know, and I'm sorry," Jaye said and put the first part of her plan into action. "But I really want to get better."

"If you practice, you will get better."

"I need lessons, too. That's what you told Uncle Connor."

Abby hesitated. "I'm sure he'll get you another private teacher if you ask him. I can give you a sheet with names and phone numbers."

"I don't want another teacher. I want you. Can't I come home with you today after school?"

The corners of Abby's mouth turned down. "You know you can't."

"We don't have to tell," Jaye said. "You can drive me back to after-school care just before he picks me up."

Abby sighed heavily. "That won't work, Jaye."

"Yes, it will. Uncle Connor won't know I'm not going. Not if you tell the ladies there I only need to be watched for a couple minutes a day."

"That's not what I meant, Jaye. It won't work because it's wrong. We've talked about this before, and you promised to stop lying. And that's what you're suggesting we do. We are not going to mislead your uncle about where you are, and that's final."

The stupid tears formed in her eyes again, making it hard to see. "But don't you want to be with me?"

"Of course I do, but it's not that simple."

"But I don't care what your brother did. It doesn't have anything to do with you."

"Your uncle thinks differently."

Jaye felt her face heat. "I hate him."

Abby put a hand on her arm. "Don't say that, Jaye. He's only doing what he thinks is right for you."

Jaye angrily shook off her hand. "I hate you, too. If you really wanted me with you, you'd find a way."

Tightly clutching her violin case in one hand, she got to her feet and started to walk toward the classroom exit.

Abby stepped in front of her, stopping her progress and looking nearly as unhappy as Jaye felt. "We can't leave things this way, Jaye. I'm worried about you."

"I need to go," Jaye said. The next class started in minutes.

She walked around Abby and out into the hall. She didn't hate Abby, not really. Already she was sorry she'd said she did, but she couldn't take it back now, not when the tears she'd been trying so hard to hold back fell down her face like rain.

THE APARTMENT SMELLED of the spaghetti sauce Abby was stirring, a fragrant mixture of tomatoes, basil, oregano and ground beef.

Her mother peered over her shoulder into the pot. "Mmm. That looks good. You're a much better cook than I am."

"I was a better cook than you when I was thirteen," Abby said without thinking. She sensed her mother stiffen and turned around to see that her smile had faded.

"You're right," her mother said in a flat voice. "You were. And Drew had to learn to cook at an even earlier age. I still feel bad about that."

Abby put a hand on her arm. "I wasn't trying to hurt your feelings, Mom. It just came out. I understood that we had to cook our own dinner because you were working to support us."

Her mother sighed. "Then I should be the one cooking you dinner now."

Abby made a face. "No offense, Mom. But after that charred turkey you served last Thanksgiving, I'll pass."

Her comment had the desired effect. Her mother laughed. "I'd always heard you needed to cook turkey for a long time. I didn't know it could burn."

"Lucky for us that you had those TV dinners in your fridge."

"I always have those. That's why I'm so happy when you invite me to dinner."

Abby checked on her pot of water, verified that it had

begun to boil and broke strands of pasta in half before adding them to the water. "I love having you over, and this way I don't have to be alone Friday night."

"What about the man you went out with last weekend?" her mother asked, a twinkle in her eye. "Is he busy on Fridays?"

Pain shafted through Abby, barely dulled since their last encounter five days ago. To buy herself time before answering, she went to the refrigerator and took out the bag of cut greens for the salad. Keeping her eyes averted, she said, "That didn't work out."

"What do you mean it didn't work out? You called when you got home from your date and said he was wonderful."

Abby had forgotten about that. She'd been so jazzed after their cosmic bowling date that she hadn't been able to go to sleep immediately. Remembering that her mother worked a late shift at the hospital, she'd phoned just as her mother was arriving home. And gushed.

"He wasn't as wonderful as I thought." A wonderful man wouldn't have allowed his mother to yell at her and kick her out of his home. A wonderful man wouldn't have treated her like a pariah when he found out she was in touch with her brother.

"What about his niece? Weren't you babysitting her after school?"

"I was." Abby dumped some of the salad greens into a bowl. "I'm not now."

"But you went on and on about that girl and her violin. And him, too. He sounded like such a good man, taking care of his niece when nobody else would."

Abby said nothing because her mother's impressions

mirrored her own. But people had layers. No man was one hundred percent good, just as no man was entirely bad. With Drew as a brother, she knew that better than anyone.

"What happened, Abby?" Her mother's voice was gentle, inviting confidences Abby wasn't ready to share.

"I went to see Drew on Monday," she announced.

Her mother's winged eyebrows, so like Drew's, rose. Abby wasn't sure whether her reaction was due to the abrupt change of subject or because of the subject itself. "You did? On a weekday?"

"Yes."

"That's not like you. And didn't you visit a week ago Sunday, too? You never go that often."

Neither of them stated the reason for Abby's infrequent visits. Only fifteen when Drew had been convicted and sentenced to a maximum-security facility, Abby had bravely insisted she accompany her mother the first time she'd visited Drew in prison. That was as far as her bravery had taken her.

Abby hadn't been able to overcome her growing panic as she and her mother had passed through metal detectors, endured a pat-down search and had steel doors close behind them. Before they'd seen Drew, Abby had begun to hyperventilate. Her mother had taken her home, and Abby hadn't visit Drew again until they'd transferred him to a medium-security prison five years ago.

"I had some things I wanted to talk to him about," Abby said. She opened a kitchen cabinet, took out two ceramic plates gaily decorated with tiny yellow flowers and set them down on the kitchen table.

"What things?"

"The lead I have for a job for him, for one thing," she said, then realized she'd mentioned a job to Drew but hadn't gotten around to discussing details. "The custodian at school has a brother who owns an auto-body shop. He says his brother might have an opening."

"Does the custodian know Drew's in prison?"

Abby pressed her lips together. She hadn't been able to get that part out. "No, but he's not the one who owns the shop. I'm going to stop by and talk to his brother. I figured he'll be more understanding if I see him in person."

"He'll probably say no, Abby."

She paused in the act of removing napkins from a nearby closet. "I won't know that until I try."

"A lot of employers won't hire ex-cons."

She placed the napkins to the right of the plates and went to the silverware drawer for forks. "Why are you being so negative, Mom?"

Her mother's chest rose, then deflated. "I'm sorry. I know you're trying to help your brother. But I'd hate for you to go through all this trouble for nothing."

"It's not for nothing." She took out the forks and shut the drawer with a bang. "His parole hearing is soon. The better formed his plans, the better his chances of getting out. You heard he's lined up a place to live, right?"

Her mother nodded shortly. Even if Dee Dee's apartment had more than one bedroom, Drew couldn't have stayed with her. Parolees were required to live in the state in which they'd been incarcerated.

"Did he tell you who offered him a place to stay?" her mother asked.

Abby tried to remember what her brother had said

as she returned to the table with the forks. "Not by name. I think he said it was a friend of a friend."

"I wonder which friend." Her mother sounded worried. "Drew had a habit of hanging out with a bad crowd."

"Not all of his friends were like that," Abby said. "Sometimes good kids hang out in bad crowds. Look at Drew."

"Drew's in jail, Abby. He killed somebody."

"That's the other thing I wanted to talk to Drew about." She stirred the boiling pasta with slow strokes before fastening her gaze on her mother. She couldn't think of a tactful way to raise the question so she blurted it out. "What do you think really happened that night J. D. Smith was killed?"

Her mother sighed. Abby couldn't see anything in her eyes but her pupils. "I think your brother stabbed the boy, and he died."

"But why? Why would Drew do something like that? I still can't believe it was over a girl. I know there had to be more to what happened."

Her mother kneaded her forehead, suddenly looking older than her forty-five years. "It serves no purpose to dredge this up. Even if you're right and the whole story hasn't come out, what good would it do to learn it now?"

"Drew's worried about the opposition to his parole."

Her mother was silent for a moment. "He should be, judging by the ad in this morning's paper."

"Ad?" Abby's heart hammered with dread. "What ad?"

The newspaper lay on a chair in the corner of the kitchen. Abby had hurriedly leafed through it this morning after sleeping late but hadn't yet had the chance to get back to it.

Her mother picked out one of the sections and turned to an inside page. She spread the paper open on the empty side of the table and gestured to a sizeable ad.

DON'T SET THE KILLER FREE, the big type screamed.

Abby's stomach pitched. She covered it with her hand and hurriedly scanned the rest of the ad, which told of Drew's upcoming parole hearing and urged newspaper readers to write letters of protest to the parole board.

"Who placed this?" Abby asked.

"It's in the small print at the end of the ad," her mother answered.

Abby didn't realize she held her breath as she searched for the source until it left her lungs in a whoosh. The ad had been placed by Elaine Smith. Connor's name wasn't mentioned.

"See what I mean about trying to find out the rest of the story about what happened that night? It might make a difference to Mrs. Smith if she knew the whole truth."

Her mother shook her head. "We might already know the whole truth. And I remember Elaine Smith from Bentonsville. If you'd met her, you'd understand how much she hates your brother."

"I have met her," Abby said quietly.

"Where? When? How could you have met her?"

The preparations for the dinner forgotten, Abby blew out a breath. Now there could be no dodging the question of why she and Connor were no longer seeing each other.

"There's something I haven't told you," she said.

"That man I went out with last Friday, his name is Connor Smith. Elaine Smith is his mother."

Her mother's hand flew to her throat. It was unnecessary to add that she was no longer involved with either Jaye or Connor Smith because of Drew. Because of Drew, they'd already had too many bad things happen.

"How could that be?" her mother asked. "How could you have gone out with this man?"

"I didn't know who he was until I met his mother," Abby explained in a calm voice at odds with the roiling of her stomach. It still rankled that Elaine Smith had accused her of trying to deceive Connor. "I met him through his niece, Jaye, the one I was babysitting after school. Neither of us talked about our families."

"You can't see him," her mother stated, her voice louder than was customary. Abby stared at her in surprise. Her mother had never been the type to issue ultimatums. "It won't do anyone any good."

Something that felt suspiciously like rebellion boiled up in Abby. But that was crazy because continuing a relationship with Connor Smith was a moot point.

"There's nothing to worry about. It's not like he has any interest in seeing me." In an attempt to hide how much that bothered her, Abby turned to the stove.

The phone rang, a welcome diversion. She picked it up with her right hand while stirring the sauce with her left. "Hello."

"Abby, is Jaye with you?" It was Connor's voice, so filled with panic that she squeezed the receiver.

"No, she's not. Why?"

"She hasn't been at after-school care today. They have a note that says she's with you."

"I didn't sign a note, Connor."

Beside her, she was aware of her mother growing very still.

"That's what I was afraid of. It doesn't look like an adult's handwriting." Controlled panic laced his syllables. "Did she say anything about coming over to your place after school?"

"She did. She had this crazy plan about having me return her to school before you were due to pick her up. She was pretty upset when she left my class. But then I contacted the guidance counselor, who talked to her and told me everything was okay."

"Evidently not."

"School let out at three o'clock," Abby said, thinking aloud. "I stopped at the grocery store on the way home, but I've been here since three-thirty. If she took the Metro, that would have been plenty of time to get to my place."

There were a few seconds of silence at the other end of the line. "I think I should go to the police."

"I think so, too," Abby whispered, her heart seizing. *Please, God,* she prayed. *Please don't let anything bad have happened to Jaye.*

"You have my cell number. Call me if you think of anything."

"Okay, but I—" She stopped in the middle of her thought as another occurred to her. "Wait. Don't hang up. I might know where she is."

"Then I'll pick you up in front of your place in about five minutes."

The drive from the school took longer than that. "But aren't you still at after-care?"

"I was so sure Jaye was with you, I called en route to your place. Five minutes. Maybe less. Be ready."

He rang off. She hung up the phone and hurried to the corner of the kitchen where she'd dumped her purse.

"Abby? What's going on?"

She'd forgotten her mother's presence in her haste to get out the door. "Jaye's missing. I've got to go."

She shoved her feet into the medium heeled dress shoes she'd worn to work, vaguely noting they didn't match her lightweight pair of red sweats and short-sleeved T-shirt.

"With Connor Smith? Is that who you're going with?"

"I have to go with him, Mom. Jaye's only nine years old."

"I know, honey," her mother said.

Abby slanted her a grateful look, then opened the door and waited until Connonr's expensive Porsche drove up to the duplex. She ran for the idling car, her thoughts fixed on finding Jaye before danger did.

CHAPTER NINE

CONNOR'S HEART RACED, the sensation similar to how it felt when he did interval work on the high-school track near his home. But fear instead of a desire to keep in shape propelled his heart now.

He watched Abby rush out of her apartment and over to his car, her short hair rustling in the light wind.

A middle-aged woman opened the door and watched her go. Even from a distance and after ten years, Connor recognized her as the woman who'd sat behind Drew Galloway in the courtroom: the killer's mother. Also Abby's mother.

But he couldn't think about that relationship now, not with Jaye missing. Abby had barely stepped into the car when he asked, "Where do you think she is?"

"The public library." She shut the door and pulled on her seat belt. "Not the one around the corner. The branch a few blocks from the elementary school."

He peeled away from the curb, squashing the urge to speed through the parking lot, and retraced his path, winding through her neighborhood, frustrated that he couldn't drive faster because of its residential nature.

"The library has listening stations where you can put on headphones and sample music to check out," she explained as he turned south on still-busy Georgia Avenue toward Silver Spring. Here, he sped. "We went there a couple weeks ago and she'd been agitating to go back before…"

She didn't finish the sentence, but he knew what she'd been about to say. *Before I met your mother and everything imploded.*

"Did you call the police?" she asked.

He shook his head. "Not yet. They'll want me to come to the station and file a report and that'll take time. I thought it'd be better to check out the places she might be first. God, I hope you're right. I hope she's there."

Her hand, soft and warm, briefly covered his on the steering wheel.

"We'll find her, Connor. I know we will."

His racing heart calmed. Not a lot, but enough that he no longer heard the rush of blood in his ears. He nodded. The hurt and the anger that had been in her voice when they'd last been together was gone, replaced by concern.

"It should have occurred to me that Jaye would do something like this," Abby said. "I had a problem with her in class today. She threw her bow, not out of malice but because she was frustrated. I talked to her, but she was too upset to listen."

"You couldn't have known what would happen. You told the school counselor. What else could you have done?"

"I could have found Jaye after school, checked to see if she was ready to talk."

"Jaye hasn't talked much all week," he told her. "She

shuts herself in her room, but I don't know what she's doing in there other than playing her violin. I doubt it's her homework, because I've been getting e-mails again from her teachers saying she isn't turning it in."

"Did you talk to her about it?"

"Me and the school counselor both. It's like talking to a stone. I can't help thinking I did something wrong. If it's anybody's fault that she's missing, it's mine."

"You're doing the best you can," Abby said softly. "It's not your fault."

But it was his fault that Jaye no longer had Abby in her day-to-day life. That had been his decision, and he knew in his gut that decision had led Jaye to run away.

If that was what she'd done.

Panic gripped him again. Jaye was out there somewhere all alone, a vulnerable young girl who thought she knew how to take care of herself but didn't.

Please God let her be in the library.

"The library's up ahead on the left," Abby instructed. "The parking lot's on the far side of the building."

Connor had never been to this branch of the library. It was a ubiquitous two-story structure that blended into the surrounding scenery so that it was barely noticeable. Connor noticed it tonight. Nightfall was still a few hours away, but clouds obscured the sun. Lights were visible from every one of the library's many windows, causing it to shine like a beacon.

He pulled into the parking lot, almost choking in frustration when he didn't immediately spot an empty space. He'd decided to damn the consequences and double park when Abby cried out, "There's a space."

He swung his Porsche into the last spot at the end of

the lot, and they both hopped out of the car. He extended Abby a hand as they rushed together toward the front door. The contact felt so reassuring that he didn't let go as they entered the building.

The hushed atmosphere inside the library seemed wrong. He wanted to hear a television blaring, children laughing, Jaye playing the violin.

A fair number of patrons milled about, some standing patiently at the checkout counter, others perusing the aisles of books, still others seated at the computers that held the library catalog.

Jaye was nowhere in sight.

"The listening stations are on the second floor," Abby told him in a loud whisper.

He let her take the lead as she headed for a staircase. A mother and her child descended the steps in the opposite direction, and she dropped his hand so they could pass.

"This way," she said when they reached the top of the stairs.

His heart lodged halfway between his chest and his throat, he followed her into the area where the library had set up the listening stations. They were nothing more than posts equipped with headsets positioned next to cushy orange chairs.

A long-limbed teenage girl with her eyes closed swayed to music only she could hear. A man in tweed leaned his head on the back rest, a smile of his face. A young boy listened with a curl to his lip.

Jaye wasn't there.

"I was so sure this is where she'd be," Abby said, the bitterness of disappointment thick in her voice. "When we came here before, she loved listening to the classical CDs. She said she could have stayed here for hours."

Frightful scenarios played out in Connor's mind—Jaye snatched by a stranger, hurt in a hospital, unconscious in a ditch. He tried to draw a deep breath but couldn't. Forcing the images from his mind, he considered their next step.

"Now we need to go to the police."

Abby's soft sob cemented the seriousness of the situation, except when he looked at her, she wasn't sobbing.

"Did you hear that?" she asked.

He nodded, and by silent agreement they grew quiet. They heard the sob again, muffled but definitely a sob. A young girl's sob. The sound seemed to come from the audio books section.

They ventured forward together, but a quick scan of the section showed no weeping girl. Connor saw no one at all.

But there was the sob again, louder this time. It seemed to be coming from the end of the aisle. He zeroed in on the location, covering the ground with long steps. And there was Jaye, curled up in a miserable ball.

He nearly dropped to his knees in relief.

"Jaye." The name burst from him, a rough, guttural sound.

The girl's blond head jerked up, the tears damp on her face. She focused first on him, then on Abby, before trying to back up against the shelf. But there was nowhere to go. "Get away from me."

"You're already in a lot of trouble, young lady. Don't make it worse." He knew it was the wrong thing to say as soon as the words left his lips, but it was too late to take them back.

Her young face filled with a combination of misery and defiance. "I don't care what you do to me. Do you hear me? I don't care."

Abby crouched down beside Jaye, her eyes steady on his niece's face. "What your uncle means is that he was worried about you, honey. We both were."

"Liar," she said, the tears streaking down her face. "You said you didn't want me at your place."

"I said we couldn't lie to your uncle about where you were after school."

"Why not? He doesn't want me at his house." She wiped the tears from her cheeks with an angry motion. "My mom doesn't want me, either. Or else I wouldn't even be here."

Connor stood speechless, shocked into silence by her onslaught of emotion. She resembled a cornered, injured animal, ready to strike out at anybody who tried to help her.

"That's not true, Jaye," Abby whispered in a soothing voice. "Both your uncle and I care about you and want you with us. That's why we argued."

Jaye's short-lived bravado crumpled, and her lower lip trembled. Abby drew her into her arms, and then the tears came, streaming unchecked down Jaye's face.

"So scared, Abby," she said between hiccupping sobs. "Couldn't figure out how to buy a Metro ticket. Walked here. Nobody talked to me. So alone."

"It's okay, honey." Abby smoothed the hair back from the girl's despondent face as she made soothing noises. "Connor and I are here now. Everything's going to be all right."

Something thickened in Connor's throat as he watched

them, the innocent girl who'd been abandoned by her mother and the woman who refused to desert her guilty-as-sin brother.

But at that moment, Abby Reed didn't seem like the half sister of the man who'd murdered his brother.

She seemed like somebody who was on their side.

ABBY SOFTLY CLOSED THE DOOR of the guest room where Jaye was staying while she lived with Connor. The room was beautifully decorated, no doubt by the skillful hands of an interior designer. The quilt on the bed was a tasteful blend of earth tones, which complemented the creamy curtains and highly polished mahogany furniture.

A nine-year-old girl should be sleeping somewhere heavy on frills and the color pink, with clutter on every available surface and posters of teen heartthrobs adorning the walls.

But Connor was doing the best job he could, Abby reminded herself. Despite today's high drama, that was pretty darn good for a man who hadn't expected to find himself as guardian to a niece he barely knew.

Holding onto the wooden railing, Abby descended the steps to the ground floor. Since she'd given in to Jaye's pleas to stay until the girl's bedtime, she'd have to call a cab to take her home. But first, she needed to deal with Connor.

He was in the family room where she and Jaye had left him, sitting on his burnt orange leather sofa and reading a copy of *Sports Illustrated*. As soon as she entered the room, he put down the magazine.

"Is Jaye okay?"

"As okay as can be expected, considering everything

that happened tonight. She's pretty worn out, so I think she'll drop right off to sleep."

He didn't take his eyes from her as he digested the information, and she realized they hadn't been alone since their anxiety-filled car trip to the library.

The entire night had been almost surreal. After they'd found Jaye in the library, the girl had clung to Abby, tearfully begging her not to leave them. Inviting Jaye and Connor to her apartment, where a spaghetti dinner and her mother waited, had been out of the question. But so had abandoning them.

She'd called her mother to apologize and inform her that they'd found Jaye, but she wouldn't be back until late, keeping her plans for the rest of the evening as vague as possible.

Then she'd let herself get talked into accompanying Jaye and Connor to his town house, where they'd ordered take-out pizza and watched a DVD Connor had picked up earlier in the week for Jaye.

In the movie, an awkward teenager being raised by a single mother discovered the father she'd never known had been royalty and she was a real-life princess. While they watched, Abby wondered what was going on inside Jaye's head. Was she envisioning a fairy-tale background for the father she didn't know?

Abby didn't find out because the fantasy playing out on Connor's high-definition television set had effectively allowed them not to talk about reality. Either the reality of Jaye's parentage or of what had happened tonight.

"You disapprove of the way I'm handling Jaye, don't you?" Connor asked, his gaze intent.

She hesitated. "I didn't say that."

"Then I will." He crossed then uncrossed his legs. He had on the same cream-colored dress shirt he'd worn to work, but he'd removed his tie and unfastened the first few buttons, revealing the strong column of his neck. "I don't know what the hell I'm doing."

"You shouldn't be so hard on yourself. You're doing the best you can." She hadn't been aware of moving toward him, but suddenly she was standing beside the sofa.

"My best doesn't seem to be good enough." Lines of worry etched his face. "I don't know anything about raising a nine-year-old girl, especially one as unhappy as Jaye."

Abby sat down beside him on the buttery-soft sofa and angled her body toward him. "I know she's seeing the school counselor, but maybe it's time to get some outside help."

"I've thought the same thing myself. Apparently she doesn't say much to the school counselor."

"Does the counselor have a theory about why?"

"She thinks it's a passive-aggressive response. She says that Jaye is an angry little girl." He sighed. "But I already knew that much."

"Having her mother leave like that couldn't have been easy on her. Neither can not having a father."

He peered at her, his eyes troubled, the softening of his mouth causing him to appear vulnerable. "Has she talked to you about her father?"

"The only time she mentioned a father was when she tried to get me to believe you were him. But I know first hand that it's not easy to grow up without one. Mine left my mother when I was a baby."

"That must have been rough."

She'd come to terms with the situation a long time ago but found it still hurt to talk about. "Not as rough as some kids have it. He made it crystal clear he had no interest in being a father so that made it easier for me in the long run."

"Easier? How could your father abandoning you make your life easier?"

If her brother hadn't been such a hot-button issue, she would have told Connor about Drew's dad. A warehouse foreman on the waterfront of Baltimore, he'd been killed on the job when a crane swung wide and he didn't jump back quickly. Drew once told her he believed his life would have gone differently if not for that crane.

"I never had false expectations," she said instead of relating the story. "Since Jaye doesn't know who her father is, she probably fantasizes that, if he knew about her, he'd love her and want her with him. The higher she builds those hopes, the farther she'll fall if they don't come true."

"You mean when they don't come true," Connor said. "Diana doesn't know who Jaye's father is, so Jaye will never know, either."

"Exactly," Abby said, sympathy for the child taking the place of her personal pain.

Connor gazed at her with such intensity, it seemed as though he was trying to see inside her. "There's something I don't understand. If your father left your mother when you were a baby, you never really knew him. So why didn't you have those fantasies?"

"I knew of him," she said. "Don't get me wrong, my

mother never bad-mouthed him. But as I got older, it became pretty clear she'd married him on the rebound after her first husband died."

"You never tried to contact him?"

She started to give her stock reply about there being no point in it, but found she couldn't dodge his question. "Once. When I was seventeen," she said quietly. "I tracked down his phone number. I was so nervous when I dialed that I had to start over three times."

The old hurt rose up and grasped her by the throat, cutting off her narrative. She'd never before confided this story to anyone. Not to Drew. Not even to her mother.

"What happened?" Connor prompted.

She affected a shrug. "He told me never to call him again and hung up."

She stated the conclusion as matter of factly as possible, but Connor's eyes reflected the emotions churning inside her. Anger, pain, regret. She saw something else in his expression, too: understanding. Because her vignette went a long way toward explaining why she'd been so disapproving when she believed him to be Jaye's absentee father.

He gently squeezed her shoulder and looked deep into her eyes. "I'm sorry."

"It was a long time ago." She blinked, deliberately breaking eye contact, and changed the subject. She needed time to rebuild her armor. "Speaking of Diana, have you heard from her?"

He didn't immediately answer and she feared he might try to continue the conversation about her father. But then his hand fell away from her shoulder.

"She's left messages on my answering machine at work letting me know she's okay. But it's clear she doesn't want to talk to me. Otherwise, she would have called during business hours." He tapped his chin. "I'm thinking of hiring a private investigator to find her."

"You can't force her to reclaim custody of Jaye."

"No, but I can make sure she really is okay." The firmness of his voice contrasted with the worry lines that appeared around his mouth and between his brows. "It's still hard for me to believe her life has gone the way it has. She was such a sweet, happy kid before…"

His voice trailed off, but Abby easily finished the sentence. Before Drew murdered their brother.

Connor had told her before about his sister's life spiraling out of control. She'd felt badly for the girl Diana had been, pregnant and alone, without the support of either her parents or her baby's father. But the blame for what had happened to Diana shouldn't fall on Drew's shoulders, too.

"Some smart women just make poor choices," she said. "You can't be sure things would have been different for Diana even if your brother hadn't died."

He sucked in a breath. "You can't really believe that."

"Why not? Take my mother, for example. She's a good woman, with a good head on her shoulders, yet she had a baby by a man who left her, then moved from state to state so the law couldn't find him and make him pay child support."

"You said your mother married on the rebound."

Abby sighed, dismayed that she couldn't get her point across. "She did. But that was a choice, too. I'm trying to say that everybody needs to take responsibility for themselves and their choices. Me. You. Diana. My mother. It's too easy to blame somebody else when things go wrong."

"My brother's dead." His voice was flinty. "By your logic, does that mean I shouldn't blame your brother for murdering him?"

Abby rose from the sofa, finishing the job of putting distance between them. He'd done it figuratively. Now she was doing it literally. The chasm between them that had closed earlier tonight gaped open like a yawning crater.

"Talking about this isn't getting us anywhere. I should call a cab," she said, backing away from the sofa. She felt his bitterness toward her brother filling up the room and had to suppress an urge to rush out the door. But she had something she needed to say first, something she owed to his niece, who had gotten caught up in a silent war a child couldn't begin to understand. "About Jaye. You should make other arrangements for her. If you send her back to the school-based program at Blue Moon Elementary next week, she won't stay."

"What about you?"

"I suppose I can ask around and find out what kind of child-care arrangements the parents of my other students have. Maybe I could get you some referrals."

"That's not what I meant." He got to his feet, and she was struck by how tall he was, easily eight or nine inches taller than her. "Would you be willing to resume our previous arrangement?"

She felt her mouth drop open, but no sound escaped.

"I know it's a lot to ask after what happened the other

day…." He glossed over the ugly incident with his mother. "But we both know Jaye won't be happy unless she's with you."

Abby was well aware of that. Connor tried his best, but the girl was emotionally fragile after all that had happened. Jaye's grandmother, obviously, hadn't helped the situation.

"I don't see how it could work," Abby said. "Your mother made it clear she didn't want me around Jaye."

"Jaye's in my care, not my mother's."

"Your mother will make your life miserable if she finds out I'm spending time with Jaye outside of school."

"She won't find out," he said stubbornly. "She still lives in Bentonsville."

"But what will you tell her when she comes to visit?"

"She hardly ever visits."

"How about when she calls to check on her grand-daughter, then?"

"She doesn't ask about her," he said flatly. "She has other things on her mind."

Abby had claimed that talking about their brothers was futile, but she couldn't let his comment pass.

"Like the ad she took out in the *Washington Post*?" Merely thinking about it made Abby's temples throb. She couldn't imagine how terrible it would be to lose a son, wanting to believe she wouldn't be as vindictive as Elaine Smith. Destroying another woman's son wouldn't bring her own son back to life.

"Yeah," he said without emotion, "like the ad."

Abby should let the matter drop, but couldn't, not when she'd lain awake at night wondering about the answer to her next question. "Did you have anything to do with it?"

He didn't avoid her questioning gaze. "Her reason for coming to see me last Sunday was to ask for the money to pay for the ad. I gave it to her."

"So you knew what the ad would say before it appeared in the newspaper?"

"Not exactly. But I had a general idea."

The answer cut into her, but it was a shallow cut. She reminded herself that her brother's knife had slashed much deeper, not only on his victim but his victim's family.

"I don't see how this can work," she repeated.

"I said I'd take care of my mother."

"I'm not concerned only because of your mother. It's because of a lot of things. My mother, for instance. I told her about you before you showed up tonight."

"What did she say?" he prompted.

"She advised me to stay away from you and Jaye. She said no good could come of me associating with you," Abby answered. Drew had said the same thing, but mentioning her brother's feelings on the matter would be like throwing a match at tinder.

"Your mother's wrong." For the first time since they'd begun talking about their mutual problem, she heard passion in his voice. "Being with you is good for Jaye."

"Not if you and I can't get along. That's the main reason resuming the arrangement we had won't work."

"We can make it work." His jaw had a stubborn tilt, and again she noticed the five o'clock shadow that made him seem less like the physically perfect male specimen she'd originally thought him to be and more like a mere man. "There's no reason the two of us need to have much contact."

She bit her bottom lip. Just last week, she'd been optimistic that she and Connor would have a lot of contact. The full-body kind. A flush traveled over her skin. Her mind had started to accept that she shouldn't get involved with him, but now that she'd experienced what it was like to kiss him, her body needed a longer adjustment period.

"But aren't you still concerned that the subject of my brother will come up and I'll stick up for him?"

"Not if I ask you not to talk about Galloway with Jaye."

"What if my mother's visiting? I can't control what she says."

"Then keep Jaye away from your mother."

Abby exhaled through her nose, frustrated by his answers. Her mother was a major part of her life, closer to her than even Rae Ann. "But what if Jaye asks about Drew?"

"Change the subject."

If he thought she could indefinitely avoid talking about her brother with Jaye, he was fooling himself. The child would be curious, and Abby wouldn't be able to let her believe that her brother was a ruthless killer.

"Please, Abby." He spoke the words softly, persuasively. If he'd talked to her that way a week ago, she'd have done anything for him. "Please do it for Jaye's sake."

She might have found the will to refuse if he hadn't added the qualifier. She'd certainly refused a myriad of requests from a lot of other men in the past, careful not to repeat her mother's blunder of getting too close to the wrong man. But something about Connor Smith tugged at her. She wanted to believe her inability to refuse him stemmed from a desire to help his niece, but feared the reason was much more complicated.

"Okay," she answered just as softly. "I'll do it for Jaye's sake."

If not for her own.

CHAPTER TEN

CONNOR DRUMMED THE FINGERS of his right hand on the mahogany surface of his desk as he listened to his mother's voice through the earpiece of the office phone.

It was nearing four o'clock, and he still had to make a fair number of calls before his business dinner this evening. One of the calls was to Daniel Mann, the bank president who'd nearly dropped his pharmaceutical stock almost six weeks ago. Since then, it had more than doubled in value.

His mother had nothing new to report, but he'd let her talk as long as she needed. He always did.

"I was thinking about having the *Washington Post* rerun my ad next month and then coming up with a new one to run before the parole hearing in June," she said. "What do you think?"

He thought she was fooling herself if she believed the ads would make a difference in whether Drew Galloway was granted parole, but telling her so wouldn't do any good.

Elaine Smith heard only what she wanted to hear, and that didn't include her surviving son's contention that she was spinning her wheels like a hamster in a cage.

"Let me know how much it'll cost and I'll give you the money," he said. Advertising space in the *Post* wasn't cheap, but he was accustomed to spending money on his mother. She received a monthly check from the divorce settlement, but Connor covered her mortgage, power bills and car payment.

"I'll get you a total by tomorrow," she said. "Can you drive to Bentonsville this weekend and give me the money?"

Just once he wished she'd issue an invitation that had no ulterior motive. She wasn't always angling to keep Drew Galloway in prison. Sometimes there were things around the house that could use fixing. Other times she needed him to take her car in for maintenance or drive her to a doctor's appointment. At still other times, she was in a nostalgic mood and wanted him to listen while she talked about how much she missed J.D.

It had been a very long time since she'd requested his presence simply for the pleasure of his company.

"I'm afraid I can't make it down there this weekend. I have a business dinner tonight with the president of a Wall Street firm." He paused so she could ask him for more details, but of course she didn't. He mentally chided himself for hoping she'd be proud of him for attracting the notice of such an important company. "And I promised Jaye I'd take her to the National Aquarium in Baltimore this weekend."

That should peak her interest. Their family had enjoyed traveling to the aquarium on Baltimore's Inner Harbor when Connor, J.D. and Diana had been children. Not only that, she must have been wondering how things were going with Jaye.

It was mid-April, nearly three weeks since her confrontation with Abby. His mother had made it her business to assure that Jaye was being cared for after school by someone besides Abby, going so far as to call the director of the school-based program at Blue Moon Elementary.

But once she'd determined that Jaye was reregistered, she forgot about her. Connor hadn't needed to lie when he'd resumed his arrangement with Abby because his mother hadn't asked about her grandchild. But now that he'd brought her up, surely she'd ask.

"Then could you call the newspaper and give them your credit-card information? The last time I was there, they told me you could pay for an ad that way, too."

He sighed. "Sure. Just tell me who to call."

"I will," she promised, then hardly took a breath before she resumed speaking, this time about tracking down the writer of an old newspaper column that had advocated lethal injection for Drew Galloway. Maybe he'd write a letter to the parole board.

Connor listened to his mother talk for another ten minutes before she finally rang off. As soon as he hung up the phone, his secretary, Mary Beth, stuck her head around the door frame.

"A Mrs. Piper called while you were on the phone," she announced, all business as usual.

Mrs. Piper was the widowed neighbor who was available to babysit Jaye on occasion. They'd arranged it that she would pick up his niece from Abby's at six, then drive back to his town house and stay with her until Connor returned from his business dinner.

"She can't babysit tonight, because her friend was

in a car accident. Nothing serious, but the friend's pretty shaken up so Mrs. Piper thinks it's best if she stays with her tonight."

He grimaced, then tried a long shot. "I don't suppose you babysit?"

"Not when I have a date, I don't." She flashed him a thank-God-it's-Friday smile, and he had to reassess his opinion of her. With her below-the-knee skirts and long-sleeved blouses, she'd seemed asexual, as though dating was far from her mind.

But she obviously dated more than Connor, who'd been out exactly once since he'd broken up with Isabel.

He could blame the drought on a lack of babysitters but the truth was that the only woman he had any interest in dating was the half sister of his brother's murderer.

"Have fun," he told his secretary.

"Believe me, I plan to," she said.

He glanced at the wall clock when she was gone. Four-thirty, ninety minutes before both his business dinner and pickup time for Jaye. And the only person who could help him out was the one with the best reason not to.

He dialed her number. He listened to the phone ring four times before the answering machine switched on, an eventuality he should have expected. Abby didn't answer the phone during lessons, and she'd switched Jaye's lesson time to four-fifteen to five on Fridays.

"Abby, it's Connor. I know I don't have any right to ask, but I need a favor...."

ABBY STOOD IN FRONT of the answering machine, listening to Connor's message. He sounded contrite, which saddened her. In the two weeks since she'd resumed taking Jaye home with her after school, Connor hadn't asked for a thing.

He'd talked to her, but only about matters related to Jaye, such as his decision to hold off on taking her to a child psychologist. The average number of minutes he spent in her apartment when he came to pick up his niece was four. She knew. She'd timed it.

"You'll say yes, won't you?" Jaye asked from behind her. The girl's approach had been so silent, Abby hadn't known she'd listened to Connor's request about keeping her later tonight.

"That might not be such a good idea," Abby began.

"Don't you want me here?" That shadowy look Abby hadn't seen lately returned to Jaye's eyes.

Abby didn't hesitate in wrapping the young girl in a warm hug. Jaye had shied away the first time Abby had embraced her, but now hugged her back tightly. Abby wasn't sure whether to be heartened by the return of affection or troubled that Jaye was getting too close to her.

"It's not that, silly," Abby said. "You know how I feel about you. But my mother is coming over for dinner tonight."

"You don't want your mother to meet me?" Jaye didn't raise her head from Abby's shoulder, but her voice sounded hurt.

Abby released her and drew back so she could see into her face. She needed to tread delicately here. "Your uncle doesn't want you to meet my mother."

"Because of your brother?"

"Yes," Abby said, "because of my brother."

"That's just stupid," Jaye cried with all the heart-felt emotion of a youngster who didn't bother to hide what she was feeling. "I want to stay here. I want to meet your mother."

"I know you do, honey." Abby ran an affectionate hand over the top of her head and made a decision. "Tell you what. Let's compromise. I'll call my mother and ask if she'd mind terribly if we had dinner together another night. If she doesn't, we'll call your uncle Connor and suggest that you spend the night."

"You mean, like a sleepover?"

"Exactly like a sleepover," Abby said. "We can paint each other's nails and make tacos and eat ice cream and watch movies. We'll have a blast."

Jaye clapped her hands. Her eyes lit up. In her excitement, she'd obviously forgotten all about meeting Abby's mother. But Abby hadn't forgotten. The phone call to her mother would be difficult to make. Not because her mother wouldn't be understanding, but because she'd understand all too well why Abby was canceling their plans.

Nothing good can come of this, her brother had said, words that her mother had echoed. But Abby couldn't regret making Jaye's life a little easier.

She playfully tugged a lock of Jaye's blond hair. "Why don't you check the freezer and see if I have any ice cream while I make those phone calls? If I don't, we'll make a quick trip to the grocery store."

"You bet." Jaye's smile grew broader until she looked exactly the way she should, like a young girl with no worries. "Mint chocolate chip's my favorite, but I'll eat anything. As long as it has chocolate."

"I liked you the first time I saw you, and now I know why. One chocolate lover instinctively recognizes another."

The sound of Jaye's answering giggles faded as the child left the room, and so did Abby's smile. Because no matter which way she turned it over in her mind, she couldn't justify the call she was about to make.

Something was inherently wrong with telling her mother that she was welcome to visit any time. Except when the Smiths were around.

"JAYE'S GETTING HER STUFF together now." Abby greeted Connor not with a hello, but with a pronouncement.

She didn't have on any makeup and the capri-length gray sweatpants she wore with a nondescript T-shirt were nothing special, but her beauty shone through, as bright as the April sun on his back.

"I can't thank you enough for watching Jaye last night," he said. "I was in a real bind."

She didn't ask for details, but he found himself explaining after she let him into her apartment. "A Wall Street firm contacted me before Jaye came to live with me. Some of their executives were in town yesterday on a short business trip and squeezed in a meeting with me."

They'd done more than meet him. They'd taken him for Italian food at one of Georgetown's see-and-be-seen restaurants, wined him, dined him and promised him riches if he came to work for them.

"Are congratulations in order?" she asked, but the frown lines that appeared on her forehead told him his news troubled her. Because she had no cause to miss him if he took a job in New York City, he pinpointed Jaye as the reason.

"It's premature for that. Working on Wall Street certainly has its allure, but now isn't the right time to make any big changes. It's something I need to think about, but for down the line."

She didn't appear convinced, but let the subject drop. "Jaye's in the kitchen, eating her cereal. But she should be about finished."

"Was she any trouble?" he asked as he followed her deeper into the apartment.

"Of course not," she said quickly, believably.

Jaye appeared from the direction of the kitchen, looking no happier to see him than she would have a dentist with a needle full of Novocain.

"Hey, Jaye. Did you have a good time?" he asked.

The girl nodded, but didn't elaborate. She dropped to her hands and knees in the middle of the living room and began to roll up a pink-and-purple sleeping bag he'd never seen before. A dark green sleeping bag was open beside it.

"We had a great time," Abby said when it became obvious that Jaye wouldn't fill him in on what had happened the night before. "We made popcorn and watched movies and slept on the floor so it would seem like a real sleepover."

"Sounds like fun," He suddenly wished he'd been invited, although he'd rather sleep in Abby's bed than on the floor. He shook off the thought, which was entirely inappropriate considering all that had gone on between them.

Jaye finished shoving the sleeping bag into a matching pink-and-purple sack and stood up, the bag in hand.

"You should leave the sleeping bag here," Connor told her.

Jaye clutched the bag tighter. "Abby bought it for me last night. She said every girl should have one."

Since the sentiment wouldn't have occurred to Connor, that showed how little he knew about young girls. He slipped his leather wallet from his back pocket. "How much was it?"

"It was my treat." Abby waved off the money he offered. She smiled at Jaye the way he suddenly wished she'd smile at him. "I had an absolutely enchanting time, which I'll remember ever after."

They giggled in unison. Abby nodded toward the coffee table, on which sat a couple of DVDs. "We watched *Ella Enchanted* and *Ever After* last night," she explained.

Girl movies. Although Abby had included him by explaining the inside joke, he felt like an outsider. Unfortunately he felt like that a lot around his niece.

"Come on, Jaye," he coaxed when the girl didn't budge from her position in the living room. "We should be going."

"But I don't want to go. I want to stay with Abby."

Those were the lines he'd been subconsciously waiting for since entering Abby's apartment. His relationship with his niece had taken a hit after the incident with his mother, but Jaye grew closer to Abby with every passing day.

"We have plans." He always had weekend plans now, a so-far-unsuccessful quest to find ground he and Jaye could share. The weekend before last, he'd taken her to a model-train exhibit that she'd pronounced boring. Last Sunday, they'd gone to a Washington Nationals baseball game, during which she'd opined that April was too cold for baseball. "Remember? We're driving to the National Aquarium in Baltimore."

"Oh, yeah," she said, but without a trace of the excitement she'd exhibited Friday morning when he'd come up with the idea.

He'd lost his taste for the outing, too. What had possessed him to suggest a seventy-mile round-trip drive with a child who had very little to say to him?

"Can Abby come with us?" Jaye asked, her tone infused with hope. "We don't have to go to the aquarium. We can go to the zoo, like we planned before."

"No, Jaye," Abby interjected quickly, shaking her head to underscore her point. "This is your time with your uncle. I'd be interfering."

"But that day my grandmother was here, you said maybe we could go to the zoo another time. This is another time," Jaye implored with a child's simple logic.

Abby glanced at him, her eyes pleading for help. But the solution Jaye proposed was perfect. It was one of those glorious April days that should be spent outdoors. And Abby could act as a buffer between him and Jaye, smoothing the rough edges and allowing them to interact without awkwardness.

"You wouldn't be in the way, Abby," Connor said. "I'd like it if you came."

Visible shock entered her eyes. He didn't blame her. He was the one who'd suggested they have as little contact as possible. But what purpose did it serve to deprive Jaye of Abby's company? To deprive himself, for that matter?

Her family connections were still problematic, but it was hardly as if Drew Galloway was her favorite topic. She hadn't mentioned him a single time before his mother had recognized her and forced the issue. As long as she continued her policy of silence about her half brother, they'd all get along fine.

She opened her mouth, then shut it, her doubts clearly on display. Just as apparent was her desire to come with them.

"Please," Jaye said, perhaps sensing that Abby was weakening.

"Yes, please come," Connor said, backing up his niece. "It won't be as much fun without you."

Abby's capitulation was in her smile. It started slowly, a slight curving of her lips, then grew until it lit her entire face. In that moment Connor admitted to himself that he'd used Jaye as an excuse to get what he wanted, which was time with Abby.

"Okay, then," she said, her eyes still on his. "I'll come with you."

Connor didn't join Jaye in outwardly cheering Abby's decision, but he smiled back at her. Wide and slow and celebratory.

LOOKING BACK ON IT, Abby thought the thaw between her and Connor had started as they'd watched the animals at the zoo. The four-ton Asian elephant that swung its trunk like a huge gray pendulum. The orang-utans with the orangey-red coats that resembled acrobats as they traveled the four-hundred-foot over-head rope between their two habitats. The black-tailed prairie dogs emerging from their underground tunnels.

How could she be at odds with a man when so many of nature's wonders surrounded her? Especially when she was coming to love his niece?

Since that sunny Saturday, when they'd marveled over the zoo's ever-expanding baby panda, things between Abby and Connor had changed. He no longer bolted from her apartment as soon as he arrived to pick up Jaye. Most of the time, like tonight, he lingered. And if the subject of their conversation was usually Jaye, that was to be expected.

His niece wasn't in the apartment at the moment, having asked permission to play a little longer with one of the neighborhood kids. Connor leaned against the counter in the kitchen and crossed his long legs at the ankles, watching Abby sort through the pile of junk mail she'd let accumulate.

"What's the name of this girl Jaye is playing with again?" Connor asked.

"Kendall." She separated a flyer advertising a pest control business called Rid It into the discard pile before giving him her attention. "And Kendall's not a girl. He's a boy."

She could swear his face paled. "What's she doing over there with a boy?"

His question was so pregnant with worry that Abby laughed. "They're playing video games. Kendall's nine, like Jaye."

He ran a hand over his lower face, a habitual gesture she'd come to recognize that meant he was troubled about something. "I hear this boy-girl stuff starts young nowadays."

"Not that young," Abby said, laughing. "But I have to say, you're starting to sound just like a parent."

"I'm starting to feel like one. It's amazing how much one ninety-pound girl can change your life. Not to mention how many times a day she has to eat."

"You mean like breakfast, lunch and dinner?" She returned to the mail, discarding an offer for yet another credit card, this one with a ridiculously high credit limit considering how much money she made.

"Don't forget snacks. I pack her one every day to eat mid-morning, because her class has the latest lunch."

"But she buys her lunch at school, right?"

"Depends on whether she thinks it's yucky or not. Did you know we're teaching each other to cook? Or maybe she's teaching me. She has a pretty good foundation."

"I gathered that the other day when she helped me make brownies," Abby said. She put the mail down again. When Connor was in the room, it was difficult to pay attention to anything but him. "She told me about your efforts. Something about burned eggs and boiling cookies."

His grimace was comical. "Who knew eggs burned? And the cookies were Jaye's fault. She read the amount of flour wrong in the recipe. But I'm getting there. I make a mean hot dog, and last night's grilled-cheese sandwiches were pretty good."

"So you and Jaye are okay?"

"For the most part," he said. "It helps that you check her homework. She gets tense when I do it."

"She says that's because you expect a lot from her."

"You bet I do. She's a smart girl. She should be getting As and Bs instead of Cs."

"I think she's doing great, considering the circumstances," Abby said. "Coming to a new school late in the year is never easy. But it's doubly hard for Jaye, because she's away from everything she's ever known."

"You mean she's away from my sister," Connor said. "But I'm starting to think she'll have to get used to it."

"Have you hired that private investigator yet?"

He straightened from the counter, crossed to one of the kitchen chairs and sat down heavily across from her, as though from the weight of his worries. "Not yet. I did try phoning the last number she called from. It turned out to be a pay phone in Knoxville."

"Is that where your sister lived before she left Jaye with you?"

"No. From the transcript Diana left, I know that Jaye's last school was in a town outside Nashville. Jaye won't talk much about where she's been, but I gather she and Diana moved around a lot, mostly in Kentucky and Tennessee, after my aunt died."

"What does Diana say in her messages?"

"Mainly that she's all right and that she appreciates me taking care of Jaye." He pursed his lips. "I'm not sure how much good it would do. I can't make Diana take Jaye back."

"Then it's fortunate for Jaye that she has a stable home here with you."

"Yeah, right." He snorted. "A bachelor with no child-care experience."

"An uncle turning his life upside down to provide for his niece," she immediately corrected.

He studied her, his expression thoughtful. "Is that really how you think of me?"

One of his large, strong hands rested on the table. Without conscious thought, she covered it with hers. "I think of you as one of the good guys."

He smiled at her. It made her feel special, confident even. Then his gaze dropped to their linked hands. When he lifted his eyes, the smile was gone, replaced by something more urgent. "Abby—"

The door to her apartment burst open. Jaye rushed in, followed by Kendall.

Abby jerked her hand back from Connor's, then felt silly. It wasn't as though they were doing anything wrong. They were friends. Nothing more.

"Hey, Uncle Connor." Jaye's cheeks were flushed the same pink tint as her shirt. "Can Kendall come over to our place and sleep over?"

Abby watched Connor give the boy standing next to Jaye a long, slow perusal. Kendall was tall for his age, a handsome boy with night-dark hair, pale skin and clear blue eyes.

"Not on your life," Connor said.

CONNOR WOULD NEVER reverse his position on boy-girl sleepovers, but as the weeks passed he began to accept Kendall as part of Jaye's life. Just as Abby had become a part of his.

He came to collect his niece from Abby's apartment one Friday in May, only to hear that Kendall's parents had taken Jaye out for burgers and laser tag.

"I hope you don't mind that I gave her permission." Worry lines appeared between Abby's brows. "I tried reaching you at work, but you must have already left. I tried your cell, too, but the call didn't go through."

"The battery died." He stroked his chin, feeling the beginnings of the beard he was forever fighting. "That boy Kendall really has it bad for Jaye, doesn't he?"

Abby rolled her eyes. "You're being silly about this. That boy is a child. He likes that Jaye gives him a run for his money when they play Halo."

"What's Halo?"

"A video game. From what I understand, it involves a futuristic super-soldier who fights to save mankind from evil aliens. Believe me, at this age Kendall's more interested in the aliens than he is in girls."

Connor knew that. Sort of. He also wasn't the least bit miffed at Abby for allowing Jaye to go with Kendall's family. He was glad Jaye had made a friend, no matter what his sex. But he couldn't resist teasing Abby.

He deliberately slid his gaze over her. The thermometer had hit eighty today, and she'd dressed appropriately for the warmer-than-average day. She looked casually feminine in worn blue-jean shorts that showed off the shape of her legs and a pale yellow short-sleeved top that clung to her curves. Her dark hair was a little longer than when he'd first met her, its fly-away quality adding to her appeal.

"I don't know about that," he said lazily. "I'd have noticed you when you were nine."

"You were fourteen when I was nine. Teenage boys notice swimsuit models, not flat-chested girls."

"You may be right about that." He winked at her. "But I still bet you were awfully cute."

She actually blushed, proving she was still cute.

"Hey," he said impulsively, "how would you like to go out to dinner with me tonight?"

She didn't answer immediately, and he understood why. They'd spent a fair amount of time together since she'd resumed caring for Jaye, but they'd never been truly alone. If Jaye wasn't present, she was nearby.

Jaye didn't stand between them now. Abby's half brother, behind bars at a Maryland prison fifty miles away, did.

"I'd understand if you didn't want to go," he began. He realized what he was about to say wasn't fair, but it was crunch time. "But if you say no, I'll have to spend my birthday alone."

"Your birthday! Why didn't I know this? Why didn't you tell me? Why didn't Jaye?" Her string of rapid-fire questions slowed while she took a breath, then she asked, "Jaye doesn't know it's your birthday, does she?"

"Nope."

"Then no one made a fuss over you today?"

He shrugged. He'd gotten over expecting others to make a big deal out of his birthday a long time ago. "My dad sent a card."

"How about your mom?" She must have read his expression because she added with sudden insight, "She forgot, didn't she?"

"Yeah." His mother's failure to acknowledge his birthday had hurt more than it should have considering he hadn't thought she'd remember, but Connor automatically made an excuse for her. "She has a lot on her mind."

Abby didn't comment on what was on his mother's mind, although the subject was patently obvious.

"I know it would be late notice, but why don't I try

to round up a group of my friends?" she asked. "We can have an impromptu celebration somewhere."

Connor nearly groaned. He hadn't revealed it was his birthday because he was angling for a party. "I'm not much for public celebrations. You going out to dinner with me is the only gift I need."

She looked doubtful. "Are you sure?"

"Very," he answered with alacrity.

"Okay," she said, just the way he'd planned. "I'll go to dinner with you. Just let me change first."

His eyes drifted over her. The shorts she wore left her legs bare and nicely outlined the shape of her rear end. "What you're wearing now is fine."

Her eyebrows rose. "I'm in jean shorts, and you're in the suit you wore to work. I'm changing."

She flashed him a smile and left the room before he could tell her that he liked all of her just the way she was.

CONNOR WOULD HAVE PREFERRED to take Abby to one of Washington, D.C.'s better restaurants. Perhaps 1789 in Georgetown, which served modern American cuisine in a renovated federal house. Or the Willard Room, with its French-inspired menu in the historic landmark hotel a few blocks from the White House.

But in the absence of both a reservation and time, he settled for a popular sandwich place on Ellsworth Avenue in the heart of the new downtown Silver Spring shopping and entertainment district. Part of a chain of stores gaining a foothold in the northeast, the restaurant featured oven-toasted sandwiches served in a cozy, rustic setting.

They stood in a surprisingly fast-moving line, deciding what they wanted from the menu board mounted on the wall behind the counter, and carried made-to-order sandwiches to a lacquered wooden booth with a candle glowing in its center. He'd barely taken a bite of his roast beef and provolone sandwich before she brought up his birthday.

"So, for the record, how old are you today?"

He finished chewing before he answered. "Thirty-one."

"Did you get anything besides that card from your father?"

"You mean besides a date with you?" He grinned at her, then found he wanted to share his news. Perhaps that was his motive for asking her out in the first place. "Actually, I did get something else. A job offer."

She paused in the act of bringing her chicken salad sandwich to her mouth. Before replying, she set it back on the plate. "A job offer from that Wall Street brokerage?"

"The vice president called today with a firm offer," he said, wondering why the prospect didn't bring him more joy. "They want a decision by the beginning of summer."

"And you're considering it?"

"I'd be a fool not to, but obviously there are extenuating circumstances. Jaye, most importantly. I know New York City is teeming with day-care options and that I could even hire an au pair. But I couldn't see bringing Jaye to Manhattan with me. It wouldn't be fair to her. I'd be working such long hours that we'd barely see each other."

She still didn't touch her sandwich. "It sounds like you do want to take it, though."

"I probably would if I didn't have Jaye to consider." He sipped from his bottled cream soda, futilely wishing they'd gone to a place that served beer. This conversation would be easier over a few cold ones. "Wall Street has always intrigued me. To quote a line from an old song, 'If you can make it there, you can make it anywhere.'"

"But haven't you already made it? Your company's Web site says it's this region's leading financial services firm, and your bio makes you sound like a whiz kid."

He grinned at her. "You looked me up on the Internet?"

She gazed down at the table. "I was curious." Her eyes rose, determination shining from them. "And don't change the subject. I want to know whether you're a whiz kid."

"I'm too old to qualify for kid status, but I'm considered quite good at what I do. All that's left is to prove myself on Wall Street."

He could tell she didn't understand. He couldn't explain it any better than he already had without mentioning his father. While his mother seemed uninterested in what he did for a living, his father, a former CPA, asked him about Wall Street all the time.

"Then it sounds like getting the job offer is a big deal," she said. "Congratulations. I'm happy for you."

He attributed his sinking feeling at the thought of leaving Maryland to the uncertainty surrounding Jaye. "Thanks, but congratulations are premature. I have two months to decide whether I'll accept the job. I won't take it if I'm not sure Jaye's in good hands."

"Is her mother an option?"

"I don't know," he said. "I did hire that private investigator, but he hasn't figured out where Diana is yet."

"Then you can't make any decisions about your own future until you find her," she said thoughtfully.

"Exactly." He took another swig of cream soda. "So how about if you tell me more about what drove you to look me up on the Internet?"

She looked at him from under her long, thick lashes. "Is it really your birthday? Or did you get me to agree to this dinner because you have ulterior motives?"

"You wound me. I wouldn't lie about it being my birthday." He raised his eyebrows. "So in the spirit of truthfulness, I should confess that, yes, I do have ulterior motives."

Their lighthearted flirting continued as they munched on their sandwiches while comparing taste in music, books and movies. She confessed a startling fondness for country music while he preferred rock and roll. She read mainly romance and suspense while he was a science-fiction aficionado. But surprisingly they both leaned toward the same types of movies.

"I still can't get over you being a fan of romantic comedy," she told him. They'd finished eating and were strolling past the interactive fountain with the colorful mosaic-tile bottom.

He took her hand, not because he was afraid they'd get separated, but because it seemed completely natural. She'd changed into a rosebud-print skirt topped by a creamy blouse with lace accents at the sleeves and neckline. A willowy blonde with a look-at-me body and face to match passed within a few feet of them, but he barely glanced at her.

"Why does it surprise you that I enjoy romantic comedy?" he asked Abby.

She wrinkled her nose. "I guess because you're a stockbroker and…"

He elbowed her gently in the side when she didn't finish her thought. "And stockbrokers are so stuffy," he said.

She laughed, a throaty, sexy sound. "I didn't say that."

"But you were thinking it," he said. "Stockbrokers have to laugh, too, you know."

"So who do you laugh at? Hugh Grant? Sandra Bullock? Kirsten Dunst? Orlando Bloom?"

"Sometimes, but my taste runs more toward the old stuff. Like *Bringing Up Baby, The Seven Year Itch, That Touch of Mink.* Stuff like that."

"I've never seen any of those movies."

He stopped dead and turned to her. "Then it's lucky you met me so I can introduce you to the classics. There aren't many theaters that do revivals, but there's always the video store."

The smile on her face faded. The spray from the fountain misted the night air, but he could see well enough to tell she was searching his eyes. "Then you see this becoming a regular thing? You and me together?"

He hadn't planned on it. A month ago, when he'd discovered that Drew Galloway was her half brother, he couldn't have predicted it. But he suddenly grasped that it was what he wanted. That *she* was what he wanted.

"You and me together. I like the sound of that."

"But your mother—"

He put a finger to her lips. "I'm an adult and can decide for myself who I spend time with."

Her expression grew troubled.

"I told my mother," she announced, then fell silent, as though reluctant to finish the thought. "She said the same thing she did the first time she found out about you and Jaye, that nothing good could come out of me associating with you."

He tunneled his fingers through the hair at her nape so that his hand cupped the back of her head.

"Ah, but there's where she's wrong." He lowered his head and kissed her, gently but thoroughly, right there in the middle of downtown Silver Spring.

She kissed him back so sweetly that his blood shouldn't have flowed in a heated rush through his body, but it did. Something about this woman had touched a chord deep inside him from the start. Even while they were at odds with each other, the air around them sizzled with suppressed energy.

He felt a little dazed when he finally summoned the will to raise his head. She looked equally bewildered, her lips dewy from his kiss, her eyes slightly glazed, her body still leaning toward his.

Wanting to lighten the mood, he breathed, "Happy birthday to me."

She threw back her head and laughed. He did, too, thrusting their mothers and their brothers to the back of his mind and letting himself take joy in her company.

DEE DEE REED WAS WORRIED about her daughter, but she wasn't half as anxious about Abby as she was about her son.

Abby had never been able to successfully hide anything from her, so it hadn't been difficult to figure out she was growing far too close to J. D. Smith's brother. Dee Dee had tried to warn her to steer clear of the man, but Abby had closed her ears. Sadly, Dee Dee understood why. Abby was falling in love. She didn't welcome hearing that hate could one day put a wedge between her daughter and Connor Smith.

Dee Dee rubbed her forehead, temporarily blotting out Abby's situation to concentrate on Drew's. It had come as a blow to learn that somebody she'd never heard of named Rico Shaw had offered him a place to live. A decent place, from what she could see of it from her car.

She'd wormed the name out of Drew and was now parked across the street from the upscale bungalow where Rico lived, her car windows rolled halfway down to let in the warm breeze and the flowery smell of spring.

Rico's neighborhood, although situated in Maryland, was barely on the outskirts of the nation's capital. The community wasn't as well groomed as some of the places in Silver Spring, but the houses were decent and well cared for. The tiny pink flowers of the occasional cherry tree the city was famous for vied for attention with the white blooms of the dogwoods and the colorful seasonal flowers.

Rico Shaw's house stacked up to the best of them on the block, which was puzzling since Drew had told her he was a construction worker. Equally baffling was the late-model motorcycle in the driveway with the personalized plates that read RICOS. Dee Dee had gotten the impression he was an unskilled laborer; he shouldn't have been able to afford a place like this or a motorcycle like that.

But then she didn't know much more than his name and age: twenty-two. Perhaps a relative had left him some money or somebody else was paying the rent on the house.

A small, white car with Maids to Order stenciled on the side in red lettering pulled up in front of the opposite curb. Two young women wearing matching white pants and red shirts got out, carrying with them a full arsenal of cleaning supplies. Dee Dee guessed that they were headed for Rico Shaw's place even before they unlocked the door and disappeared inside.

She frowned. Would Drew be subsidizing someone living beyond his means? And how did Rico know her son, anyway? He would have been only twelve years old when Drew had gone to prison. Drew would only say what he'd told Abby, that Rico was a friend of a friend.

She was about to conclude she'd seen all she was going to see when a shiny red sports car pulled into the driveway. A man in his twenties with a dark complexion and a mustache that matched his black, untidy hair got out of the passenger seat.

Rico Shaw, Dee Dee presumed.

He took the steps to his house two at a time while the driver of the car that had dropped him off executed a U-turn, which took him past Dee Dee's car.

The sunlight streamed down on the driver, catching the familiar spider scar slashing his right cheek. He'd shaved off his lank, blond hair, but Dee Dee would have recognized his hawk-like face and prominent chin even if it hadn't been for the scar.

Spider Strickland.

She didn't know Spider's given first name but remembered Drew saying Spider Strickland was the main reason she'd packed up Drew and his sister and moved them out of Baltimore a decade ago. His juvenile record stretched a mile long. Assault and battery, public drunkenness, shoplifting and marijuana possession were the offenses she knew about, but Dee Dee suspected he'd also been selling drugs.

She'd tried forbidding Drew from associating with him, but that hadn't worked and she'd lived in fear that Drew would get caught up in Spider's trouble. She almost laughed at the irony: Spider walked the street whiles Drew was the one in jail.

But she'd bet everything she owned that Spider not only had a record, but was still up to no good. She'd also wager that he was the friend who'd put Rico Shaw up to offering Drew a place to live.

With more questions than answers, Dee Dee started her car and drove away. But this wasn't the end of it. She'd been a rotten mother, so busy with work that she'd failed to keep abreast of what was happening in her son's life.

She hadn't absorbed that an involved parent made the best parent until Drew had landed in prison, but she'd learned her lesson well. Her next step was to find out whether Spider Strickland had an adult record to go along with his juvenile rap sheet. It was the kind of preventive step she should have taken before when Drew was a teenager, a failure that would forever haunt her.

If she could verify that Spider's life of crime had

continued into his adult years, she'd take steps to assure Drew didn't go anywhere near him.

Or near Rico Shaw, for that matter.

CHAPTER ELEVEN

CONNOR CRINGED AS JAYE wheeled the grocery cart around the corner of an aisle so fast she'd have flattened anyone with the bad luck to be traveling in the opposite direction. He could have sworn the wheels screeched.

"Careful," he told her. "I didn't take out collision insurance on that cart."

"What?" She gazed at him in confusion, her eyes wide and innocent.

"Never mind. Just go slower. And watch so you don't crash into anyone."

She nodded her head, her eyes perusing the shelves. "Hey, look. Oreos. Can we get some?"

"Sure." He watched as she dropped the cookies into a cart that already contained double-chocolate-fudge ice cream and Doritos. So far, he was making precious little progress on buying the ingredients for the healthy dinner he planned tonight.

She swung the cart back into the flow of traffic, carefully avoiding another cart nearby filled with the healthy foods he should have been buying—skim milk, yogurt and a brand of cereal low in sugar.

"Jaye. Imagine running into you here, sweetie," the cart's driver exclaimed with a broad, Southern drawl.

She was tiny, sandy-blond, full of energy and looked to be in her thirties. "I just tried calling your mother to see if you could come to Ashley's sleepover tomorrow."

Jaye's eyes cut to Connor's when the woman mentioned Diana, but then grew round and excited. "Really? Ashley really wants me to come?"

"Of course, silly. What kind of a party would it be without you there?"

Jaye turned to him, her excitement palpable. "Can I go? Please?"

The woman seemed to notice Connor standing beside Jaye for the first time. "Oh, my goodness. Pardon my manners for not introducing myself. I'm Susanna Gibbons, the room mother for Jaye's fourth-grade class. That's how I know Jaye."

"Nice to meet you. I'm Jaye's uncle, Connor Smith."

"Her uncle?" Susanna Gibbons looked disappointed. "Then you can't give her permission, now can you? I'll try her mother again when I get home. It was naughty of me, but I talked the school secretary into giving me the phone number from Jaye's file even though she wasn't supposed to."

"That's my phone number," Connor explained. "Jaye lives with me."

"But where's her…" The woman's voice trailed off, having caught herself before she asked a question that was none of her business. "So I gather you're the one who can give Jaye permission after all?"

"Yeah," he said, "and it's fine with me if Jaye wants to go."

"I want to go," Jaye said, but some of the excitement had leeched out of her voice.

After bidding Susanna Gibbons goodbye, they finished their grocery shopping, settling on rotisserie chicken for a main course. The meal was more appetizing than Connor's usual fare, considering that preparing the chicken consisted of warming it up, but Jaye didn't seem to have much of an appetite when they finally sat down to dinner.

"Is something bothering you?" Connor finally asked, although he already had a good guess as to what it was.

Her eyes downcast, she picked at her chicken but didn't actually eat any. She was silent for so long that Connor thought she wouldn't answer.

Then her eyes lifted. In them, he spotted sorrow. "Where's my mom, Uncle Connor?"

He inhaled deeply, catching the scent of the roasted chicken. To give himself time to compose an answer, he released his breath slowly. "She's somewhere in Tennessee. I told you about the messages she leaves me at work so we know she's okay."

"Where in Tennessee?"

"She didn't say," Connor hedged, although he knew exactly where she was after this morning's report from his private investigator. Murfreesboro, a town on the outskirts of Nashville, where she had a month-by-month lease on an apartment.

"When is she coming back?"

"She didn't say that, either."

Jaye's eyelids drooped, concealing whatever else she might be feeling. Rejection. Confusion. Concern. Despite what Diana had done, Connor sensed that she'd been a good mother to Jaye. That could be why her sudden absence had hit Jaye so hard.

"Can I be excused?" she asked in a small voice.

At a loss as to how to make things better, he answered, "Sure. I'll clean up tonight."

He waited until the sounds of the violin drifted from her bedroom, figuring he had thirty minutes with little likelihood of Jaye interrupting him. Locating the notes he'd taken when the P.I. had called, he punched in a phone number.

"Hello." It was a female voice, impatient, slightly out of breath and very familiar.

"Hello, Diana," he greeted his sister.

"Connor!" She was clearly stunned. "How did you find me?"

"Not easily. I had a private investigator track you down."

"Is Jaye okay?" Panic laced her question. "Please tell me she's okay."

He didn't let her concern for her daughter sway him. "As okay as she can be considering you deserted her and never left a number where you could be reached," he said harshly.

"You don't understand."

"You're right." He didn't mask his disapproval. He'd always had sympathy for her situation, but he was angry, as much for Jaye's sake as his own. "I don't. So why don't you explain it to me?"

"I don't think I can." Her voice was little more than a whisper. "Let's just say I'm trying to get myself together, to find out who I really am."

He kept a lid on his temper, but only barely. "You're Jaye's mother."

"I know that. But until I get a few things straight, I can't be the mother she deserves."

He grew silent, trying to figure out what he could say to get through to her. "Jaye was asking about you tonight. She wants to know when you're coming back."

There was a long pause on the other end of the line, then she said, "I hope you didn't say it would be soon."

"Listen to yourself, Diana. This is your daughter we're talking about. Aren't you worried about her?"

"Why should I worry? She's fine as long as she's with you."

That hadn't been what he'd meant. He'd been referring not to Jaye's physical well-being but to her state of mind. Though trying to talk sense into Diana was like talking to a wall.

"I can't take care of Jaye indefinitely."

"I'm not asking you to. I'll be back for her, Connor. I swear I will."

He was about to tell her about the Wall Street firm that had given him until the beginning of summer to accept its job offer, but there were more important things to discuss. "Jaye's upstairs right now. I can get her so you can talk to her, let her know you're all right."

"No." The refusal was instantaneous. In a softer voice, she asked, "Can't you let her know I love her and that she shouldn't worry about me?"

"Jesus, Diana. Don't you see there's something wrong when you won't even talk to your own daughter?"

"It won't make any sense to her now. What if she asks when she'll see me?"

"What am I supposed to say when she asks *me* that?"

"You're better at this stuff than me. You'll think of something." Her voice seemed to crack before she said, "I'm sorry, Connor. But I've really got to go."

"But what about—"

She hung up before he could finish his question. *What about Jaye?*

The blaring dial tone sounded in his ear. He depressed the button, shutting off the phone, and put it down on the nearest counter.

He kneaded the space between his brows. He could call his sister back, but didn't see the point. From the way Diana had talked, she had no immediate plans to reclaim her daughter. At the moment, Connor was providing his niece with what the state of Maryland called "informal kinship care." Diana was still legally the decision maker, responsible for decisions about Jaye's medical care and her education.

But if a time came when his sister was unwilling or unable to decide what was best for Jaye—which could easily have happened when her whereabouts had been unknown—Connor or another relative would have to petition the court for legal guardianship.

As well as Connor and Jaye were getting along now, they both knew the arrangement was temporary. The child deserved a permanent home, one that would provide a more stable environment.

Abruptly making up his mind, Connor picked up the phone again and dialed. It shouldn't be difficult to wrangle an invitation to visit, especially if he didn't mention that he was scoping out a possible new living arrangement for Jaye.

"Okay. What's my surprise?"

Abby lasted about five seconds inside Connor's town house before asking the question. It was his fault. He'd called earlier that Saturday to say a surprise would be waiting if she arrived at his place around eight o'clock.

It was exactly eight o'clock now.

He folded his arms over his chest, his amusement evident in the curve of his lips. He wore a black T-shirt with lightweight elastic-waist gray shorts, clothes that made him look more like a jock than an office worker. He obviously worked out. His upper body was leanly sculpted, with nicely defined biceps. His legs, covered with a healthy sprinkling of dark hair, had great definition.

It occurred to Abby that Connor, looking like this, was surprise enough.

"You don't have any patience, do you?" he asked.

"None, especially considering I passed up a girls' night with Rae Ann and company," she confirmed, listening for Jaye. She half expected to hear the girl's surprisingly heavy footsteps thundering down the stairs. "Where's Jaye? She better show her face soon, because I'm dying to find out what my surprise is."

He laughed, rich and low and seductive. Placing a warm hand at her back, he gently propelled her through the living and dining rooms into the family room, where his oversize, high-definition television was located.

"This is half the surprise." He picked up a stack of DVDs from the glass-top coffee table and handed them to her. The movie on top was *Bringing Up Baby,* but it was only one of a wide selection of classic romantic comedies.

"These look terrific," she said as she shuffled

through them, "but there must be a half dozen here. Do you really think we'll have time to watch them all?"

"If we get bored, I can think of other things we could do." He encircled her waist and nuzzled her neck, sending goose bumps quivering across her skin and making her giggle.

"Stop that." She halfheartedly pulled away from him. "Jaye might walk in on us."

"That's the other half of the surprise," he said, holding her loosely in the circle of his arms. "Jaye got invited to a sleepover. I don't have to pick her up until noon tomorrow."

The fact that she and Connor were truly alone and would be all night hit her like spray from a waterfall, although she wasn't sure if the temperature of the water ran hot or cold. Her body already tingled from where it was in contact with his, but their relationship felt so tenuous that she wasn't sure she was ready to take the next step.

"So Jaye's making more friends," she remarked to buy herself some time. "That's wonderful for her."

"I think it's kind of great for us, too," he said, his gaze steady, his meaning unmistakable. He must have picked up on her uncertainty because his voice abruptly lightened, and he let her go. "But the night's young. So what do you say we watch Katharine Hepburn and her pet leopard?"

Relief coursed through Abby, nearly making her swoon. "Why would she keep a leopard around her baby?"

He shouted with laughter. "Baby is the leopard's name. Hepburn's a free-spirited heiress pursuing Cary

Grant, who's a stuffy paleontologist. We're talking screwball comedy here."

"This I've gotta see," Abby said, aware that their ease with each other was back. She got comfortable on his sofa while he cued up the movie.

When the movie ended with the mismatched couple embracing after Hepburn accidentally crumbled a dinosaur skeleton that Grant had spent years assembling, Abby leaned her head against the back of the sofa and turned to gaze at Connor. He sat next to her, his arm around her shoulders, where it had been throughout most of the movie.

"I wondered about your taste in movies but now I understand," she said. "I've never heard you laugh like that."

"After the week I had, I needed to laugh."

She was instantly alert. "But I thought you and Jaye were getting along better now."

"We are," he hastened to reassure her. "It's not that."

He grew silent, prompting her to ask, "Do you want to talk about it?"

"Yes. But not right now."

"Why not now?" she persisted.

His eyes danced. "Because now I have you where I want you."

"And here I thought you were going to introduce me to another of your favorite flicks. Maybe explain how you came to be the only little boy in your neighborhood who could pick Cary Grant and Spencer Tracy out of a lineup."

He ran his knuckles gently down the side of her face and laughed. "I didn't watch these kinds of movies back then. I liked violence as much as the next kid."

"But you don't now?"

He shook his head. "I never watch violent movies. I won't even put on a TV cop show. I haven't since…"

"Since when?" she asked again when he grew silent.

His brows drew together, he removed his arm from her shoulders and sat up straight. When he spoke, he was staring off in the distance instead of at Abby. "Son of a bitch. I never put it together before now."

"Put what together? Your choice in movies?"

He nodded, the expression on his face pained. "Yeah. What I liked to watch changed right after the plea bargain. A psychologist would have a field day with that, don't you think?"

She absorbed the meaning of what he'd revealed in silence, understanding that he'd been turned off by depictions of violence because of what had happened to his brother. Of what her brother had done to his.

"No less of a field day than he'd have with me," she said quietly. "I didn't pick up the violin until I was fifteen."

That was how old she'd been the year Drew had gone to prison.

"Why the violin?"

"Fate, maybe. It was my grandmother's. She died when I was a baby, so I can't be sure how good she was or how much she played. She left the instrument to my mom, who was divorced and raising two kids by herself. My mom needed money, but never sold it because she remembered her mother playing it."

"How did the violin get to be yours?"

"I found it in a hall closet after it happened. Things at school, well, they weren't good. We were still relative newcomers so I didn't have all that many friends to begin with. Then, well, let's just say I had even fewer friends. Finding somebody who'd eat lunch with me was especially, um, difficult."

He winced. "That wasn't fair."

"That's just the way life works out sometimes," she said, summarizing the lesson it had been so hard for her to learn. "Anyway, something about that violin stuck with me. Looking back on it, I think it was fate that I found it. I needed something to lose myself in, and the violin turned out to be that something."

"How'd you learn to play?"

"Trial and error, mostly. I spent a lot of time by myself back in those days. After we moved from Bentonsville, I lucked out. We didn't have money for private lessons, but the music teacher at my new high school took an interest in me."

"The way you've taken an interest in Jaye."

She nodded. "I could tell she needed something to care about, something to take her mind off her troubles. I thought she might be able to lose herself in music, too." She grew thoughtful, wanting to know more about him. "What did you lose yourself in, Connor?"

"The real world," he said. "I was a junior in college when it happened. I temporarily dropped out so I could help my parents, then took out a loan and waited tables so I could afford to go back."

"I can't imagine you waiting tables." Working in a restaurant didn't fit with the suave, moneyed image he presented to the world, but Abby had already realized that image was at least partially an illusion. "How about your parents? Didn't they help you out financially?"

"My mother never worked outside the home. Dad was a CPA. He had a business in Bentonsville, but stopped going to work after J.D. died. I tried to keep the business afloat but didn't have enough experience. Dad finally sold the business for much less than it was worth. He managed to pull it together and became successful again, but not right then. So paying for college was up to me."

"Didn't you get scholarships?" Abby asked. The cost of her own education had been largely covered by grants based on both academic merit and financial need.

"I was a good student in high school, but not good enough to stand out. Things were different when I got to college. I pursued a business degree because it seemed the most practical route to take and surprisingly I was good at it."

"Why surprisingly?" she asked. "I'm sure you're good at a lot of things."

"Not when I was growing up, I wasn't," he said. "Not as good as I wanted to be, anyway."

"Oh, come on," she chastised. "I bet you were one of those impossibly popular kids who captained the high-school football team and always got the girl."

"Hardly," he said. "I played football but tore up my knee at the end of my sophomore year."

"I thought I noticed that you limped sometimes."

He indicated a slight scar below his knee, barely visible and whitened with age. "It doesn't usually bother me except when the weather changes or I'm tired. But it was a steep price to pay to play football, especially since I was only an adequate player, not like my…"

His voice trailed off, but she filled in the blank. Not like his brother. She wet her lips, her heart aching for his loss and for what might have developed between her and Connor if not for the past. The incident between their brothers had already torn them apart once and might well do so again.

"Why does everything always have to come back to our brothers?" she whispered.

He didn't say anything for a long moment in which he gazed at her as though trying to see inside her soul. Then he traced the curve of her cheek, very gently.

"It doesn't," he said. "Tonight is only about us."

She attempted a smile and failed. "That's easy to say now, when we're here alone. But what about tomorrow when we have to deal with our families?"

"This is our business. It has nothing to do with our families."

That wasn't true, of course. People didn't exist in a vacuum, where their choices affected only themselves. Humans, by their very nature, were social creatures with ties binding them to family and friends. Actions had consequences, with any single event holding the possibility to cause a domino-like reaction.

Abby could have told him as much, but her need to go along with the fiction he'd proposed was stronger.

"I want to believe that," she said, unable not to touch him. She traced the shape of his beautiful mouth with two fingers.

"Then do," he said and kissed her.

They'd kissed twice before, the first time when they hadn't known much more about each other except that they could generate this searing heat. The heat was present this time, too, but so was an appreciation of this moment. Because each time they kissed, there was no guarantee that they'd ever kiss again.

He kissed with his eyes open, which was somehow sexier, because it meant he acknowledged exactly who he was kissing: Abby Reed, a woman with a past that had tragically entwined with his. She wished they could erase that unfortunate tie between them and that it was only the present they shared. For tonight, she thought that might be possible.

She breathed in his scent, clean and male, along with his breath so that it mingled with her own and became indistinguishable. Angling his head and opening his mouth, he deepened the kiss, stroking her tongue with his, causing a tense heat to coil deep within her body.

She braced one of her hands on his shoulder and buried the other in his thick hair. But she couldn't get close enough to him, not as close as she wanted. No, needed.

He trailed his mouth from her lips to her throat, and she arched her head back to give him access. Shivers cascaded down her body like raindrops as his warm hand traced her collarbone, then moved lower to stroke the softness of her breast.

"I want to make love to you," he breathed against her neck in a low voice.

"Then do." She repeated what he'd told her a moment ago, her words like pieces of breath.

"Not here." He drew back so he could look her in the eyes. His pupils were constricted, his breathing out of sync. "In my bed."

The import of what he was asking struck her. Making love here on the sofa could be explained away as an act of passion. But their lovemaking would take on greater meaning if she went to his bedroom. This wouldn't be a one-night stand.

In the silence while he waited for her answer, she thought she heard her heart beat. Fast, faster, faster still. She couldn't attribute her reaction to his touch because no part of his body was in contact with hers, perhaps because he wanted her to make a decision not clouded by lust.

Recognizing they were at a turning point in their relationship, she tried to think about the choice she had to make. But her hammering heart had already made it for her.

Wordlessly, she put her hand in his—and her trust in him.

THE SUN THAT SLIPPED through a gap in his bedroom blinds shone on Connor, gradually pulling him from a deep, satisfied sleep.

He slowly cracked open his eyes, instantly aware of the feeling that swept over him. He recognized it, even though it had been a very long time since it had burned this brightly.

Happiness.

He turned over to locate the source of his contentment. She was lying on her side facing him, her features soft in sleep. The sheet covering her had slipped, exposing a creamy shoulder and one beautiful bare breast. His body responded to the sight, instantly growing hard.

Smiling slightly in bemusement that he could want her again so quickly after the passionate night they'd shared, he kissed her soft lips. He coaxed and cajoled until she came awake and kissed him back with a sweetness that stole his breath.

His eyes were open so he saw the instant her eyelids lazily lifted, revealing eyes already darkening with passion.

She was still naked under the sheet and he gathered her body to his. She couldn't miss the unmistakable truth that he was ready for her. Again.

He felt her smile against his lips. He drew back slightly and smiled. "Good morning."

He cupped her bare breast, enjoying the weight of it in his hand and her little gasp of pleasure as he gently rubbed her nipple until it hardened.

"Mind telling me what you're doing?" she asked huskily.

"Making sure you don't have morning-after regrets," he said and kissed her again. Not sweetly this time, but druggingly, sweeping his tongue inside her mouth.

Her arms slipped around his neck, and she molded the length of her body against his as they put the things they'd learned about each other to good, carnal use.

When his need for her became too great to delay any longer, he reached for the condom on the bedside table and realized a truth: He could make love to this woman a thousand times, and it still wouldn't be enough.

"Did it work?" he asked her much later as they sat across from each other drinking coffee on the tall stools in his kitchen nook. He'd already cleared their plates, empty of the cheese omelets and toast he'd prepared for breakfast.

She lowered her coffee mug, a small smile on her well-kissed lips. Her dark hair was wet from the shower and her skin glowed. "Did what work?"

"My way of convincing you not to have regrets."

"Oh, it worked all right. You can be very convincing," she agreed.

"Good, because there's something else I need to convince you of."

He got down from the stool, crossed the kitchen to the counter where he'd written the information the private detective had faxed him and handed it to her. She looked it over, her eyes tracking from line to line.

"This is about your sister," she said. "This is the reason you had a tough week. The private detective found her."

"Outside of Nashville," he said. "She's living in an apartment where she has a short-term lease and working as a secretary for a temp agency."

Her eyes lifted from the paper. "Have you spoken to her?"

"Yesterday. It wasn't encouraging. She wouldn't talk to Jaye. She said she needed time to get her life in order and sort out who she is."

"She's a mother," Abby exclaimed.

"That's what I said, but it didn't make any difference. The bottom line is that she's not coming back for Jaye any time soon." Connor blew out a breath and sat down. "You see why I didn't want to talk about this last night? It's depressing."

"It's heartbreaking for Jaye, is what it is. Does she know?"

Connor shook his head. "She knows her mother's been in touch and that she's all right, but that's it."

"So what are you going to do?"

"The only thing I can do. I'm going to find Jaye a more permanent living arrangement."

A MORE PERMANENT living arrangement.

Abby struggled to process the meaning of Connor's statement, the omelet she'd eaten for breakfast settling uneasily in her stomach. Her eyes, she realized, hadn't been as wide open as she'd believed when she'd gone into Connor's bed.

She'd chosen to forget about the job offer on Wall Street and that his time here in Maryland— his time with her—was finite.

"Don't worry. I won't say anything to Jaye about her mother or anything else yet," he said, evidently misinterpreting her stunned reaction. "I need to make sure what I have in mind will work."

Abby's thoughts returned to Jaye, a horrifying idea striking her. "Please tell me you're not thinking of having Jaye live with your mother."

He stiffened. "My mother's not as bad as you think. You'd know that if you'd met her before she lost a son."

Realizing she'd struck a nerve, Abby tried to phrase her next sentence more diplomatically. "Your mother doesn't seem like the best person to take care of Jaye."

"Don't you think I know that?" he asked rhetorically. "She wouldn't give Jaye the attention she needs."

"Then what do you have in mind?"

"My father," he answered.

She searched her mind for what he'd told her about his father. It wasn't much. He was a CPA who'd sold his business after his son had died. Abby didn't know where he was working now or even if he was still married to Elaine Smith, which seemed doubtful.

"Does your father still live in Bentonsville?"

"He hasn't for years. My parents divorced about a

year after J.D. died. Dad moved to Richmond to be near his parents. He's still living there, though not with his parents. He has a second wife and a young son. Ben's seven, I think."

"You don't know how old your stepbrother is?"

She could almost see him turning dates over in his mind. "Yeah, he's seven. I haven't seen him in almost a year, but I call my father every month or so. He and Shannon have been married for eight years. It sounds like they're happy. They could provide exactly the kind of environment Jaye needs."

If it had been a year since Connor had seen his father, they hadn't gotten together for the traditional family gathering times of Christmas or Thanksgiving. She knew his father had sent him a birthday card. But how close, she wondered, could they be?

"Does your father agree with you?" she ventured.

He hesitated. "Dad hasn't seen Jaye in years, so I haven't told him what I have in mind yet. I need to see how it goes. He invited us to spend Memorial Day with him."

Tomorrow was Memorial Day, a school holiday and, she concluded, a day off for Connor. Abby mentally questioned Connor's use of the word *invited.* She suspected he'd phoned his father and suggested he and Jaye drive down to Richmond for a visit. The entire scenario sounded anything but promising.

"This is about the Wall Street job, isn't it?" she asked abruptly.

He stared at her mutely for a moment, and it was impossible to tell what was going on in his head.

"You're wrong," he said finally. "This is about what's best for Jaye."

"Why are you so sure you're not what's best for her?"

He paced from one end of his kitchen to the other. "We've talked about this before, Abby. I feel like she's missing out. I'm not a father, and I sure as hell don't stack up to a mother. You see how she comes alive when she's with you. She should live in a house where there's another woman."

"Not all women are the motherly types."

"Dad's wife is. Shannon quit her job to stay home with Ben. Dad says she volunteers for everything."

Abby grew silent, not convinced he'd described the ideal situation for Jaye. "When will you tell your father and his wife what you have in mind?"

"I'm not sure I will tell them. I want to get an idea of whether things would work out first."

"And how are you going to do that?" she challenged.

He took her hand, turned it over and drew lazy circles on her palm. Her body responded to even that slight touch, remembering the pleasures of the night before.

"I need a second pair of eyes," he said, still drawing the circles. "That's why I'd like you to come with us to Richmond."

The enormity of what he was asking registered, and she pulled her hand away. "That's a very bad idea."

"It's not only for me," he said cajolingly. "It's for Jaye, too. I can't bring up the subject of her living with my father until I'm sure there's a possibility it could happen. She already has a complex about nobody wanting her."

Abby completely agreed with his instinct to use caution. Another rejection would devastate Jaye, but surely Connor must understand why Abby couldn't help. When he didn't state the reason, she did. "You know I wouldn't be welcome in your father's house."

"That's not true," he countered. "I called while you were in the shower and asked if he'd mind if I brought you along tomorrow. He's fine with it."

That she found hard to believe, unless... "Did you tell him who I was?" she challenged.

His gaze slipped away before returning to hers. "I told him you were Jaye's violin teacher and a close friend of mine."

"But you didn't mention who my brother is." She stated it as a fact.

"That's irrelevant."

"Your mother doesn't think so," she retorted. "What if your father recognizes my name like she did?"

He sighed, making it clear he didn't want to talk about this. "He won't. I referred you by name when I talked to him just now, and he didn't react."

"What if your mother tells him about me?"

"My parents don't talk to each other," he insisted. "Besides, Dad's very different than my mother."

She wasn't convinced his father wouldn't throw her out of his house the instant he discovered her family connections. He'd also lost a son that dark day, and Drew, whatever the extenuating circumstances, had admitted to being responsible.

Connor reached for her hand again. "You'd know

better than anyone else whether my father's family would be a good fit for Jaye. Please, Abby. I need you. And so does Jaye."

His plea for the little girl who had come to mean so much to both of them superseded, but didn't erase, Abby's lingering doubt. But there was still only one answer she could give.

"Okay," she said softly, "I'll come with you to Richmond."

CHAPTER TWELVE

THE CONTRAST BETWEEN THE HOUSE where he'd grown up and the one where his father now lived in Richmond with his second wife and young son struck Connor as he walked through the French doors onto an impressive wooden deck.

His father's four-bedroom colonial opened onto a stunning backyard with a view of a beautifully landscaped golf course. The rear porch of the much-smaller house in Bentonsville provided a sightline into the neighbors' cramped kitchen.

"It's gorgeous out here," Abby told Shannon Smith.

"We like it." Shannon giggled although nobody had said anything remotely humorous. When his father had married her, Connor had attributed her out-of-context laughter to her youth. She'd been twenty-two, a year younger than he'd been. It made sense that she was nervous around her new husband's family and friends. But eight years later, Shannon was still laughing at nothing.

She was also the only one of the three Smiths living in this showpiece of a house who was currently at home. She'd served them lemonade and suggested they sit outside to enjoy the sunshine.

"The view is what sold Denny on the house." Shannon squirmed in her teak chair and fiddled with the set of diamond rings on her left hand. Fair-haired and petite with freckles sprinkling her nose, she looked much younger than her twenty-nine years.

If she'd broken up his parents' marriage, Connor would have resented her. But she'd arrived on the scene after they'd split up. Since it seemed as though she was in over her head, he'd always felt somewhat sorry for her.

"Denny said having a golf course nearby could inspire Ben to become a better player," Shannon said.

"Isn't your son only seven years old?" Abby asked.

"Oh, yes. But he's very athletic. A natural, Denny calls him."

Once upon a time, his father had said the same thing about J.D. Connor had been a decent athlete, but he couldn't compete with a brother who drove a golf ball three hundred yards, hit a baseball out of the park and threw a football for touchdowns.

Shaking off the memory, Connor turned from the railing where he'd been gazing at the perfectly groomed grass of the fairway and addressed Shannon. "You said my dad took Ben to a basketball game. I didn't know teams played on Memorial Day."

Her giggle this time wasn't as pronounced. "Oh, yes. They play all the time. So many AAU teams have sprung up in the last couple years that gym space is an issue."

"AAU?" Abby asked. "What's that?"

"Amateur Athletic Union. It's the highest level of youth competition. You know, for the serious player."

Abby raised her eyebrows. "There are serious basketball teams for seven-year-olds?"

"Not for every seven-year-old. But Ben's good

enough that he can play against older kids on an under-nine team."

Connor, who'd heard all this before, also perceived something else in Shannon's explanation. "So my father knew Ben had a game when I called and set up the visit?"

"I don't think so," Shannon said. "Ben's team usually plays three or four games a weekend, but we were supposed to have this weekend free. This is a scrimmage that came up at the last minute."

"A scrimmage," Connor repeated, not able to keep the edge from his voice. He hadn't seen his father in almost a year, and Dad wasn't home to greet him because of a practice game. "Do you know when they'll be back?"

"Hopefully soon," she said, "but you never can tell about these things."

Abby slanted him a look that spoke volumes. Jaye had been unusually chatty on the two-hour drive to Richmond, mostly about her new friend Ashley but also about getting reacquainted with the grandfather she didn't remember. Now she sat silently in one of the deck chairs, her lemonade untouched.

A yapping sounded from inside the house. For the first time since they'd arrived, Jaye perked up. "Is that a dog?"

"It's Ben's golden retriever," Shannon said. "I shut him away in the game room when we're having visitors."

"Can I play with him?" Jaye asked, hope written clearly on her face.

"I'm afraid not. Denny doesn't like it when strangers play with Ben's dog. Goldie can be kind of excitable. I'm sure you understand."

Connor could tell that Jaye didn't understand why

her grandfather would object to her playing with the dog. Neither did he. "Jaye's not a stranger, Shannon. She's family."

"Oh, yes. Of course. I know that." Shannon sounded as if she were spouting words she didn't believe. Relief suddenly appeared on her face, and she leaped to her feet, the subject of the dog forgotten. "There they are now."

Connor assumed she'd heard the front door opening, but wasn't sure how. He hadn't detected a sound. His father came through the French doors onto the deck a few moments later. The gray was gone from his hair that was no longer brown but auburn.

He'd lost weight, too, although his athletic shorts and T-shirt still revealed a blocky, almost square, build.

"Hello, Dad," Connor said.

"Connor," he exclaimed with a grin, enthusiastically shaking hands. His eyes, Connor noticed, were the same shade of green as Jaye's. The same shade J.D.'s had been. They shifted to his granddaughter. "And you're Jaye, of course. I haven't seen you since you were a couple years old, but you're even prettier now than you were then."

"Hello," Jaye said shyly. She half rose, her hand starting to stretch toward his. But his father was already turning away from her and toward Abby.

"Speaking of pretty, you must Abby." He bestowed upon her the full force of his smile. "I can't fault my son for his taste in women."

Connor nearly interrupted his father to tell him he'd gotten the wrong impression of their relationship, but realized that wasn't true. He and Abby were sleeping together. The fact would take some getting used to, but he liked the sound of it.

Abby's gaze flicked to his, and Connor knew the same thoughts must have crossed her mind. He smiled at her, and she in turn smiled at his father. "Thank you. It was nice of you to let me come along, Mr. Smith."

"Happy to have you here. And, please, call me Denny." He glanced over his shoulder. "Where is that son of mine? Wait till you see how big he's gotten, Connor. He was a brute in the basketball game today. Scored twelve points, all in the paint."

"It's amazing how accomplished children are today. Jaye plays the violin beautifully, especially for a beginner," Abby said in an obvious attempt to bring his father's attention back to his grandchild. Jaye, who had reverted to sitting quietly, looked at Abby adoringly, her face beaming with pride.

"That's nice," his father said absently, then bellowed, "Ben. Get out here. I want to show you off."

Wearing a Richmond Running Rebels basketball uniform and carrying a half-finished sports drink, Ben walked slowly onto the deck. He was a few inches taller than when Connor had last seen him, but appeared thinner, partly due to the long, baggy shorts that made his legs look even skinnier than they were. He had his mother's sandy hair and long, thin face, but his father's green eyes.

"Hey, buddy," Connor said, and the boy smiled hesitantly at him.

"This is my boy, Ben. Isn't he something?" his father told Abby and Jaye, hugging the child against his side with one arm. "The pretty lady over there is Connor's girlfriend, Abby, and that's your cousin, Jaye."

Technically, Jaye was Ben's niece, but Connor didn't correct his father. Both children mumbled greetings but barely glanced at each other. So much, Connor thought, for connecting right off the bat.

"I like the name of your team," Abby told Ben. "The Richmond Running Rebels has a good ring. Did the team members get to pick it out?"

"The entire AAU club is called the Running Rebels," his father answered before Ben could speak. "I tell you, it's an honor to be on one of these teams. Tryouts are brutal. Anybody can play winter basketball but only the best of the best play club ball in the spring."

Ben said nothing, but stood in the circle of his father's arm, drawing patterns on the deck with the sole of his athletic shoe.

"Is basketball your favorite sport, Ben?" Abby asked.

"He likes them all. Don't you, Ben?" His father finally released the boy, chucking him under the chin as he did so. "He's going to take more golf lessons this summer, then in the fall we'll try football. I have a feeling that'll be his best sport."

Football was his father's favorite. He'd signed up first Connor, then J.D., in youth leagues as soon as they were old enough to play and had been on the sidelines at every game. That is, until J.D.'s games had conflicted with Connor's. Then he'd chosen to watch J.D. But Connor had understood. J.D. had not only been three years younger, he'd been a star.

Connor had tried to stand out in other ways. He'd majored in business in college primarily to help out at his father's accounting business. But his father had sold the business after J.D. died, stating that life was too short to spend at a career he didn't enjoy. After splitting the proceeds with the wife he was divorcing, he'd received his real-estate license and become a success.

The upshot was that Denny Smith would still rather talk sports than finance.

"Can I go play video games, Dad?" Ben asked.

"Sure, son. But only until your mother and I get things ready for the cookout."

"Hold on, Ben," Connor said before the boy could make his escape. "Maybe Jaye would like to go with you? How about it, Jaye? Why don't you get to know your cousin better?"

Jaye didn't appear thrilled at the prospect, but got awkwardly to her feet. "Okay," she said and followed the silent Ben into the house.

His father's face glowed as he watched his son leave. "You should have seen him today on the court, Connor. He had ten rebounds to go with those twelve points. Nobody could stop him. I'm sure looking forward to football."

"You don't want to put too much pressure on him, Dad," Connor said in a soft, warning voice.

"Nonsense. The boy thrives on pressure, like any good athlete." He got a wistful look on his face. "Takes after his brother that way."

Everybody on the deck knew he wasn't talking about Connor.

"Connor's job is full of pressure," Abby said, "and he handles it really well. Otherwise, he wouldn't be so good at it. Did he tell you that a Wall Street firm is courting him?"

Connor swung his gaze to Abby, surprised that

she had anything positive to say about his job. She looked as proud of him as she had of Jaye a few moments ago.

"Good for you, son," Denny said, acting as though the job offer was news to him even though Connor had mentioned it when they'd spoken on the phone. "You'll have to tell me all about it, but now we've got to start lunch. Ben's sure to be hungry after that big game he had."

Abby appeared ready to say something else, but Connor beat her to it. "I'll help get the grill ready."

He saw Abby's chest rise, then fall in a silent sigh. "And I'll see if Shannon needs help in the kitchen."

"Do me a favor and make sure she doesn't overdo it," his father said, then slapped his forehead when they looked at him quizzically. "Me and my big mouth. I keep forgetting she wants us to wait before we tell anybody."

"Tell anybody what?" Connor asked.

"What the hell. You're my son. I'd have told you soon anyway." His chest puffed out, peacock style. He waited a beat, increasing the drama. "Shannon's pregnant."

ALL THOUGHT OF BEING EXPOSED as Drew Galloway's sister vanished as Abby registered the stricken look on Connor's face. She hurriedly crossed to his side, lacing her fingers with his. He felt cold even though the temperature was in the seventies.

"That's wonderful news," she said, filling the silence. "We're both very happy for you."

Connor slowly emerged from his trance and offered his father the hand Abby wasn't holding. "Yeah, Dad. Congratulations."

"We don't know the sex yet." His father winked as he heartily shook Connor's hand. "But I'm hoping for another boy. Don't know a thing about raising girls."

Abby thought first of what that meant to Jaye, but asked, "What about Diana?"

"Diana proves my point. I tried to get her interested in sports so we'd have something in common, but it didn't work. She was closer to her mother."

A mother who'd turned her back on her pregnant daughter at the time she'd needed her most. Abby wondered what, if anything, Denny had had to say about the pregnancy.

"Having a girl around can be wonderful," Abby said, with Jaye in her thoughts. "I understand you were disappointed your daughter wasn't into sports, but every child is good at something."

"Yeah," Denny said, scratching his chin thoughtfully, "looking back on it, I should have encouraged Diana to be a cheerleader. Who better to lead the cheers for her brother?"

The rest of the afternoon passed slowly, in much the same vein as it had started. Shannon faded into the background, and Denny did most of the talking. He was silent long enough to listen to the details of Connor's Wall Street job offer, but soon changed the subject to the high-end real estate he sold.

After their cookout, Ben asked if he could play in the yard with his dog and the neighbors. Jaye went with him, but soon joined the adults in the expensively-finished downstairs game room where, at Denny's suggestion, the adults had retreated for a game of pool.

"Why don't you be on the team with me and Connor,

Jaye?" Abby suggested. "That way, it can be the three of us against Denny and Shannon."

"I've never played before," Jaye said quietly.

"Then it might be best if she watched," Denny cut in. "She won't—"

"I think it's a great idea," Connor interrupted, and Abby could have kissed him for it. "How will she learn if she never plays?"

"Okay, but don't expect me to take it easy on you because you've got beginners on your team," Denny said before he racked up the balls and lined up his pool cue for the break.

Thirty minutes later, she, Connor and Jaye were down two games to none.

"I'm not very good," Jaye murmured after she knocked the cue ball into a corner pocket.

"Me, neither," Abby volunteered, although she was easily better than Shannon, who had knocked in about as many balls as Jaye. The difference was that Shannon had a partner with the ability to run the table. "Besides, it takes time to learn a new skill. You know that because of the violin. I wish we'd thought to bring it along so you could have shown everybody how nicely you play."

"That's right," Denny spoke up, focusing on Abby instead of Jaye. "Connor did say you were Jaye's violin teacher."

"I am," Abby answered. "We've worked it out so Jaye comes home with me after school, and Connor picks her up at my place after work. We've managed great."

Jaye made a face. "Except when Grandma found out about it and tried to stop you from teaching me."

Denny directed a sharp look at Jaye. "Why would your grandmother do that?"

Abby knew what was coming but couldn't stop it.

"Because of Abby's brother," Jaye replied.

Denny turned to Abby, his gaze curious. "Who's your brother?"

She'd decided during the drive to Richmond not to evade the question if asked directly. But that was before she'd met Denny and before finding out Shannon was pregnant.

Connor was having a hard enough time dealing with his father as it was. Telling Denny who she was would only make things more difficult for him.

Because Denny was so preoccupied with his new family, Abby figured the question wouldn't be hard to dodge. She'd give a vague answer, and in the space of a few minutes he'd forget what they'd been discussing.

She mentally prepared an unclear answer, but didn't get to voice it, because Connor answered the question for her: "Drew Galloway."

CONNOR WASN'T SURE who was more surprised that he'd made the revelation—Abby or himself.

He hadn't realized he meant to blurt out her family connection until he'd already done it, but keeping the information under wraps had seemed unfair to Abby.

She stared at him now, her face infused with wonder. His father had paled so that those green eyes he'd passed down to his dead son seemed to overtake his face.

"Who's Drew Galloway?" Shannon asked in a

chirpy voice, oblivious to the sudden tension cloaking the other adults.

Connor couldn't hide his surprise. How could Shannon not recognize the name of the man who'd killed her husband's son?

"Someone from our past," Denny said obliquely. He seemed to compose himself, then addressed his wife again. "Shannon, would you do me a favor and take Jaye upstairs for some of your homemade chocolate-chip cookies?"

Shannon didn't ask why, but nodded toward Jaye. "Sure. And when we're up there, we can see where Ben's gone off to."

Nobody left in the basement said a word while Shannon and Jaye retreated, causing the sound of their footsteps on the stairs and Shannon's laughter to sound unnaturally loud. But eventually they faded and silence ruled.

Connor spoke first. "Galloway's actually Abby's half brother. They have different fathers, which is why their last names are different."

Abby lifted her chin and Connor surmised she was bracing herself for the worst. Communicating to both her and his father that he was on her side, he gathered her to him with an arm around her shoulders.

"Abby and I met through Jaye, just like I told you," Connor continued, clueless as to what his father was thinking. "We didn't know at first that our paths had crossed before. By the time we found out, we were already involved."

His father gazed back at them, uncharacteristically saying nothing, his countenance more serious than it had been all day, causing him to appear older. Finally, in a quiet voice, he asked, "Were you ever going to tell me?"

Connor shook his head, shouldering the blame. "Abby wanted to tell you, but I talked her out of it. I was afraid you'd have negative feelings toward her."

He waited, realizing he'd clenched his stomach muscles in anticipation of his father's reaction. He still didn't have any notion of what it would be.

"Why would I blame her? Abby didn't have anything to do with what happened." He pinned his gaze on her. "You were, what, fourteen, fifteen at the time?"

Connor felt Abby's shoulders slump, as though the tension had abruptly left them. She'd been worried about his father's reaction, too, he realized.

"Fifteen," she answered. "But do you mean that? You really don't have a problem with me being in your house?"

"I have a problem with not being told who you were up front, but that's all," he said in his more customary booming voice. "Oh, don't get me wrong. I didn't always feel this way. If you'd come into my house right after it happened, I'd have thrown you out. But I've moved on. I don't see the point in holding grudges, against either you or your brother."

Connor released a short, harsh breath. His arm dropped from Abby's shoulders. He didn't hold a grudge against Abby, either. But he couldn't say the same about Galloway. "You really mean that?" he asked his father. "You don't hold a grudge against the man who murdered your son?"

"Dwelling in the past won't bring J.D. back. I've

gotten on with my life. My priorities now are Shannon, Ben and the baby."

Connor noticed that his name wasn't included on his father's short list, but then Denny Smith had shown little interest in his oldest son all day. Or in Jaye, for that matter.

If their visit to Richmond had proved one thing, it was that his father and Shannon weren't the right people to raise Jaye.

The purpose for the trip concluded, they stayed only thirty more minutes before heading back home. Neither he nor Abby spoke until Jaye put in the headphones of her CD player, leaned back against the car seat and closed her eyes.

"I liked your father," Abby announced.

He wasn't surprised. Denny had treated Abby no differently after he'd discovered her connection to Galloway than he had before. "Most people do. He's a likeable guy. Although I can't say I liked the perfunctory way he treated Jaye."

Abby must have noticed that his father treated him in a similarly dismissive manner, but she didn't point it out. He'd claimed he needed her along to help decide what was best for Jaye, but he realized the real reason had been for moral support. Talkative or silent, she'd made it clear she was in his corner.

"In case you have any doubt, I do realize Jaye wouldn't be happy with my father and his family," he said. "It was pretty much a no-brainer."

She nodded, the brief movement enough to convey her agreement. "Then it's good that you didn't tell Jaye what you had in mind."

They traveled in silence for another five miles before she spoke again. "There's something I can't make sense of no matter how hard I try." She craned her neck so she looked fully at him instead of the road. "Why did you tell your father the truth about Drew being my brother?"

"It seemed wrong not to," he said, then lapsed into another silence. He had yet to examine his motive closely, but did now. After a few moments, he expanded on his answer. "I never want you to feel as though you have to pretend to be somebody you're not around me or my family."

He reached across the seat, picked up her hand and brought it to his lips. He took his attention briefly from the road to meet her still-doubtful eyes.

"I like who you are," he said. "Inside and out."

CHAPTER THIRTEEN

THE AUTO-REPAIR SHOP that Louis Clark's brother owned was nestled in a congested part of Rockville, on a rutted section of road that ran parallel to Interstate 270.

Abby visually canvassed the area, noting a doughnut shop, a Subway and a secondhand clothing store. She blew out a breath, relieved that the surrounding businesses were of a benign nature. She'd half feared she'd spot something that would tempt an ex-con, like a strip joint or liquor store.

"Fuzzy's Auto Repair," Jaye read as Abby pulled into the last available spot in front of the shop. "That's a funny name. Like in that rhyme about Fuzzy Wuzzy being a bear."

"Was he?" Abby asked, and Jaye giggled.

Although the girl had been good company, Abby regretted bringing Jaye along on this errand. It couldn't be helped. Today she'd realized the parole hearing was two weeks off and she'd yet to carve out the time to visit the auto-repair shop. Fuzzy reportedly didn't work weekends, so the only time Abby could manage a face-to-face meeting was after school.

"Why did you say we were coming here?" Jaye asked.

Abby hadn't said. She intended to support her

brother in any way possible, but agreed with Connor that she should avoid discussing Drew with Jaye if it could be helped.

"I need to talk to Fuzzy," Abby said, hoping Jaye wouldn't ask for a more thorough explanation. "He's the owner."

"His name is really Fuzzy? Cool." Jaye opened the car door and hopped out.

Abby suppressed a sigh. She'd originally planned for Jaye to wait in the car, but didn't feel comfortable leaving her alone in such a shabby neighborhood. She joined the girl on the sidewalk, then led her inside the shop.

The carpeting in the reception area was worn and green and the air smelled like exhaust fumes and automobile grease. Situated against the back wall were a pair of vending machines and a midsize television with poor reception. A worn wooden table piled high with magazines and some uncomfortable-looking, orange plastic chairs completed the waiting area.

Behind a waist-high counter at the head of the room, a large man with an unruly red beard talked on the phone in a language that sounded like it might be Korean.

Jaye nodded toward him and said in a loud whisper, "That has to be Fuzzy, 'cause he sure is."

Abby smiled at her. "I bet you're right."

Abby reached into the bottom of her purse for the change that always collected there and offered Jaye a handful of coins. "Why don't you get something out of the vending machines and watch television until I'm done talking to Fuzzy?"

"Sure." Jaye took the change and headed for the

machines at about the same time the big, bearded man hung up.

Before Abby could speak, a young, dark-complected man with a pockmarked face stuck his head in the room and asked the big guy a question in Spanish. The redhead answered in kind, then turned to Abby when the man retreated.

"What can I do for you?" he asked in perfect, unaccented English.

"You can tell me how many languages you speak, for starters," she said.

"Three. English, Spanish and Vietnamese although I can get by in Portuguese. I know, I know. What's a guy like me doing in a place like this?" He shrugged. "My mother would tell you I'm a classic underachiever, but I do okay. I own this place free and clear, and my kids go to private school."

"You're Fuzzy Williams, then?"

He nodded, deep furrows appearing on his forehead. "In the flesh. Who are you?"

"Abby Reed, Louis's friend. He's the custodian at the school where I work. Did he mention me?"

He scratched his bushy beard. "Reed. Reed. Yeah, as a matter of fact he did. Said you were asking about a job for your husband."

"My brother," she corrected. "His name is Drew Galloway."

"Have him stop by any time this week or next," Fuzzy offered. "Turnover's a lot higher here than I'd like. I'm always on the lookout for a good mechanic."

Abby glanced briefly over her shoulder at Jaye. The

girl sat in front of the television munching on a bag of chips and sipping a soda.

"Here's the thing. Drew's in jail, but his parole hearing is in a few weeks. It would greatly help his chances of getting out if he had a job lined up." She took a deep breath and plunged ahead even though Fuzzy had already started to shake his head. "You wouldn't be sorry. He's a good mechanic and a hard worker. He worked on cars before he went in, and he's gotten training in jail."

"Sounds like he can do the job but it's too risky."

"Haven't you ever hired an ex-con?"

"A couple of times," Fuzzy admitted. "Had good luck with them, too. But your brother's still in jail. I can't hire him sight unseen."

"I know you don't know me, but I can vouch for him. I'll get him to call so you can tell him what you'd expect. The risk to you would be minimal. If he doesn't meet your expectations, you can fire him. You wouldn't be sorry you hired him. Honest."

She stopped talking when she realized she was babbling. Fuzzy's implacable expression hadn't changed. With a sinking heart, she waited for him to refuse her request.

"What's your brother in for?" he asked instead.

Prepared for the conversation to go from bad to worse, Abby answered, "He stabbed another teenager to death ten years ago when he was eighteen."

One of Fuzzy's red eyebrows arched. "Over what?"

"An argument over a girl, the police said." She was about to explain that she'd never been convinced that was the true reason for the altercation, but the air of wariness surrounding him stopped her.

Silently admitting defeat, she drew a shaky breath, squared her shoulders and said with as much dignity as she could muster, "I'm sorry I took up your time. Thank you for talking to me."

She whirled away from him, blinking back tears. It would take a supreme acting job to fool Jaye into believing that nothing was wrong.

"I'm not done talking," Finzy announced.

Abby's head whipped back around, her tears instantly drying.

"When's this parole hearing?"

"Two weeks from tomorrow."

He digested the information in silence, then said, "If he gets out, a job'll be waiting."

"I can't thank you enough," she blurted, then quickly made arrangements with him to put the offer in writing. "You won't be sorry. I promise."

"That brother of yours is damn lucky to have you, but it's not you who has to do the promising," he said. "You never know how guys who have been in the joint are gonna turn out. Sometimes they work extra hard and sometimes they don't. It's a gamble."

She could have left well enough alone, but her curiosity wouldn't let her. "What made you take the gamble?"

"Besides being a sucker for a pretty face?" He shrugged. "Like I told you, I've had good luck with ex-cons in the past."

Abby wasn't aware that Jaye was standing behind her until she backed up and almost bumped into her. How much had the girl heard?

"Are you done talking yet, Abby?" Jaye asked. Her

lips were vaguely orange from the barbecue-flavored chips she'd been eating.

"I'm done," Abby said brightly, then addressed Fuzzy. "Thanks again. I really appreciate it."

Jaye skipped to the car, offering to share the half-eaten bag of chips she'd gotten out of the vending machine and chattering about the woman on the daytime talk show who'd lost two hundred pounds.

"They said two hundred pounds is as much as a grown man weighs," she said. "Imagine losing Uncle Connor."

Abby relaxed, fairly certain Jaye hadn't overheard enough to figure out the purpose of the visit. The light ahead of them switched from yellow to red, and Abby slowed to a stop.

After a single beat of silence, Jaye asked, "Abby, what's an ex-con?"

THE QUESTION THAT FELT as though it had been festering in Connor's brain fled when Abby opened her apartment door. Every part of her looked welcoming, from her shining eyes to her smiling lips to her reaching hand.

"Jaye's next door with Kendall." She pulled him into her apartment, shut the door and looped her arms around his neck. "So hurry up and kiss me, because she'll be back any minute."

She didn't wait for him to take the initiative, but brought his head down and eagerly claimed his mouth. The sensation of her lips on his and her soft curves pressed against him filled his senses and clouded his brain. She smelled like sunshine, clean and fresh and warm.

He lost himself for a moment, kissing her back, until he remembered what his body was trying very hard to forget. Reluctantly lifting his head, he broke their mouth-to-mouth contact.

"Connor?" There was a question in her voice. She gazed up at him, her eyes confused, her mouth dewy. "Is something wrong?"

"Yeah. Something's wrong."

She withdrew her arms from his neck and wrapped them around her midsection. "You're scaring me, Connor. What is it?"

He absently rubbed the back of his neck. "This morning at breakfast, Jaye told me about this guy named Fuzzy. She probably wouldn't have mentioned him except she thought he had a funny name."

Abby didn't reply, but her expression turned guarded.

"She said Fuzzy owns an auto shop." He watched her carefully, noticing her posture stiffen. "But she said you didn't have any work done on your car. She said you went there to talk to Fuzzy about ex-cons."

Abby grimaced, confirming his suspicions. His mother had made it her business to find out every detail about Drew Galloway, including his job history after he'd dropped out of high school. He'd worked in an auto-repair shop before his arrest and incarceration.

It didn't take much of a stretch of the imagination to conclude that Abby had been at Fuzzy's Auto Repair to line up a job for her half brother.

"How could you involve Jaye in anything to do with Galloway?" he asked, unable to stop his voice from rising. "Don't you know how I feel about that?"

"Of course I know. You haven't exactly made it a secret. But you're jumping to conclusions. I didn't involve Jaye."

"So you didn't go to that auto-repair shop to talk the owner into giving Galloway a job?"

"Yes, but—"

"That's involving her."

"Jaye didn't know why we were there," she retorted.

"She knew it was about something involving convicts. She's a smart girl, Abby." He paused. "Want to hear what she asked me this morning? She asked if I thought Galloway would get out of prison."

"I didn't realize she'd pieced it all together."

He tapped his closed fist to his mouth, trying to keep himself from saying anything he'd regret later. "Why did you take her with you in the first place?"

"Fuzzy doesn't work weekends or past six o'clock on weekdays. I assumed he'd be more receptive to what I had to say if I talked to him in person. I kept putting off the visit precisely because I didn't want to take Jaye with me. But finally I had to."

He digested the information, understanding her reasoning but loath to condone it. "Why are you the one trying to get Galloway a job?"

"You know as well as I do that a prisoner's chances of getting out on parole are better if he has a job and place to live lined up."

"But why is it your responsibility?"

"Why not me? Drew needs somebody on his side. Heaven knows there are enough people against him."

"With good reason," he muttered.

She lifted her hand, palm side up. "Let's not get into

this again. It's unreasonable of you to expect me not to help him."

"It's unreasonable of *you* to expect me to like it that you're helping him."

They stared at each other, at an impasse. He could have asked if she'd been successful in securing the job for Galloway, but the question would only stir up more resentment. Especially if the answer was yes.

He sighed heavily. "I don't want to fight with you."

"Me, neither."

He stepped forward and drew her into his arms, nestling her body against his as he rested his chin on the top of her head. She felt every bit as warm and wonderful as she had the other night when they'd made love, but something was different. Even though no space separated their bodies, he didn't feel quite as close to her.

Drew Galloway, it seemed, had found yet another way to mess up his life.

THE PUB WHERE RICO SHAW hung out was in a section of northeast Washington, D.C., where merchants put bars on the windows of their businesses and young men loitered on street corners.

Spider Strickland's flashy red convertible stuck out like a gaily dressed clown at a funeral. Dee Dee slowed her car, and saw Spider saunter out of the bar, his gold necklace catching the glint of a streetlight.

Any misgivings about what she was about to do fled. This was the second time she'd seen Spider in the vicinity of Rico Shaw. The younger man was involved with the ex-con, and she'd wager it had more to do with business than friendship.

She entered the pub, which wasn't one of the new-fangled establishments where trendy types congregated. It had a smoky, basement-type atmosphere that gave her an immediate sense of claustrophobia, a couple of pool tables, one undersized television and a bar running the length of the back wall.

Every occupant in the place looked at her when she entered, heightening her self-consciousness. The majority of the customers were male, but the few females were decades younger than Dee Dee. She searched the curious faces for Rico Shaw and didn't see him.

Disappointment nearly flattened her. She'd known it was a risk coming here, but her hopes had been high that she'd stumble upon a time when Rico was present. When she'd spotted Spider outside the bar, she'd been sure she'd timed things right.

She'd have to stop by the bar another time. Or go by Rico's house and knock on the door. Or… A man sitting alone at the bar turned to say something to the bartender, bringing his profile into stark focus and halting her thought.

The man was Rico Shaw.

Her pulse jumped and her stomach churned, but she ignored the physical signs of nervousness. She was here, and so was Rico. She'd be damned if she let anything stop her from what she had to do.

She walked directly to the bar and sat down on the stool next to him. His gaze shifted to her. His ordinary features were pleasant enough but she glimpsed something hard in his eyes before he looked away, automatically dismissing her.

"What can I get for you?" asked the bartender

gruffly. He was a big man with a shaved head and a tattoo of an eagle on his forearm.

"Tonic water," she said, and ignored his small snort of disgust.

She waited until he delivered her drink before speaking to the young man beside her. "Your name's Rico Shaw, isn't it?"

He didn't look up from the mug of beer he was cradling. "Who's asking?"

"My name's Dee Dee Reed. I'm Drew Galloway's mother."

A wariness settled over him as tangible as the smell of smoke in the air. He turned to her and regarded her from under hooded, dark eyes. "What do you want?"

"I want to talk to you," she said, trying to figure out the best way to approach the subject. "Do you have a child of your own, Mr. Shaw?"

He threw back his head and laughed, revealing a chipped front tooth. "I hope not, but a man can't never be sure."

"You probably won't be able to understand what I'm doing here until you do." She formed her words carefully. "If my son gets out of prison, I want him to have the best possible chance to succeed."

"Why you telling *me* this?"

"I think that Spider Strickland asked you to offer my son a place to live."

He frowned and repositioned himself on the bar stool. "What's it to you if he did?"

That was all the confirmation Dee Dee needed. She already knew from calls to friends in the old neighborhood that Spider had just served three years in prison for possession of marijuana with intent to distribute. The rumor was that prison rehabilitation hadn't worked on him.

Dee Dee looked Rico Shaw straight in the eyes. "I want you to withdraw your offer for Drew to live with you."

He snorted. "Why would I do that?"

"Because I'll pay you if you do."

His already small eyes narrowed. "I've got enough money."

"I don't think so," she ventured, ignoring her damp palms and pounding heart. "I think someone like you can never have too much money."

"What do you mean by someone like me?"

She thought he had a drug habit. She also thought that Spider was supplying him with drugs to sell on the street, but of course she couldn't prove any of that. She could, however, make an anonymous call to the police department's narcotics unit.

"A businessman," she said. "A man who doesn't want any trouble with the authorities."

His faint smile disappeared, his expression growing dark, his voice menacing. "Are you threatening me?"

She locked gazes with him, refusing to let him see how nervous she was, glad for the girlfriend who'd taught her poker and the fine points of bluffing. "Not if you take my money, I'm not. My only stipulation is that you don't tell either Spider or Drew I talked to you."

"And all I gotta do for this money is tell the guy in prison I changed my mind about him living with me?"

"That's all," she said.

He stared at her for a moment longer, his eyes not nearly as cold as Spider Strickland's. Then he shrugged. "What the hell, I'm not hot on having a roommate anyway. How much you offerin'?"

CHAPTER FOURTEEN

THE END-OF-THE-YEAR ORCHESTRA concert was a full week before classes let out for the summer. Abby had discovered over her years of teaching that students were so eager for summer vacation that they accomplished little in the waning days of the school year.

She bustled from student to student in the designated warm-up room, helping tune one out-of-key instrument after the next. The familiar flare of excitement that always preceded a performance lit her belly.

The flame grew dimmer when she noticed Jaye sitting at the edge of the room. She was dressed in the same cheery blue orchestra T-shirt as the other students, but the similarity ended there. Her violin was on her lap instead of perched on her shoulder.

Abby passed a half dozen other students, offering encouragement and smiles, before she reached her. She bent down so that they were at eye level. "Jaye, why aren't you warming up? Do you need me to help you tune your instrument?"

A quick shake of the head, then she said, "I don't feel so good, Abby."

Frowning, Abby pressed a hand to the girl's forehead. "You don't feel hot."

"My stomach hurts. It feels like it's jumping up and down inside my body."

The mysterious malady suddenly made sense. Hiding a smile, Abby drew a chair over to the girl's side and sat down. "Have you ever heard of pre-concert jitters?"

Jaye shook her head, her pretty face solemn.

"It's an anxious feeling performers get before taking the stage, but you know what? It's completely normal."

"It is?"

"Sure is. There are a couple of things you can do to make it better. First, take some deep breaths. Like this." Abby breathed deeply in, then out. Jaye's thin chest rose and fell in unison with hers.

"Good. Then remind yourself that you know your stuff. You've practiced these pieces so many times, they'll become second nature when you're onstage. And finally, make your nervousness work for you. It can give you the energy you need to dig deep and do a good job, just like I know you will." Abby ended her speech with a full smile.

"I'm not nervous about that, Abby," Jaye said. "I know I can play the songs."

"Then why is your stomach jumping?"

Jaye's lower lip trembled, and she caught it with her upper teeth. She didn't say anything for a long moment, then blurted, "Because I don't know if anyone will come watch me."

"Do you mean your uncle Connor?"

The girl nodded wordlessly, her head bowed so her blond hair nearly covered her face.

"He said he'd come, didn't he?" Abby asked.

"My mom used to say that, too," Jaye whispered, "but half the time she didn't show up. She always had a good excuse, like her boss wouldn't let her leave work, but I didn't care about that. I wanted her there."

"Of course you did." Abby's heart felt as if it were splitting in two, not only for Jaye but for her mother. Diana Smith had made plenty of mistakes and was still making them, but raising a child alone when she'd been little more than a child herself couldn't have been easy. "But, even if no one else comes tonight, I'll be there, honey."

Her statement didn't have the desired effect. Jaye sniffed and blinked rapidly so her tears wouldn't fall. "So you don't think Uncle Connor will come, either?"

"I didn't say that," Abby said quickly. She took Jaye's small hand, squeezed it gently and put her faith in Connor. "Your uncle will be there, Jaye. Trust me on that."

Jaye's slight nod was almost imperceptible. Unshed tears swam in her eyes, but her lips curved into a ghost of a smile. "I trust you, Abby," she whispered.

Abby's stomach was the one doing flip-flops after that. What had possessed her to promise Jaye that her workaholic uncle, who'd had her feed his niece dinner because he needed to catch up at the office, would attend the concert? If she was wrong, Jaye would feel betrayed not only by Connor, but by Abby, too.

A dozen small tasks required her attention before the students could take the stage. She did them automatically, her mind on the promise that hadn't been hers to make.

The time finally came to line up the students and steer them toward the middle-school auditorium they'd borrowed for the concert. She brought up the rear, then broke off from the group and waited in the wings while they filed onto the stage.

The auditorium was a nice size for a concert, with ascending seats that overlooked the curved stage. The lights had yet to dim, providing her with a good view of the audience. She scanned the crowd of parents and relatives, searching for one face. Feeling sick to her stomach, she scanned the audience again.

Just as she was about to survey the group for the third time, a door at the top of the auditorium opened and her eyes verified what her heart had known all along.

Connor hurried inside wearing one of his expensive suits, this one in navy blue. Abby had never been happier to see a man. He smiled and waved toward the stage. Jaye was standing in front of her seat, waiting for Abby, the conductor, to take the stage. Jaye smiled and gave the tiniest wave back.

Abby watched the interplay between uncle and niece, knowing that the uncle had just claimed a little bit more of her heart. She delayed taking her position behind the conductor's stand, wanting to give Connor time to find a seat.

He surveyed the crowd before moving toward a section of seats less crowded than the rest. She stifled a gasp as she recognized her mother, sitting alone in the center of them. Dee Dee hadn't been sure she'd be able to attend the concert, and somehow Abby had missed her when she'd scanned the crowd earlier.

Didn't Connor see her mother, either? Or had he somehow failed to recognize her? The possibility grew less likely as he passed one empty seat after another until he reached her mother. He said something, then sat down beside her.

Abby's eyes brimmed with happy tears. She blinked them back, optimistic that things were not only going to work out between Jaye and Connor but for her and Connor, too.

With a smile wreathing her face, she walked onto the stage to a smattering of applause from an audience that included two of the people who meant the most to her.

WITH DEE DEE REED SITTING perfectly motionless beside him, Connor listened to the student orchestra play a surprisingly competent version of a musical selection by Mozart.

He felt as though he'd been plunked into the middle of a Fellini movie, where the surreal reigned supreme. Abby's mother could probably identify with the feeling. He'd read shock on her face when he'd asked if she'd mind if he sat next to her.

He'd recognized her instantly, having gotten a clear view of her standing on the doorstep that night Jaye had gone missing. He'd surmised from the rigid set of her shoulders when he'd approached that she'd known who he was, too.

Since she couldn't have gotten a good look at him as he'd waited in the car for Abby, he wondered if she recognized him from the courtroom ten years ago or because he looked like his dead brother.

The song ended. Somebody had dimmed the auditorium lights, rendering it impossible for Jaye to see him. He clapped loudly and long, hoping she could hear him.

Mrs. Reed leaned slightly toward him. She smelled

of peppermint breath mints, the same way his own mother often did. "Which one is your niece?"

"The pretty blonde in the first row who already has her bow in position for the next song." He heard the pride in his voice and was unashamed. Jaye had practiced for many hours to get ready for the concert and the result was worth the effort.

"She's beautiful," Mrs. Reed said.

"Thank you," he said, and sat beside her through lively, simplified selections by Tchaikovsky and Bach. Then Abby took her bow, the amateur musicians lapped up the enthusiastic response from their adoring friends and family and Connor was alone with Abby's mother.

The lights flickered on. The shape of Dee Dee Reed's face and slant of her nose were so like her daughter's that it struck him that Abby would look very much like her mother in twenty years. Abby, he thought, would be lovely.

"There's something I need to say," she suddenly announced, her face pinched with tension. "It's something I tried to say to your mother a half-dozen times. I even wrote her a letter, but she sent it back unopened."

His gut clenched and he put up a hand. "You don't need to say anything."

"Oh, but I do." She blinked back a shimmer of tears. "I'm truly sorry for your family's loss and for the heartache you endured because of my son. Not a day goes by when I don't say a prayer for your brother."

He swallowed the lump that threatened to clog his throat. He didn't want to talk about J.D., but had to say something. "No one blames you," he mumbled.

That wasn't true, he realized even as he uttered the

words. His mother blamed her. One of her common rants was that J.D. might be alive today if Dee Dee Reed had been a better mother.

Dee Dee's smile turned watery. "I can understand what my daughter sees in you. A good man is one who can find it in his heart to forgive."

Except he wasn't the man she thought he was. He could only accept Mrs. Reed's apology because, unlike his mother, he thought she had nothing to apologize for.

He didn't feel the same way about her son. Some actions were so unconscionable that words could never atone for them. Had Drew Galloway claimed he was sorry, Connor would have thrown his apology back in his face.

Abby's mother, obviously, couldn't know what was running through his head. "It was a pleasure to sit next to you, Mr. Smith."

"Please, call me Connor."

"Okay, then, Connor. And you can call me Dee Dee." She smiled again, and the way her eyes crinkled at the corners was so like Abby's that his breath caught. She picked up her purse from the empty chair next to her.

He angled his head. "Are you leaving?"

"Just as soon as I get the chance to tell Abby what a great job she did." She paused. "I know the two of you must have plans."

The hour was too late for dinner, but Connor had promised to treat Jaye and Abby after the performance. Dee Dee obviously concluded she wasn't welcome.

"We're only going out for ice cream." He hesitated slightly before asking, "Would you like to come with us?"

Surprise registered on her face. "Are you sure you want me to come?"

He'd issued the invitation before he'd consciously thought about offering it. But now that it was out in the open, he realized it was the right thing to do. "Yes, I'm sure."

Her smile was all the thanks he needed. "Then I'd love to."

He stood up and offered her a hand. She put her much smaller hand in his, and he helped her to her feet. Shame swept through him for asking Abby to keep her mother away from Jaye.

Even before he'd met Dee Dee, he should have known better.

Dee Dee might be Drew Galloway's mother, but she was Abby's mother, too. And any mother who had raised a woman as fine as Abby was a person worth knowing.

"YOU, CONNOR SMITH, are an amazing, amazing man."

Abby dropped down next to Connor on the leather sofa in his living room, wrapped her arms around his neck and plastered his face with kisses. His forehead, his cheeks, his chin, his lips. She was an equal-opportunity kisser.

They'd shut the door to Jaye's bedroom only minutes ago. Abby was fairly sure the child, exhausted from the concert and the extra fun afterward, would fall asleep quickly. But if she walked in on them, Abby could deal with that. It was about time Jaye knew the full extent of how her teacher felt about her uncle.

Connor laughed, letting her do with him what she willed. "And you, Abby Reed, are a crazy woman."

Crazy in love with him.

The words thundered through her brain, the full

import hitting her. She stopped planting kisses, drew back and stared at him as the newfound knowledge registered. It had happened so gradually that she hadn't realized until just now that the feeling was sneaking up on her. But now that the thought had invaded her consciousness, she knew it was true.

She was in love with Connor Smith.

His sensuous mouth curved in a half smile. "Why are you looking at me like that? Do I have chocolate ice cream on my face?"

His mention of ice cream vividly reminded her of the invitation he'd extended to her mother to join them for a post-concert treat.

The four of them—she, Connor, her mother and Jaye—had gathered around a circular red table at a brightly lit ice-cream parlor digging into their treats. A hot-fudge sundae for Jaye, a root-beer float for Abby and chocolate-fudge ice-cream cones for Connor and her mother.

Abby had been afraid that the conversation would be punctuated by long, awkward pauses, but it had flowed seamlessly. They'd talked about everything from the concert to Jaye's rapid improvement on the violin to elementary school classes to the minimally invasive procedures the surgeons operated under at George Washington University Hospital.

Through it all, Connor had treated her mother—the mother of the man who'd killed his brother—with the utmost respect. It had even seemed to Abby as though he liked Dee Dee.

Is that when she'd fallen in love with him? Or had it been earlier, at the concert, when he'd kept his promise to Jaye to be in the audience? Or even earlier than that, at his father's house, when he'd been the one to reveal that Abby was Drew Galloway's sister?

"If your face was smeared with chocolate, I would have kissed it off by now," she said, recovering her voice and making an effort to keep the mood light. She obviously fell shy of the mark.

"Then why were you staring at me like that?" he asked. "You looked, I don't know, like you had something you wanted to say."

That wasn't quite true, Abby realized. The knowledge that she loved him was so new she wasn't ready to share it. But there was something she had been meaning to ask him.

"I know that it wasn't an accident that you sat beside my mother at the concert. I spotted you arriving and saw you approach her. I've been wondering why you did."

"I hadn't realized you saw that," he said, almost to himself.

She said nothing, waiting for his answer. He rubbed his chin, as though trying to figure out his own motivation.

"She's your mother," he said simply.

It should have been enough of an explanation, but it wasn't, not taking into account their history. "But you told me to keep her away from Jaye. More than once."

"I was wrong." His eyes met hers, and she read sincerity in the dark depths. "I know that now, and I'm sorry for it."

She touched his face, aware that the conclusion couldn't have been easy for him to reach. Could he know that accepting her mother was a gift more precious than diamonds?

"There's something I need to tell you." His eyes had grown as soft as his voice. She held her breath, hoping he'd say the three words crowding her brain.

"I called that Wall Street firm today to say I didn't want the job."

Her mouth dropped open. "But I thought Wall Street represented the pinnacle of success to you. When we talked about it last weekend, I got the impression you were leaning toward accepting the offer."

"I was, but I belatedly understood that a desire to impress my father wasn't a good enough reason to uproot my life and move to New York City."

Abby didn't think so, either. Any pride Denny Smith felt in his son's accomplishment would be fleeting. The man was too focused on his new life to pay much attention to someone who reminded him of his old one, even if that someone was his son.

"I didn't realize that impressing your dad was the reason you were interested in Wall Street," she said.

"It took me a while to figure that out, too. When I did, I accepted that it wouldn't work, anyway. Dad's much more impressed at the way Ben can score points in a basketball game. The same way he used to be in awe of J.D. and the way he played football. That used to be all he talked about."

Abby could well imagine it. She could also envision Connor futilely vying for attention in a house where the youngest son was the obvious favorite, with both his father and mother. "Were you jealous of your brother when you were growing up?"

"Jealous?" He said the word as though it had never occurred to him. "No way. I was proud of J.D., too. We were only three years apart in age, but that was far enough that I never felt like I was competing with him. And he was a really likeable kid. He used to tell these stupid jokes that weren't funny, but he'd laugh so hard at the punch lines that you'd find yourself laughing, too. I couldn't have asked for a better kid brother."

He grew silent, and she acknowledged the enormity of what he'd lost when J.D. had died. No wonder his animosity toward her brother ran so deep that she could feel it even now, when he said nothing. But the focus of their discussion wasn't J.D.; it was Connor's dynamic with his family.

"Still, it wasn't fair of your dad to put so much emphasis on one child when he had three of them," Abby said.

"No, I guess it wasn't," Connor agreed. "But I never blamed him for that. Dad was a football player too when he was in high school. The way he tells it, he dreamed of the pros but wasn't even good enough to play in college. I think he's living vicariously through his athletic sons."

"Your accomplishments are every bit as impressive as anything your brothers have done. More so, even. Your father should recognize that," she said with heat, angry at his father on his behalf. "Your mother should, too. She's blind not to recognize what a good son you are."

"I appreciate you saying that," he said, "but I realized something else during that trip to Richmond. Making my parents proud isn't nearly as important as making you and Jaye proud. Taking that job on Wall Street won't accomplish that, but staying here just might."

Her heart felt so full it was as though somebody had pumped it with helium, because he was right. The measure of a truly successful man wasn't what he achieved at work but what he accomplished outside of it. She swallowed, afraid to ask her next question but more afraid not to.

"Are you sure that staying in Maryland is what you want?"

He tenderly cupped her cheek and smiled into her eyes. "I'm sure of this much. Wherever you are is where I want to be."

"That's what I want, too," she whispered.

She longed to tell him that she'd move in with him, that she'd marry him if he asked her, that she couldn't imagine living the rest of her life without him. But she said nothing because another hurdle was still in their path.

He squinted, seeing more than she wanted him to. "What's wrong?" he asked.

"The parole hearing. It's next week. I can't help but think it's bound to cause trouble between us."

"We'll get through it." Confidence radiated from him. "Because whatever happens, it won't change one basic truth. And that is I'm in love with you."

She gaped at him, stunned to hear the words in her heart on his lips. The silence stretched, and he blew out a breath, appearing more unsure of himself than she'd ever seen him.

"It's okay if you don't say anything," he said. "But my heart's taking a battering here, so you could try to look a little less shocked."

Surprised at his interpretation of her reaction, she

gently cupped his face. "Silly man. I'm only shocked that you had the courage to say what's echoing in my head."

His smile started slowly and spread until it reached his eyes and lit up his entire face. "And what's that?"

"I am so in love with you, I can barely think straight." She stroked his cheek, trailing her fingers across his lips. "Why did you think I called you an amazing, amazing man?"

He grinned. "I'm not sure about the terminology, but I can't fault the sentiment."

She met him halfway in a kiss heavy with promise and passion. But even as she kissed him, she knew there were things they hadn't said to each other, things they wouldn't say until after her brother's parole hearing.

His kiss grew more urgent, his tongue thrusting deeper, his hand skimming up her rib cage to find her breast.

And then, blessedly, she couldn't think at all. Not about the hate he still harbored for the brother she loved and not about what would happen if Drew was granted parole.

She could only feel. And what she felt was love.

"WELL, WHAT DID YOU THINK?"

Abby was so eager to hear her mother's impressions of Connor that she asked the question before Dee Dee Reed was barely inside the apartment. Her mother's eyebrows raised the way they did when Abby had done something not to Dee Dee's liking.

"Hello, dear. It's nice to see you, too."

Abby giggled before wrapping her mother in a quick hug. Dee Dee was an inch or so shorter than Abby and finer boned, but there was nothing frail about her. "You know how I feel about you, Mom. Of course I'm glad to see you."

That said, Abby grasped her mother's right hand and pulled her along to the small patio outside her ground-floor apartment. The fenced backyard wasn't big enough for a good pace, but Abby had turned it into a sanctuary by adding a wrought-iron table with two chairs and gracing the entrance with hanging flower baskets.

"Sit," she instructed her mother. "And tell me what you thought of Connor."

Her mother rolled her eyes, but obligingly sat in one of the chairs. "Don't I even get a glass of water?"

"Yes." Abby sank down in the chair kitty-corner from her, leaned forward and perched her elbows on her knees. "But not until after you tell me what you thought of him."

"Is my opinion really that important to you?"

Surprise rattled through Abby at the question along with a heavy dose of apprehension. "I wouldn't ask if your opinion wasn't important. Why? Don't tell me you didn't like Connor."

"Of course I liked him," her mother said, and the heaviness that had settled over Abby lifted. "He's quite a charmer, not to mention articulate and attractive."

"He is, isn't he?" Abby clasped her hands together and grinned. A yellow butterfly with black-spotted wings crossed her field of vision and landed on the rose-colored trailing verbena in her hanging basket, reminding her of something else. "And he's thoughtful, too. Those flowers he presented to Jaye after the concert? I didn't tell him to buy them. Did you see how thrilled Jaye was? She told me it made her feel like a real musician."

"Jaye seems very attached to him."

"She wasn't at first. But now they're getting along great, and that's to Connor's credit." The butterfly flew away from the hanging basket, over the fence and out of sight. "I can't believe how wrong my first impression of Connor was. I mean, he's a stockbroker. I thought all he cared about was making money. But he's not like that at all. He's everything I could want."

Abby crossed her arms over her chest and hugged herself. The afternoon sun shone down on her, but the warmth spreading through her originated from inside.

"He seems like a good man," her mother said, but her tone was flat.

Some of the apprehension that had so recently lifted settled back over Abby. "But?"

Her mother's gaze dropped to the wrought-iron table, another bad sign. She heard her mother's sigh over the coo of a nearby morning dove and the sound of a car engine starting on a nearby street. "Does he discuss Drew with you?"

She hesitated, reluctant to admit that she and Connor dealt with the terrible tragedy by not talking about it. "There's nothing to discuss."

"I was afraid of that," she said. "I could tell how uncomfortable he was at the concert when I apologized for the heartache Drew caused his family."

"That's only natural, Mom," Abby said. "It's a difficult subject."

"Do you know how he feels about his mother's efforts to keep Drew in prison?"

Abby swallowed. "I know he doesn't want Drew to get out of prison."

"If Drew does get out, have you considered how that would affect things between you, Connor and Jaye?"

"We'll get through it," Abby said stubbornly.

"How can you know that when you haven't even discussed the possibility with him?"

"Why are you being so negative?" Abby asked. "You were the same way when I told you I was dating him. Remember what you said? That nothing good could come of it. You were wrong. Connor and I are in love."

Her mother's shoulders sagged. "I was afraid of that."

"That's your response? You can't say you're happy for me?"

"I want to be happy for you," her mother implored. "More than anything, I hope things work out. But you need to be wary."

"Of what? The man who loves me?"

"Of the inescapable fact that the man who loves you is the brother of the boy Drew killed."

Abby sprang up from her chair so fast she got lightheaded. She braced a hand on the table, feeling sick to her stomach as well. She and Connor were dealing with what had happened between their brothers in their own way. Why couldn't her mother accept that and leave well enough alone?

"I'll get that glass of water for you now." She moved to the door with alacrity so her mother couldn't stop her.

She opened the sliding glass door to the welcome ring of the telephone, a valid reason to delay returning to the patio until she could get her emotions under better control.

"I need to get that," she told her mother, slid the door closed and hurried to her wall phone in the kitchen. After she said hello, an operator asked if she'd accept a collect call from Drew Galloway.

Such calls weren't unprecedented. Since Drew had been moved from the maximum-security prison, he'd enjoyed limited telephone privileges. The calls were subject to monitoring, but that was a small price to pay for the opportunity to keep in touch.

"Yes, I'll accept the charges," she said.

Her brother's familiar voice came over the line a moment later. Even though he'd finished going through puberty more than a decade ago, he still sounded like a young boy. "Hey, sis. What's going on?"

"Drew. It's good to hear from you. Mom and I were just talking about you." She winced, instantly regretting sharing that information with him.

"Mom's there?"

"Out on the patio," she answered.

She braced herself for him to ask what they'd been talking about, but he announced, "I've got a problem. Rico Shaw says I can't live with him if I get parole."

She instantly switched mental gears from her own problem to his. "Why not?"

"I don't know, but the reason doesn't matter. I've got to find another place to live, and I only have a couple days to do it."

"Do you have any ideas?" she asked.

"Yeah. One," he said. "With you."

"Me?" She sank into one of her kitchen chairs.

"You have an extra bedroom, right? It would only be till I was on my feet and could get a place of my own."

The possibility of Drew living with her hadn't occurred to Abby before this moment, but she wasn't sure why. Unlike her mother, she lived in Maryland. She was the logical solution.

"What do you say?" he prompted.

She said the only thing she could: Yes.

ABBY HAD BEEN GONE SO LONG that Dee Dee jumped at the sound of the sliding glass door opening. She intended to apologize for the things she'd said about Connor, but her daughter spoke first.

"That was Drew. Rico Shaw withdrew his offer of a place to live."

Relief coursed through Dee Dee. Even though Rico had taken the money she'd offered, she hadn't trusted that he'd follow through on their bargain.

"I suppose he wanted help in lining up another place to live," Dee Dee said. It was a problem she'd been working on solving since her confrontation with Rico. "What about this? Between us, we could probably come up with enough money for a security deposit and first month's rent on an apartment."

Abby shook her head. "We don't have to. The problem's solved. I told Drew he can live with me."

Dee Dee's heart felt like it stopped beating. Had she gotten her son out of a potentially explosive situation only to thrust her daughter into one? She didn't trust Drew not to keep out of trouble, not after she'd discovered that he'd been in touch with Spider Strickland.

"You can't let him live with you, Abby."

"Why not? I have a spare room."

"He's been in prison for ten years. That changes a

man." Dee Dee's head pounded. There were things about her brother that Abby didn't know, things Dee Dee suspected but couldn't prove. But maybe it was time Dee Dee stopped protecting her daughter from the truth. Abby wasn't fifteen years old anymore.

"There's something you should know," Dee Dee said, then plunged ahead. "Drugs were found on J.D.'s body the night he died. The police thought they may have played a part in what happened."

"Drugs?" Abby didn't react the way Dee Dee had anticipated. She seemed confused and surprised instead of distraught. "What kind of drugs?"

"Marijuana and PCP."

"But why did I never hear about this?"

"Because I never told you. And because Drew accepted a plea bargain. If he hadn't, it would have come out at trial."

Abby took a moment to digest what Dee Dee had told her, then said, "What would it have mattered if the information got out? You said the drugs were found on J.D., not on Drew."

Although Drew had never admitted selling the drugs to the other boy, Dee Dee had feared back then that he still had ties to some of the unsavory characters he'd associated with in Baltimore. Now that she'd confirmed he was still in contact with Spider Strickland, that long-ago fear seemed justified.

"The police would have tried to build a case that Drew sold J.D. the drugs."

"But that's crazy," Abby began, then stopped, peering intently at her mother. "Wait a minute. You can't believe that's what happened. I know Drew was no saint before he went to prison, but he wouldn't have touched drugs."

Dee Dee pinched the bridge of her nose, searching her mind for a non-inflammatory way to say what Abby needed to hear. There was none. "Before you let your brother move in with you, you should consider you might be wrong about that."

"I can't believe what I'm hearing," Abby cried. "We're not talking about some stranger. We're talking about your son. Even if you were right about the drugs, and I'm not saying you are, it doesn't mean Drew would get involved with anything like that again."

Dee Dee stopped short of telling her about Spider Strickland's reappearance in Drew's life, unwilling to confess her part in her son's housing problems. She tried a different tactic to get Abby to see reason.

"My son is a convicted murderer. It doesn't mean I love him less, but it's a fact I've had to accept. You have to face up to it, too. The parents of those children you teach sure will."

"What do the parents of my students have to do with this?"

"Do you think they'll let their children continue taking lessons from you when they find out Drew's living in your apartment?

A muscle in Abby's jaw worked. She'd always been a reasonable child. Dee Dee prayed she'd see reason now.

"I might be able to make arrangements with the school to use one of their rooms after hours."

"What about Jaye? What will you do about her?"

"She can stay with me at school until I'm through teaching. Connor can pick her up there," Abby said, clearly making up the plan as she went along. "Or, better yet, I'll ask Connor if I can teach at his place."

"So you think Connor will be okay with your brother living with you?" Dee Dee asked.

Uncertainty crossed Abby's face, but then she raised her chin and said, "Connor loves me. He'll support whatever I decide to do."

But in her daughter's eyes, Dee Dee saw the truth. Abby wanted to believe that Connor would be on her side no matter what, but she feared that wouldn't be the case.

Dee Dee offered up a silent prayer that Connor would help Abby see reason. Because if he didn't, Dee Dee would be forced to do something herself to assure that Drew didn't destroy his sister's life.

Something drastic.

CHAPTER FIFTEEN

ABBY'S MIND WAS ON SOMETHING other than the music.

Connor had sensed it while they sat in the opulent Concert Hall at the Kennedy Center listening to the symphony play selections from Beethoven, Stravinsky and Bartok.

The last time he'd watched Abby at the symphony, she'd seemed totally immersed in the music. But tonight, she'd fidgeted, made perfunctory replies to his occasional whispered comments and joined the applause at the end of a selection a beat late.

Her behavior was puzzling, since she'd been so interested in attending the concert when he'd mentioned it a few days ago. Truthfully, Connor would rather be at RFK Stadium watching the Nationals play baseball or at Ford Theater enjoying a play. He also would have been up for another cosmic bowling outing with her friends.

Classical music wasn't his music of choice except when Jaye played. Then he was so impressed with what his niece had been able to learn in such a short time that he loved listening to every last note.

"Did you enjoy the concert?" he asked Abby when it was finally over. Most of the audience members had headed to the parking garage, but he'd suggested a stroll on the River Terrace, the focal point of which was a large fountain that shot water into the night sky. He much preferred the fresh air and view of the Potomac River to sitting in post-concert traffic.

"I always enjoy the National Symphony," she said as they walked along the tiled sidewalk. In the distance, they could see the headlights of cars crossing the Roosevelt Bridge. "Jaye would have liked it, too. I'm surprised she chose a night with Ashley over music."

"I'm not," Connor said. "As much as she likes music, it can't compete with a social life. It's taken her a while to make friends."

"I'm happy for her, but I still think another nine-year-old can't compete with Beethoven's Symphony no. 9. It takes my breath away every time I hear it."

He whistled a few bars from *Ode to Joy*. "No. 9 is the symphony Beethoven wrote when he was completely deaf, isn't it?" he asked, feeling as though he were making small talk when there was something else they should be discussing.

"Millions have heard it performed, but Beethoven only heard it in his own head."

They stopped at the railing at the far end of the River Terrace. She looked beautiful tonight in a sophisticated black cocktail dress and strappy, black heels that cut the difference in their heights. He put his arm around her shoulders and gathered her close as they gazed out at the river, but still felt her distance.

"I'd like to know what's going on inside your head," he remarked. "You've been preoccupied all evening."

He heard the soft, warm wind rustle through the

leaves of the trees a clever landscaper had planted on the terrace before she answered, "I didn't realize it was that obvious."

"Only to somebody paying close attention to you, which has become my new favorite pastime."

She looked up at him and smiled before gazing back into the night. It wasn't a good sign that she'd rather not look at him when she answered his question. He felt his shoulders tense as he waited for her to speak.

"My brother called yesterday and asked me for a favor."

As soon as she mentioned Galloway, he realized that he'd been afraid her half brother was the cause of her preoccupation. Sensing he wouldn't like what she was about to say, he dropped his arm from around her shoulders. "What kind of favor?"

The night was quiet enough that he could hear her take a deep breath before she answered, "He asked if he could live with me if he gets parole."

Connor felt the rush of blood in his veins and the beat of his pulse at the base of his neck. Bile rose in his throat. He swallowed it back. There was no sense in overreacting, not when he didn't know anything definitive. Yet. "What did you say?"

"I said yes."

The answer hit him like a blow to the chest, one that was hard enough to stop his heart. His voice sounded strangled when he asked, "Why would you agree to that?"

"I didn't have a choice." She still wouldn't look at him. "The hearing's in four days, and the living arrangements he made fell through."

"You always have a choice," he snapped.

Finally she turned to face him. Her lips were set in a stubborn line, and her eyes blazed. They weren't blue like her brother's, but the shape of them was the same. "Then, fine. I choose to help my brother. It will seriously hurt his chances of getting parole if he can't prove he has a place to live."

Connor was in favor of anything that decreased Galloway's chances of getting out of prison, but said, "Then let him get a place of his own."

"He doesn't have the money for that."

"So you're going to put his needs above your own? Haven't you thought about the cost to you? You won't be able to teach private lessons at your apartment anymore, for starters."

"I realize that some parents might not want their children around Drew."

"Might not?" Connor's laugh was harsh and humorless. "*Will* not, Abby. And it won't be some of them. It'll be all of them."

"I don't have to teach at my apartment. If you're okay with it, I could give lessons at your place. That way, Jaye can go straight home after school, and you wouldn't have to drive to my apartment to pick her up after work."

He shook his head, trying to absorb what he was hearing. "Are you listening to yourself? You're talking about inconveniencing yourself so you can shelter a murderer."

She winced. "That's not how I think of my brother."

"That's what he is," Connor replied angrily. "Galloway's the reason my brother's lying in his grave."

She didn't back down from his anger, standing her

ground as she continued to face him. "We all agree that your brother's death was a terrible tragedy, and I'm more sorry about what happened than you can know. But I already told you I thought there were extenuating circumstances."

"Oh, yeah, the mysterious extenuating circumstances," he said sarcastically. "Do you have any idea what they could be?"

"As a matter of fact, yes, I do. My mother told me just yesterday that drugs were found at the scene that night."

He took a moment to digest the information, which was news to him. "You mean Galloway was high when he killed my brother?"

"That's not what I mean at all. And why did you jump to the conclusion that it was my brother who was high? There's no proof of that. The drugs were found on your brother's body."

Her suggestion was insulting. "J.D. didn't take drugs."

"Are you sure about that? You're three years older than him. You were away at college when he died."

"He was an athlete. He was going to college on a football scholarship, for God's sake. Don't you see what you're doing? You're trying to make my brother a villain so you can fool yourself into thinking Galloway is a good guy."

"What do you always refer to him that way? It's always Galloway or my half brother."

Now she wasn't making sense. "He is your half brother. You have different fathers."

"Has telling yourself that Drew's not my full brother made it easier for you to be with me? Because in my heart, where it matters, there's no distinction. Drew's my brother. And nothing you say will make me stop loving him."

He swore under his breath even though her charge had merit. He didn't like to think of Abby and Drew Galloway sharing anything, least of all blood. But that wasn't the most pressing problem they faced. The problem was that she didn't understand how having Galloway in her apartment could wreck her life.

"Okay, he's your brother. But if he gets out of prison, he'll also be an ex-con. Do you really want an ex-con living with you?"

The corners of her mouth turned down. "I want my brother to feel welcome in my home."

"How about me, Abby? Do you think I'd feel welcome in your home if the guy who murdered my brother was living with you?"

How had they failed to talk about how Galloway's possible release from prison would affect them? he wondered. Was it because they'd both subconsciously known they'd never see eye to eye on the issue? Is that why he hadn't even let himself think about it?

"I can't just dissociate myself from my brother," she said. "I won't."

"And I won't risk the possibility of Galloway coming anywhere near Jaye. If he gets parole and you insist on living with him, I'll have to find somebody else to care for her this summer."

"Are you saying you want me to choose between Jaye and my brother?" Abby asked, sounding as though he was the one being unreasonable.

The fight went out of him because he finally understood the battle was already lost. That's why they had delayed talking this out, he acknowledged. They both must have known neither of them would win.

"You've already chosen," he said sadly. "You're putting Galloway's needs above Jaye's needs. Above my needs."

"Your needs?" Her tone turned accusatory. "That's what all this is really about, isn't it?"

He considered his answer carefully before he spoke. "Maybe you're right. Call me unfair, but it seems to me that the woman I love—the woman who says she loves me—shouldn't be sharing an apartment with a man I hate."

ABBY HAD KNOWN CONNOR'S animosity toward her brother ran deep, but until this moment she hadn't allowed herself to put a label on what drove it: Hate.

It hung over them like a huge cloud, blacker than the darkest night because it had been festering inside him for ten years. Abby's stomach rolled and pitched, and she thought she might be sick.

"I thought your mother was the one who hated," she said. "I didn't know you'd let hate consume you, too."

"Galloway murdered J.D., Abby. How did you think I felt about him?"

"I thought you'd find it within yourself to have compassion for somebody who regretted what happened that night," she whispered, still unwilling to say the word murder. She couldn't think of what Drew had done that way.

The moon was bright enough that she could see flint in Connor's eyes. "I've never heard anything about regrets."

"That's because your mother returned Drew's letters unopened until he stopped sending them. She did the same with the letter my mother wrote her."

"Words on pieces of paper won't bring J.D. back."

"Neither will this bitterness you're harboring against Drew. Can't you see it's hurting you more than it is him? That it's hurting us?" She put a hand on his arm, but he felt tense, his muscles as intractable as his position.

"I can't change the way I feel."

"No, I suppose you can't," she said, removing her hand. Sadness welled in her, and she feared it might never go away. "But deep down I must have hoped that getting to know me would make a difference in how you felt about my brother."

The night was warm. But when he didn't reply, she hugged herself to ward off the chill that had settled over her. It stemmed, she realized, from despair.

She'd naïvely believed that she and Connor had gotten past the unfortunate connection that linked their pasts, but she'd been fooling herself. They'd merely swept the past under the proverbial rug, where it had waited until it could leap out and deal their relationship a killing blow.

She had to face facts. No matter what happened at the parole hearing, it was over between them.

This time when they walked together past the fountain that lit up the night and through the doors to the Grand Foyer, their bodies didn't touch. Hopelessness settled over her, growing as thick as the silence between them as they walked to the parking garage and he drove her home.

"What happens now?" he asked after he'd walked her to the door.

She gazed her fill at him, this man with whom she'd fallen in love despite knowing what stood between them. She still loved him. She probably always would.

"It's over, Connor. You know that."

"Because I can't forgive a murderer?" He sounded incredulous.

"No. Because you can't let go of your hatred." She swallowed the sudden lump of emotion in her throat. "Goodbye, Connor."

Before he could say another word, she opened the door to her apartment and slipped inside. Only after she'd shut the door did she give into the weakness that had overtaken her, slumping to the floor and letting the tears run unchecked down her face.

HAD DRUGS PLAYED A PART in what happened to J.D.? Connor couldn't banish the question from his head, partly because obsessing over the possibility Abby had raised helped him avoid thinking about Abby. She'd broken up with him two days ago, and it still felt as if it had happened only moments ago.

Even Jaye had noticed something was off, sweetly asking if he wished to talk about what was bothering him. Unburdening himself would have meant hurting Jaye, so he'd kept quiet, although he'd be forced to come clean about the split very soon.

The question of why Abby no longer figured into their child-care plan would eventually come up. Ashley's mother had agreed to look after Jaye this week, an arrangement his niece viewed as a treat. But the Gibbons' family planned to spend the bulk of the summer at their house in coastal Maine.

Okay, so Connor couldn't completely dodge thoughts of Abby or deny she'd ravaged his heart. He couldn't miraculously fix things between them, but there was a place he could go to get answers about his brother.

Using his key to enter the house in Bentonsville where he'd grown up, he stepped inside and let his eyes adjust to the gloom.

He remembered the house as being filled with light, but shadows predominated on this overcast, rainy Monday afternoon. The weather fit his mood. He switched on a light in the hall, but the interior appeared no cheerier than the outdoors. The walls needed painting, and every available surface was filled with clutter and coated with a fine layer of dust.

It hadn't always been that way. His mother used to clean with a pink feather duster. In the kitchen, where she'd whip up recipes she'd invented, she worn an apron. Sometimes, she hummed cheery tunes to herself. He remembered one of her favorites as "You Make Me So Very Happy," but this house hadn't seen any happiness for a very long time.

"Mom?" he called. "It's Connor. Are you home?"

Silence greeted his question even though Elaine Smith's car was in the garage. Where could she be?

He wandered through the house, checking the various rooms for a sign of his mother, growing more sure she wasn't at home despite the presence of her car. Wherever she was, she couldn't have gone far.

He probably should have alerted her that he was coming, but he hadn't known himself until an hour ago when he'd instructed his secretary to cancel the rest of the day's appointments.

He headed downstairs, which was also deserted, so he climbed the steps to the second-floor bedrooms. Every interior door yawned open, save the one to his dead brother's bedroom.

A sign reading Enter at Your Own Risk hung on the door, as it had for more than a decade. Connor took the risk, pushing open the door and stepping back in time.

The room was exactly as J.D. had left it, with a poster of a bikini-clad Pamela Anderson from her *Baywatch* days hanging over the bed and his football trophies proudly displayed on the shelves their father had built.

Connor wandered over to the trophies, picked up the largest and read the inscription: Most Valuable Player, Maryland State Football Championship.

Medals hung from hooks, not all of them for what J.D. had accomplished on the football field. He'd excelled in basketball and baseball, too.

A navy-blue Penn State banner with white lettering yellowed with age took up a portion of one wall. A framed photo of J.D. with Joe Paterno, the college's legendary football coach, graced the bedside table.

Connor picked up the photo. His brother stared back at him, a huge grin splitting his open, handsome face. The photo, Connor remembered, had been taken during a recruiting trip to Happy Valley, after which J.D. had verbally committed to attend the school. His brother, easily a head taller than Paterno, looked young and eager, as though he had his whole life ahead of him.

Three months after the photo had been taken, J.D. was dead.

Connor always believed the case had been clear cut, with one boy coldly and calculatingly stabbing the other because of an argument over a girl. But if what Abby had said was true and drugs had been involved, Connor would have to reassess his thinking.

"What are you doing here, Connor?"

His mother's voice. She stood in the doorway, dressed formally in a stiff-collared blouse and skirt, no smile of welcome on her face. He'd been so absorbed in the past, he hadn't heard her approach.

"Hello, Mother. I came to talk to you."

She strode across the room, took the framed photograph from him and set it back down on the bedside table, carefully arranging it exactly the way it had been.

"Let's go downstairs." She didn't wait for his reply before leaving the room.

After a moment, he followed. But when he pulled the door closed on J.D.'s old room, he wondered if he'd misinterpreted his mother's initial question. She could have been asking not what he was doing in Bentonsville, but what he was doing in his brother's room.

In the kitchen, his mother turned on her electric kettle, telling him, "The water for the tea will be ready in a few minutes."

"None for me," he said. It was always what he said when she offered him tea. No matter how many times he refused, she never remembered that he wasn't a tea drinker.

"I was at Margaret Poole's house," she stated, naming one of her longtime neighbors. "I've been trying to locate Barb Wilson, and it just occurred to me that Margaret's daughter June might know how to get in touch with her. June and Barb used to be friends."

Barb Wilson, with her natural good looks and

position as the school's head cheerleader, had been the girl J.D. and Drew Galloway reportedly fought over.

"I'm going to talk Barb into sending the parole board an email. It's already too late to write a letter, seeing that the parole hearing is in two days," his mother continued. "I only wish I'd thought to try June for her number earlier."

She dug into the pocket of her skirt and pulled out a piece of paper. "According to June, Barb's living in Boston now. Since time's so short, I need to call her right away."

A sense of purpose in her step, his mother moved toward the streamlined phone hanging on the kitchen wall.

"Could you wait until we've talked before you call, Mother? I can't stay long. I need to get back to town by six to pick up Jaye."

His mother fidgeted with the paper in her hand, her mind on J.D. instead of Jaye. "But I just told you time was short. I have to call Barb now."

"I'm only asking for a few minutes. Surely you can wait a few minutes before you make the call."

She didn't pick up the phone, but neither did she move away from it. "Okay, but only a few minutes," she said, her gaze shifting longingly to the phone.

"Something's been bothering me about Wednesday," he began. "I've heard you say a thousand times that ten years isn't much time to spend behind bars for taking somebody's life?"

"It's not," she said forcefully.

"Then explain something to me that never made sense. Why did you and Dad agree to that plea bargain?

Why didn't you push the state's attorney to take the case to trial?"

Her eyes slid away from his. "We've talked about this before, Connor. Douglas Benton wasn't sure he could get a conviction."

"Why not?" Connor pressed. "I thought it was an open-and-shut case. I thought the evidence was clear-cut."

"Galloway was willing to confess to second-degree murder. He wouldn't go for anything more serious."

Or could it be, as Abby had suggested, that there were things Connor didn't know about the crime? Could drugs have played a part? Had the defense attorney alerted the prosecution that the court might show leniency because Galloway hadn't been in his right mind when he'd stabbed J.D.?

"Were drugs found at the scene?" he asked directly.

She winced. Something flashed in her eyes before a curtain closed over her face. But Connor had seen enough to know that his question was on the mark.

"Who told you that?" she asked sharply.

"It doesn't matter who told me. All that matters is whether it's true."

"I don't know."

"Yes, you do." Connor rose to go stand in front of her. "You know everything about the case, Mother. It's all you've thought about for the past ten years. Don't tell me you're not sure if drugs were involved."

"So what if they were?" his mother asked defiantly. "That just proves what a terrible person Drew Galloway is."

"But if Galloway was high when he stabbed J.D., why haven't you mentioned it before? Why keep it quiet?"

Silence, except for the hum of the refrigerator and the patter of raindrops on the window. Finally, his mother broke it. "Galloway wasn't high."

He remembered the accusation Abby had hurled at him, which he'd dismissed as ludicrous at the time. "Was J.D. high?"

The defiance fled from his mother's gaze. She looked away. "I don't think so."

"You don't think so? That means you believe it's a possibility. How can that be? I never heard anybody say J.D. was using drugs."

"And we're going to keep it that way," his mother said fiercely. "That's why I agreed to the plea bargain. Douglas Benton said that if we went to trial, the information would come out that J.D. hadn't gone to the football field that night to fight over a girl."

"Then why did he go there?" Connor asked even as the answer occurred to him. He rubbed his forehead, trying to erase the thought, but it persisted. "He was buying drugs from Galloway, wasn't he?"

His mother nodded, her face miserable. "We can't let that get out, Connor. I never wanted you to find out. J.D.'s reputation is all he has left. I want people to remember him as he was, a wonderful son, an outstanding athlete, a fine young man."

A fine young man with a drug habit that had gotten him killed.

"What are you thinking?" his mother asked anxiously. "Because whatever it is, you can't let it cloud the way you remember your brother. This doesn't change anything."

But as Connor walked to his car a short time later, he admitted the knowledge changed everything.

He racked his brain, wondering if he'd missed a sign that would have alerted him that his brother had been in trouble. But, no, he'd been away at college at the time. When he'd come home for a visit, he'd seen the J.D. he always saw—the kid brother with the athletic swagger, the one projecting confidence with every step he took.

Had hidden insecurities propelled J.D. to use drugs? Or had it been pressure to live up to his all-American image? Or a weakness of character Connor had never noticed?

Whatever it was, his brother hadn't been a blameless victim. Nobody deserved to be murdered, but J.D. had played a part in what had happened to him.

The rain had stopped. Connor gazed up at the sky to see the cloud cover dissipating. It was a fitting metaphor for the hate he'd harbored for so many years. In order for the sun to shine on his life, he needed to let the hate go.

The hate wouldn't bring his brother back. Its only purpose had been to tear apart his relationship with Abby and blind him to something he should have clearly seen. That she loved her flawed brother, the same way he still loved his.

He stood on the damp grass in front of the house where he'd grown up, remembering the little brother who'd sung at the top of his lungs along with the radio while he washed the car and playfully squirted anybody who got too near with the hose.

Connor had already forgiven that young man for his tragic mistake with drugs. It was time he fixed what was wrong between himself and Abby and forgave the man who'd killed J.D.

CHAPTER SIXTEEN

WHEN SHE BOLTED AWAKE EARLY on the morning of the parole hearing, Abby's first thought was of Connor. A sense of loss swept over her so profound that she felt like weeping. She touched her cheeks, discovered they were already damp and realized she'd been crying in her sleep.

She'd dreamed of him. They'd been inside a train station, their arms around each other's waists, their spirits high. Even bumping into each of their mothers in turn hadn't dampened their enthusiasm. Elaine Smith and Dee Dee Reed, finally agreeing on something, had admonished them in strong language not to take the sightseeing trip of the Maryland countryside.

She and Connor disregarded their warnings, bought two round-trip tickets and settled in for the journey by a wide, clear window. Holding hands, they'd enjoyed each other and the passing scenery—the lush greenery of the trees and fields, the shimmering blue of a lake, the varying hues of the flowers.

When panicked cries swept through the train about broken track ahead, they'd steadfastly ignored them—until the train derailed, wrenching their hands apart and hurtling them into chaos.

It was only a dream, Abby told herself now, trying to slow her breathing and stifle her panic.

But she couldn't ignore the obvious symbolism between the train ride in the dream and her relationship with Connor: both had been doomed from the start. Pain lanced through her. Connor was as lost to her as the man in the dream.

She got out of bed, trying with some success to turn her mind to Drew. If things went well today, her brother could be a free man soon. She ate some cereal and toast, showered, got dressed and noticed it would be an hour before her mother picked her up for the parole hearing.

Taking out her violin, she spent the time lost in her music, burying the knowledge that today she and the man she loved would be on opposite sides of the issue being decided.

Eventually her mother arrived in her Chevy Cavalier. Abby settled into the passenger seat and the miles of highway passed as the two of them drew inexorably closer to the prison.

In less than an hour they drove up the long road that led to the main gate, gave their names to the unsmiling guard who checked that they were on his list, and entered the parking lot.

Abby scanned the rows of cars for Connor's silver Porsche and found it immediately, its waxed finish gleaming in the sun. She felt the pulse in her neck jump, even though she'd expected him to be here. Elaine Smith had requested the hearing be open, which meant a limited number of spectators could be present.

An audible sigh escaped, but her mother was the one who made it.

"Is something wrong, Mom?" Abby asked.

Her mother attempted a smile and failed. She'd been largely quiet during the drive, talking about anything but the hearing when she did speak. "It's the prison. It's never pleasant coming here."

"If things go well today, we won't have to come back," Abby said. "They'll transfer Drew to a prerelease center, and then hopefully none of us will ever step foot in a prison again."

Her mother didn't answer until after she parked and they were walking toward the prison's main entrance. "Don't get your hopes up too high, Abby. This hearing might not go the way you want it to."

Dee Dee squeezed Abby's hand, then together they endured the familiar process of getting checked into the prison. After they'd passed through the metal detector, had their handbags searched and presented their identification at the visitor's desk, the guard directed them to the meeting room where the hearing would take place. Along the way, Dee Dee excused herself to go to the restroom.

"I'll wait out here in the hall for you," Abby said.

No more than a few minutes passed before Abby heard the clacking of heels on the linoleum floor. She looked up to see Elaine Smith walking toward her, wearing a funereal black dress that brought out the stark unhappiness on her face.

Abby started. She'd assumed Elaine had driven to the prison with Connor, but she'd obviously just arrived. She and her mother must have missed seeing Elaine in the parking lot by seconds. Recognition passed over Elaine's face and her step faltered, but then she recovered her poise and prepared to sweep past Abby to the meeting room.

"Mrs. Smith, wait." Driven by an impulse too strong to control, Abby was as surprised at the sound of her own voice as she was sure Elaine Smith must be. "There's something I need to say to you."

Elaine stopped and pivoted, ice in her glare. "Nothing you say will stop me from getting justice for J.D."

"This isn't about J.D., Mrs. Smith. It's about your living son." Abby took a breath, composing the words that had been formulating inside her for so long. She only wished Denny Smith were also present because her words also applied to him. But she doubted Connor's father would even attend the hearing. "I think you should take a good look at Connor and acknowledge what a fine man and good son he is. He's not only been there for you, but for your granddaughter."

"What are you talking about? I know he's a good man," Elaine said angrily.

"Then show him. Remember his birthday. Invite him to dinner. Ask him how things are going with him. No matter what happens today, he needs you in his life. And so does Jaye."

"They have me in their lives," Elaine snapped.

Abby refused to let herself be intimidated by Elaine's anger. "Not the way they need for you to be there."

Elaine stared at her mutely for a moment, then spoke, "How dare you try to tell me how to treat my own son and granddaughter. This conversation is over."

She continued to the meeting room at a brisk clip,

disappearing inside. Abby swallowed her distress, hoping her failure with Elaine wasn't a precursor of equally disappointing things to come.

She pasted on a smile when her mother emerged from the restroom, even though her insides were jumping. Connor was in the meeting room, and he might not be any happier to see her than Elaine Smith had been.

"Are you feeling okay, Abby?" Dee Dee asked. "You look pale."

"I'm a little nervous is all," Abby said truthfully, then braced herself for the sight of Connor.

She'd initially thought the hearing would take place in a courtroom, but reality was a small, ordinary meeting room. Connor and his mother were the only two people already present. As she'd expected. Connor's father was absent. Elaine Smith glared at her, but Abby's gaze went past her to her son.

His solid frame looked too big for the chairs that had been set up in the room for spectators. He'd gotten a haircut since she'd seen him last, the thick strands falling well shy of his collar. With his tailored khaki-colored suit, he should have looked like a yuppie. Instead, he looked like the man she loved.

She steeled herself not to react, but her heart thudded ponderously when his gaze met hers. His eyes no longer looked angry, but that was probably her imagination conjuring up what she wanted to see. He nodded in greeting, then extended the same courtesy to her mother.

His mother nudged him sharply in the side with her elbow. "Ignore them, Connor," she said in a loud whisper. "It's best to have nothing to do with them."

He mouthed a silent apology, then leaned toward his mother and whispered in her ear. Judging by the resulting curl of Elaine's lips, whatever he said wasn't to her liking. Abby didn't attach any more significance to the gesture. Even if he was taking Elaine Smith to task for her rudeness, she was well aware of where she stood with Connor.

"Let's sit over here," Dee Dee said, indicating the two chairs farthest from the Smiths.

They were saved from enduring an awkward silence by the opening of an interior door. A middle-aged woman with a weathered face and her gray hair swept into a bun entered the room alongside a portly man with a mustache and neatly trimmed beard. Abby assumed they were the parole-board commissioners because she recognized the man following them as Drew's institutional case worker. Drew and an armed guard brought up the rear.

Her brother caught her eye, winked and progressed to the front of the room. His prison-issued jumpsuit seemed to swallow him, making him look smaller than he was. His hair was close cropped and what little facial hair he possessed shaved clean.

She stole a glance at Connor and his mother. Connor's expression was bland, concealing his emotions, but ill will emanated from Elaine Smith like smoke from a campfire. Her features were contorted in a fierce scowl.

After calling the hearing to order, the female commissioner summarized their reason for being there and asked if a representative of the victim would like to make a statement.

"I most certainly would," Elaine Smith replied. She leafed through a manila folder, removed a few sheets of paper and stood. "I have written copies of my remarks for each of the commissioners, but I'll wait to submit them until I've read my statement."

From the research she'd done on the way parole hearings were conducted, Abby knew that Elaine Smith would have the floor for up to five minutes.

"Words cannot begin to express the heartache Drew Galloway has imposed on my family," she began in a cool, hard voice. "He's served ten years of his sentence, but he sentenced my family to a lifetime without our beloved J.D. He not only robbed me of my son, he robbed J.D. of his breath, of his future, of his very life. And he did it with the cold heart of a killer.

"No matter what he says today, no matter how much he insists that he's changed, what he did was unforgivable. Prison can't change a man's heart. Drew Galloway needs to be caged, like the animal he still is."

Her mother clutched Abby's hand. Drew's only reaction was a tightening of his mouth as Elaine Smith continued to speak in the same angry vein. Abby dared not look at Connor, afraid she'd see his mother's rage reflected on his face.

The interview phase of the hearing was next, with the commissioners questioning Drew about remorse, his last ten years in prison and the plans he'd made should he get parole. He said all the right things, but in a monotonous drone that didn't have the same emotional impact as Elaine Smith's impassioned remarks.

"Not a day goes by when I don't think about J.D.

Smith. If I could, I'd exchange my life for his," he finished, the words barely more than a mumble.

Abby searched the faces of the two commissioners for empathy, but found nothing that suggested warmth. They didn't believe Drew was sorry, that was clear to her now. She dropped her head and hugged her midsection as misery gripped her. They were set to rule against her brother and she didn't know how to stop them.

"Can I say something?" Connor's voice, clear and confident, filled the small room. "I'm Connor Smith, the victim's brother."

Abby's head jerked up in time to see Connor glance at her before he stood. She blinked, certain she'd misinterpreted the encouragement she'd thought she read in that glance.

She had no idea what he meant to say, but for the first time since she'd awakened from her dream that morning, she didn't envision broken train track stretching ahead of her.

THE FEMALE COMMISSIONER shuffled the papers on her desk as Connor waited. She withdrew one of them. "We've already heard from you, Mr. Smith. I have your victim impact statement right here."

"Since I submitted that, I've learned some things about my brother and come to some new realizations," he said, gathering courage from Abby's silent presence on the other side of the room. "I'm only asking for a few minutes."

He remained standing while the commissioners conferred with each other on his request.

"What things? What realizations?" his mother asked

in a low, worried voice. "The hearing is going fine. Take it back. Tell them you don't have anything to add."

"I'm sorry, Mother, but I can't," he said, bending to answer her. His conscience, not to mention his heart, wouldn't allow him to keep quiet.

"Sorry for what?" his mother demanded a moment before the commissioners finished their dialogue. Connor straightened without answering his mother.

"This is unusual, but we're going to allow it," the female commissioner announced.

"Thank you." Connor cast an apologetic glance at his panic-stricken mother before looking at Drew Galloway. He still had blue eyes, apple-red cheeks and a pale complexion, but a decade in prison had hardened his features so that Connor could no longer see the boy inside the man.

Connor cleared his throat and began. "I've hated Drew Galloway for what he did to my brother for ten long years."

The hate hadn't always bubbled to the surface, but it had always been percolating inside him—even while he was falling in love with Abby.

"I thought of my brother as somebody who could do no wrong. But now I know that J.D. wasn't perfect. He had flaws and weaknesses, just like we all do. He didn't deserve to die, but he shouldn't have been at the football field that night."

He glanced at Abby, who was gazing at him in wonder. The sight of her gave him the encouragement he needed to continue.

"Connor, don't say anything else," his mother urged. With great difficulty he ignored a lifetime of catering to his mother's needs, not wanting to hurt her but knowing he must. Drew regarded him with a tilt of his head that reminded Connor of Abby. He wasn't a monster, Connor realized, but a man who'd made a terrible mistake.

Connor took a deep breath before continuing. "Keeping Drew Galloway in prison won't bring my brother back. I think the best thing for my family would be to learn to forgive him, so I have no objection to his receiving parole."

His mother's gasp cut through him, like the knife that had slashed J.D. She stared at him as though she were Caesar and he, Brutus, had committed a terrible betrayal.

"How dare you," she spit out. "I'll never forgive him. Never."

The hate that poured off her was like a live thing, black and destructive. How could he have not realized that the same hate that had lived inside him for so long had almost devoured him?

"I'm sorry, Mother," he apologized, "but that's the way I feel."

Her face turned frighteningly red. "It's that sister of his, isn't it? She's the one who turned you against your family, against your brother. How could you have done this?"

The portly male commissioner, who'd been largely silent throughout the hearing, finally spoke. "If you don't settle down, Mrs. Smith, you'll have to leave the hearing. Your son's statement is not the final word on the matter. It's another piece of information that will help us make a determination."

"Then I have something to say, too."

Dee Dee Reed rose, but, unlike Connor, didn't wait

for permission to speak. "I respectfully ask that the commissioners deny my son parole. I believe he may still commit crimes if he gets out of prison."

Connor wondered briefly if he'd heard her wrong, but then Drew Galloway interrupted the stunned silence, yelling, "That's a lie!"

Dee Dee Reed looked directly at her son, her expression unutterably sad. "Then why did you admit yesterday, when I visited, that you were in touch with an ex-con? Why did you say you'd jump at the chance to make some easy money if he offered it to you? Even if it involved drugs."

Drew swore at her, a particularly vicious oath and pushed back his chair from the table. Before he could rise to his feet, the prison guards were upon him, containing his struggles.

"In light of this development, I'll have to ask the guard to escort Mr. Galloway back to his cell," the female commissioner said. "We'll notify the prisoner of our decision shortly."

The prison guard snapped handcuffs on the thrashing, cursing Drew. Connor's mother smiled triumphantly, but Connor was more interested in the reactions of Abby and her mother.

Her chin quivering, Dee Dee Reed walked quickly from the room. Abby's eyes met his for a pregnant few seconds, during which she seemed to ask a hundred questions. Then she rose and all but ran to follow her mother.

ABBY PUT ONE FOOT IN FRONT of the other, valiantly trying to catch up to her mother even though she longed to rush to Connor and find out why he'd spoken out in favor of Drew.

Could Elaine Smith have been on the mark? Not about Connor turning against his family, but about Abby being the impetus for him to let go of his hate? What did that mean to their future? To their love?

She put her questions on hold because first she needed to talk sense into her mother. Why hadn't Dee Dee listened when Abby had told her Drew would never get involved in drugs, not now and not ten years ago?

She needed to get to the bottom of whatever had pre-cipitated her mother's stunning statement. And fast. Before the commissioners put their ruling in writing and Drew had no chance of being granted parole.

The guard manning the metal detector confirmed that a woman fitting her mother's description had left the building, saving Abby from checking the restroom.

She exited and spotted her mother in the parking lot, heading straight for her Chevy.

"Mom, wait," Abby yelled, but her mother yanked opened the door of her car and got behind the wheel. She already had the key in the ignition by the time Abby joined her inside the Chevy. Her mother turned the key, summoning the engine to life.

"Mom, wait just a minute." Breathing hard from her dash through the parking lot, Abby covered her mother's hand on the ignition. "You can't leave things the way you did. There's no way Drew will get parole if you do."

"That's as it should be," she said, shifting the car into Reverse.

"Mom, stop," Abby cried. Deliberately lowering her voice, she pleaded, "Please just talk to me."

Abby was afraid her mother would ignore her request, but then she turned off the car with a deft flick of the wrist. The engine sputtered and died, the only sound in the car their combined quickened breathing. Through the windshield was a view of the prison where Dee Dee had likely relegated her son to spend at least one more year if not more.

Abby curbed her leap of anger; only a cool head would help Drew now. "I don't know why you said what you did, but it might not be too late to go back in there and tell those commissioners you were mistaken."

Her mother shook her head. "I can't do that."

Abby tried again. "I know what you think Drew admitted, but you must have heard him wrong. He wouldn't touch drugs."

"You have a lot of faith in him," her mother said quietly.

"Of course I do. I love him."

Dee Dee blinked a few times, then said, "I love him, too. That's why I want him to have a fighting chance to succeed when he gets out of prison."

"He could have succeeded this time!"

"No," her mother said, and Abby noticed the glint in her eyes was actually a sheen of tears. "He might even have brought drugs into your house and dragged you down with him."

"I already told you. He'd never sell drugs."

"He's done it before."

"No," Abby said, shaking her head vehemently, "I don't believe you."

"It's my fault you don't. I should have told you a

long time ago I suspected Drew had been at the field that night to sell J.D. drugs, but I thought I was protecting you. Now I can see that I was wrong."

A coldness settled over Abby, stemming from fear of what her mother would reveal. Even while she'd railed against accusations that Drew had sold drugs, a part of her must have feared it was true. Still clinging to hope, she said, "Suspicions aren't facts."

Dee Dee made a sound of dismay. "They're not suspicions anymore. Yesterday when I confronted Drew about his involvement with Spider Strickland, he told me the whole story."

Abby instantly recognized the name Spider Strickland from when they'd lived in Baltimore. Even as a young girl barely into her teens, Abby had known Spider was bad news. He'd had a juvenile record, and rumors of drug dealing had swirled around him. The first time she'd seen Drew in his company, she'd almost thrown up.

"Why do you think Drew's in touch with Spider?"

"Because Rico Shaw admitted that Spider asked him to offer Drew a place to live."

"You talked to Rico Shaw?" The answer to one of the puzzles of the last week suddenly dawned on her. "You're the reason Rico told Drew he couldn't live with him, aren't you?"

"I paid Rico to take back his offer. I had to, Abby. I don't think he works steadily, but somehow he lives very, very well. And both times I've seen him, he's been with Spider."

"That doesn't necessarily mean anything."

"But it could. Some people from the old neighborhood told me that Spider served time in prison for possession with intent to distribute a few years back."

"Maybe prison changed him," Abby said. "Maybe he cleaned up his act."

"I hoped so, because I knew if Drew got parole that I couldn't keep him away from Spider indefinitely. If Drew hadn't asked to live at your apartment, I would have let it go. But it frightened me to think of what could happen if I was wrong."

"So you went to the prison to talk to Drew," Abby said, filling in a blank.

"I asked Drew how he knew Rico, but he wouldn't say. Then I told him I'd seen Rico with Spider and that I was afraid they might be involved in something illegal. That's when Drew figured out I was responsible for messing up where he was going to live." Her mother closed her eyes tightly, almost as though she wanted to shut out the confrontation. "Drew said that I couldn't keep him away from Spider ten years ago, and I couldn't do it now, either."

Abby said nothing, afraid to hear the rest of her mother's story.

"Then I asked him point blank about the drugs on J. D. Smith's body. He was still so angry that he admitted he'd sold them to J.D."

Then Abby had been right. J. D. Smith had been a drug user.

Despite claiming as much to Connor after the symphony, it was a shock to have it verified. She'd never spoken to J.D., but everybody at Bentonsville High knew who he was. The big man on campus, the football jock headed for greatness at a

Division 1 college and a possible pro career. The all-American boy.

"After Drew sold J.D. the drugs," her mother continued, "J.D. tried to shortchange him. Drew pulled out a knife to back up his demand for more money. J.D. went for it and died in the struggle."

"Drew told you all of that?"

She nodded. "I heard a different version from the police after it happened. You know about the girl Drew and J.D. fought over a few days before the stabbing? The police believed Drew lured J.D. to the stadium on the pretense of selling him drugs, then stabbed him."

"Then you knew about the drug dealing all along?" Abby asked in a small voice.

Her mother shook her head. "I knew drugs had been found on J.D.'s body, but I didn't want to believe Drew had sold them to him."

Abby shook her head, still trying to make sense of it. "But why didn't the police's version of the story ever come out?"

"They couldn't prove it. But I suspect the main reason had to do with Elaine Smith. She would have done anything to protect her son's reputation, and she knew the state's attorney personally. I always thought that's why he was willing to offer a plea bargain."

Abby grabbed her head with both hands, fighting off a headache as she tried to process the information. She still didn't want to believe it, but it explained so much.

Her mother continued speaking. "Drew was in contact with Spider Strickland back then, despite everything I did to prevent it. He as good as admitted to me yesterday that Spider was the one who'd supplied him with the drugs."

Abby shook her head, not wanting to believe such terrible things about her brother. "But you can't know that Drew would get involved in that life again."

"Then why did he hide his involvement with Spider?" Her mother's voice broke and the tears that had been forming in her eyes fell freely down her face. "I couldn't take a chance that he'd make another mistake. I had to tell the commissioners, even if it meant Drew wouldn't get parole. Don't you see that I had to tell?"

The pain on her mother's face was so stark that Abby's own eyes welled with tears. She leaned across the seat and met her mother halfway in a hug, but wasn't sure which one of them needed comfort more.

"How could I have been so wrong?" Abby murmured as she held her mother tight. "I was so sure there was an explanation that would somehow absolve Drew. But there's not."

"No," her mother said, sniffling, "there isn't. But we believe the things we want to believe about the people we love. I always suspected that Drew sold those drugs to J.D. back then, but I couldn't make myself believe it."

"I wouldn't have believed it then, either," Abby said. "I can hardly believe it now."

"It'll be easier now," her mother whispered, "because now Connor will help you get through this."

"But I said such awful things to him." Abby drew back. "Oh, Mom. I was so wrong. How will he ever forgive me?"

"He forgave Drew," her mother said, smoothing the hair away from her face. "He'll forgive you."

What her mother said made sense. Connor had demonstrated at the hearing today that he had a remarkable capacity for forgiveness. But Abby didn't want him simply to forgive her.

She wanted him to love her. And she couldn't be sure he still did.

CHAPTER SEVENTEEN

CONNOR SAT IN THE RESTAURANT across from his mother, wondering when the day's surprises would end. Elaine had insisted they wait at the prison until they were certain the commissioners had denied Drew Galloway parole, but then she'd asked him to lunch.

He'd expected to spend the entire meal defending what he'd done at the parole hearing, but the fight seemed to have gone out of her and she hadn't brought up the subject. She'd used the time, instead, to talk to him. Asking him about his job, getting him to tell her about Wall Street and showing an interest in Jaye.

Even though Connor longed to get back home so he could resolve matters with Abby, he found himself enjoying the attention.

"I'm sorry I forgot your birthday last month," she suddenly announced. "It won't happen again."

Connor scratched the back of his head, more certain than ever that something strange was going on. "Don't worry about it. It's not a big deal."

"It is a big deal," she said, fastening her eyes on him. She looked the same as the strong-willed woman who'd spoken so forcefully at the parole hearing, but seemed softer somehow. "I'm your mother. I should have remembered."

He put his forearms on the table and leaned forward. "Where's this coming from?"

She glanced away from him. "I'd say I'm not sure, but that would be a lie. I started thinking about what Abby Reed said to me."

"Abby? When did you talk to Abby?"

"Before the hearing." She cradled her coffee cup in her hands, then lifted her eyes to his. "You've been in contact with her all along, haven't you? Even after I forbade her from having anything else to do with Jaye?"

"I'm a grown man, Mother. I need to use my own judgment and do what I think is best. Abby's good for Jaye." He paused. "She's good for me, too."

He expected fireworks, but she merely nodded. "Believe it or not, I can understand that. In the hall, before the hearing, she stopped me and told me that I needed to pay more attention to you and Jaye. She said you both needed me in your lives."

He was speechless, amazed that Abby had approached his mother before the hearing, more surprised that the subject she'd discussed hadn't been her brother.

"I was angry at the time, but at the prison, when we were waiting for the parole board's decision, I started to think about what she said." She closed her eyes, as though waging an interior struggle. When she opened them, they looked apologetic. "You know what? She was right."

He was so stunned at her admission that he didn't answer. After a moment, she said, "You're in love with her, aren't you?"

He'd decided even before his mother's question that he wouldn't hide what he felt for Abby any longer. "Yeah," Connor said. "I am."

"I won't lie," Elaine said. "I don't like it. I'd rather you be in love with almost anyone else."

Connor digested what she said, then realized a truth of his own. "I'd love to have your approval, but I don't need it. If Abby will have me, I intend to spend my life with her."

His mother took a deep, shuddering breath. "I don't think I can give you my blessing. I look at her, and I see her brother. And I know she had a lot to do with you speaking up at the hearing. You hated Galloway as much as I did."

"I spoke up because it was the right thing to do. I meant what I said. Continuing to hate him will only bring our family more pain."

"We did nothing to bring this pain on ourselves," her voice was lackluster, almost devoid of emotion. "It was all Galloway's doing."

"You know that's not true. If J.D. hadn't been using drugs, he wouldn't have been there that night."

"He still didn't deserve to die." His mother's temper flashed, but it was a shadow of what it had been at the hearing. "I'll do whatever's in my power to make sure Galloway continues to pay for what he did to J.D."

Connor shook his head, seeing his mother clearly for the first time in years. "Can't you see what hating Drew Galloway is doing to you? You won't be able to move on with your life until you forgive him."

"I can't forgive him. Forgiving him would seem like a betrayal to J.D." She seemed to have difficulty getting her next words out. "But maybe one day I'll be able to accept that Abby's in your life."

He sighed, "I'm not sure Abby will still have me."

"She'd be a fool if she didn't." She shook her head. "I've been a fool, too. Not only where you're concerned, but where Jaye is, too."

She didn't elaborate, but hope leapt in Connor that she'd cracked the door to developing a relationship with her granddaughter. He'd do his best to facilitate one. Jaye needed to feel loved, especially because he discovered last night that the phone number he had for Diana had been disconnected.

"It's not too late to make amends," he told his mother.

She covered his hand with hers, her eyes suspiciously moist. Baby steps, Connor told himself when she didn't speak. She wasn't yet ready to take the giant leap.

"I love you, too, Mom," he whispered.

ABBY'S PALMS WERE DAMP and her breaths so uneven she thought she might hyperventilate right there on the doorstep of Connor's town house.

The parole hearing had ended hours ago. After her mother had dropped her off at her apartment, Abby had waited fruitlessly for Connor to come to her. When he hadn't, she'd lifted up her sinking heart and mustered the courage to go to him.

Driving to Connor's town house had seemed to take an eternity while she'd fought rush-hour traffic and worried about why he hadn't sought her out.

She wanted to believe he'd spoken up at the parole hearing about letting go of his hate in part because he loved her. But it was entirely possible that she'd killed his love by refusing to believe in the guilt of a guilty man.

She tried to be patient after ringing the doorbell, but time passed in slow motion. She knew he was home because his Porsche was parked in his driveway. So what was taking so long?

The door suddenly swung open, and Connor stood there, tall and strong and dear. He'd taken off his suit jacket, but otherwise was dressed the same as he'd been at the parole hearing. His heavy beard had started to show through his skin, making him look like the imperfect man with whom she'd fallen in love.

"I know you might not want to see me, but there's something I have to say," she blurted out, afraid she wouldn't have the courage to bare her soul if she waited. "I was a fool for believing all those years that there was some mitigating circumstance that would explain what Drew did. There wasn't. You were right, I was wrong and I'm so very sorry for all those things I said."

He looked thunderstruck, causing her insides to twist with pain. She hadn't considered what she'd do if he didn't accept her apology, but then he asked, "Why wouldn't I want to see you? I was heading over to your place as soon as Jaye got home from her end-of-school pool party."

Abby's pain abated, replaced by hope. "You really forgive me?"

"There's nothing to forgive," he said, giving her hand a gentle tug so she came into the house. Her heart tumbled, too. "I was as wrong about my brother as you were about yours."

"But the commissioners were right to deny Drew parole," Abby said, needing to get everything out in the open. "My mother found out that Drew was in contact with an ex-con he'd known as a teenager. She said it was the same guy who provided him with the drugs he sold your brother. That's why she said what she did at the hearing."

"She's a good woman, your mother."

"A good woman with a broken heart. She's pretty torn up over Drew."

"He'll get out of prison one day, Abby. If you like, you and I can work on a plan so he'll have a better chance of being released at his next hearing."

"You'd do that for me? But why?"

"You heard what I said at the hearing. It's time for me to let go of the hate. I let it tear me apart. I even let it tear us apart. I don't want to lose you again, Abby. If that means accepting your brother, I can do that."

The tears she wiped from under her eyes temporarily choked her voice. Or maybe it was her heart, so filled with emotion it seemed to take up every part of her.

"I'm not wrong here, am I?" Connor suddenly seemed uncertain. "You do still love me, don't you?"

"With all my heart," she said and threw her arms around his neck.

Smiling, he gathered her to him. The kiss was all the sweeter because of everything they'd been through. As always, his kiss scrambled her brains but two words formed through with stunning clarity: The One. She'd been right about what Connor Smith was to her, after all.

The door banged open a few moments later, too abruptly for them to break apart, not that they would have.

"Uncle Connor, I'm ho—"

Jaye, her blond hair still wet from the pool, stopped and stared at the two of them with the eyes that were so like her late uncle's. "Were you two kissing again?" she asked, her question reminiscent of the one she'd asked the night of their first date.

"Yeah," Connor said without releasing Abby. "We sure were."

Jaye smiled, a carefree smile that made her look like the happy little girl she was starting to be. "Then you worked things out? Everything's okay between you again? And I don't have to spend the summer at day camps?"

"Everything's great," Connor said. "And you're spending the summer right here. In fact, I was just going to ask Abby what she thought about spending the summer in the same house as us."

Jaye whooped. "You mean you're going to ask her to live with you?"

"Close," Connor said, never taking his eyes from Abby. "I'm going to ask her to marry me."

"What are you going to say, Abby?" Jaye asked, her voice breathless.

"Yes," Abby said, her eyes locked on Connor's. "I'm going to say yes."

"Cool," Jaye said.

"Jaye?" Connor asked, still looking at Abby instead of his niece.

"Yeah."

"How about giving us a little privacy?"

"Sure thing," she said, then Abby heard the pounding of her footsteps as she dashed up the stairs.

"Remember what you said about love?" Connor asked her when Jaye was gone. "About how it didn't end?"

She nodded wordlessly.

"Then this is the beginning of our never-ending story," he said, an instant before he claimed her lips the same way he'd captured her heart.

Turn the page for a sneak peek
of Diana's story....

PROLOGUE

WITH ONLY THE DIM GLOW of the bathroom night light to guide her, Diana Smith moved silently through the upstairs hall of her brother's pricey townhouse. The low heels of her boots sank into the plush carpeting, muffling her footsteps.

Shifting the weight of her backpack more comfortably on her shoulder, she stopped in front of the bedroom where her nine-year-old daughter Jaye slept and carefully eased open the door. The hinges groaned in protest, the sound gunshot-loud in the quiet house. Diana froze, her breath catching in her throat.

She glanced down the darkened hall to her brother's bedroom door, waiting for Connor to emerge and find her awake and fully dressed. But the door remained closed.

She exhaled, her breath coming out ragged. Careful not to nudge the door, she peered around the crack into the room.

Jaye was still asleep but stirred restlessly, turning over onto her side. Diana stood perfectly still until the girl settled into position and her chest expanded and contracted in a rhythmic motion. Weak moonlight filtered through a crack in the blinds, bathing Jaye in soft light.

Her face was relaxed, her cheeks rosy and her full

lips slightly pursed as she slept. Her long, blonde hair spilled over the pillow like a halo.

A wave of love overwhelmed Diana. She'd decided on her course of action three days ago, but gazing upon her daughter she wasn't sure she had the strength to carry through.

She was reminded too vividly of another place, another time and a man whose features she glimpsed in the sleeping child. She'd done right by Tyler Benton, too, but the doing had nearly ripped out her heart.

From necessity and long practice, she shoved Tyler from her mind and concentrated on the here and now. Before she could muster the will to retreat, she broke into a cold sweat, her muscles and her very bones aching. She fought off a bout of nausea as her stomach pitched and rolled.

If she needed a sign that leaving Jaye was the right thing to do, her physical condition couldn't have provided a better one.

She'd felt ill since losing control of her car on a slick stretch of road and crashing into a towering oak tree, but not due to injuries sustained in the crash. She'd walked away from the one-car accident remarkably unscathed, considering she might have died if she'd struck the tree a few inches left of impact.

The police had attributed her accident to bad luck, but Diana feared the pain pills she'd popped after leaving her job at a Nashville clothing warehouse had been the true cause.

She'd been using the drug since straining her back six months before, devising new and clever ways to secure the tablets long after her prescription ran out.

Horrified that Jaye could have been in the car with her, she'd faced the fact that she was addicted. Then she'd flushed the rest of the Vicodin down the toilet, only to find a new stockpile a few days later in one of her hiding places.

Since then, she'd confronted some more harsh truths. She was in a dead-end job, her bills were mounting, she needed help to kick her habit and she wasn't fit to be around her daughter.

After much thought, she'd packed up Jaye and the child's meager belongings and boarded a bus for the two-day trip from Tennessee to Connor's townhouse. They'd arrived in Silver Spring, Maryland, not even six hours ago, surprising a brother she hadn't seen in years.

Jaye made a sweet, snuffling sound in her sleep and hugged the soft, stuffed teddy bear that Diana had bought her when she was a toddler. Diana longed to rush over to the bed and kiss her one last time, but couldn't risk waking her.

"I'm sorry, baby," she whispered.

Tears fell down her cheeks like rain as she memorized the planes and angles of the sleeping child's face before moving away from the door. She left it ajar, unwilling to risk making another sound.

She crept down the hall and descended the stairs as silently as a ghost. When she reached Connor's state-of-the-art kitchen, she turned on the dim light over the stove, dug Jaye's school transcripts and birth certificate out of her backpack and set them on the counter.

After locating a pad and pen, she thought for long moments before she wrote. *Connor, I need to work some things out and get my head on straight. Here's ev-*

*erything you need to enroll Jaye in school. Please take
good care of her until I come back. I don't know when
that will be, but I'll be in touch.*

She put down the note, read it over, then bent down
and scribbled two more words: *I'm sorry.*

A fat teardrop rolled from her face onto the note
paper, blurring the ink of the apology.

Wiping away the rest of the tears, she headed for the
front door. Her chest ached. Whether it was from being
without Vicodin or from heartache, she couldn't be
sure.

Within moments, she was trudging down the sidewalk by the glow of the street lamps toward the very
bus station where she and Jaye arrived.

She knew that abandoning her child was unforgivable, just as what she'd done to Tyler Benton ten years
ago had been unforgivable.

But it couldn't be helped.

She'd been barely seventeen when Jaye was born,
no more than a child herself, grossed out by breast
feeding, impatient with crying and resentful of her
new responsibilities.

Love for her daughter, which gathered strength with
each passing day, had helped Diana grow up fast. She
tried her best, but harbored no illusion that love made
her a good mother.

Diana waited for the sparse early morning traffic to
pass before crossing a main street, placing one foot in
front of the other when all she wanted was to turn back.
But she couldn't. Not only did she lack the courage to
confess to her brother that she had a drug problem, she
couldn't risk having him say Jaye couldn't stay with him.

Despite his bachelor status, Connor represented her best hope. Her parents, to whom she hadn't spoken in years, were out. She had no doubt that her brother would take good care of Jaye. Until Diana kicked her habit and put her life back on track, Jaye was better off with him. And without Diana.

She blinked rapidly until her tears dried, then turned her mind to her uncertain future. Once she spent a portion of her dwindling cash on a return bus ticket to Nashville, she'd need to find a cheaper apartment, search for a better-paying job and somehow figure out how to get into drug treatment.

Even now she craved a pill so badly her entire body hurt.

She reached into the front pocket of her blue jeans, her fingertips encountering the reassuring presence of the three little white Vicodin tablets left from her stash.

Despite her desire to do right by her much-loved daughter, she couldn't say for sure whether the pills would still be in her pocket by the time she reached Nashville.

HARLEQUIN® Romance

A family saga begins to unravel when the doors to the Bella Lucia Restaurant Empire are opened...

The Brides of Bella Lucia

A family torn apart by secrets, reunited by marriage

AUGUST 2006

Meet Rachel Valentine, in
HAVING THE FRENCHMAN'S BABY
by Rebecca Winters

Find out what happens when a night of passion is followed by a shocking revelation and an unexpected pregnancy!

SEPTEMBER 2006

The Valentine family saga continues with
THE REBEL PRINCE by Raye Morgan

If you enjoyed what you just read,
then we've got an offer you can't resist!

Take 2 bestselling
love stories FREE!

Plus get a FREE surprise gift!

Clip this page and mail it to Harlequin Reader Service®

IN U.S.A.
3010 Walden Ave.
P.O. Box 1867
Buffalo, N.Y. 14240-1867

IN CANADA
P.O. Box 609
Fort Erie, Ontario
L2A 5X3

YES! Please send me 2 free Harlequin Superromance® novels and my free surprise gift. After receiving them, if I don't wish to receive anymore, I can return the shipping statement marked cancel. If I don't cancel, I will receive 6 brand-new novels every month, before they're available in stores. In the U.S.A., bill me at the bargain price of $4.69 plus 25¢ shipping and handling per book and applicable sales tax, if any*. In Canada, bill me at the bargain price of $5.24 plus 25¢ shipping and handling per book and applicable taxes**. That's the complete price, and a savings of at least 10% off the cover prices—what a great deal! I understand that accepting the 2 free books and gift places me under no obligation ever to buy any books. I can always return a shipment and cancel at any time. Even if I never buy another book from Harlequin, the 2 free books and gift are mine to keep forever.

135 HDN DZ7W
336 HDN DZ7X

Name	(PLEASE PRINT)	
Address	Apt.#	
City	State/Prov.	Zip/Postal Code

Not valid to current Harlequin Superromance® subscribers.

Want to try two free books from another series?
Call 1-800-873-8635 or visit www.morefreebooks.com.

* Terms and prices subject to change without notice. Sales tax applicable in N.Y.
** Canadian residents will be charged applicable provincial taxes and GST.
All orders subject to approval. Offer limited to one per household.
® are registered trademarks owned and used by the trademark owner or its licensee.

SUP04R

©2004 Harlequin Enterprises Limited

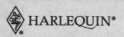

® HARLEQUIN®

American ROMANCE®

American Beauties

SORORITY SISTERS,
FRIENDS FOR LIFE

Michele Dunaway

THE MARRIAGE CAMPAIGN

Campaign fund-raiser Lisa Meyer has worked
hard to be her own boss and will let nothing—
especially romance—interfere with her success.
To Mark Smith, Lisa is the perfect candidate for
him to spend his life with. But if she lets herself
fall for Mark, will she lose all she's worked for?
Or will she have a future that's more than
she's ever dreamed of?

On sale August 2006

Also watch for:

THE WEDDING SECRET
On sale December 2006

NINE MONTHS NOTICE
On sale April 2007

Available wherever Harlequin books are sold.

Stability is highly overrated....

Dana Logan's world had always revolved around her children. Now they're all grown up and don't seem to need anything she's able to give them. Struggling to find her new identity, Dana realizes that it's about time for her to get "off her rocker" and begin a new life!

Off Her Rocker

by Jennifer Archer

Available August 2006
TheNextNovel.com

COMING NEXT MONTH

#1362 A TEMPORARY ARRANGEMENT • Roxanne Rustand
Blackberry Hill Memorial
All Abby wanted was to spend a quiet summer filling in at a small hospital in the beautiful Wisconsin woods before going back to teach nursing. But this temporary arrangement is far from quiet. Especially since single dad Ethan has the only vacancy in town.

#1363 THE HORSEMAN • Margaret Way
Men of the Outback
When Cecile meets Raul Montalvan—a mysterious Argentinian—she knows she to break her engagement with a man she doesn't love. Not that she really expects anything to happen with Raul—because as attracted as they are to each other, she can't help but sense his reasons for being in the Outback are not what they seem..

#1364 BEACH BABY • Joan Kilby
A Little Secret
Nina Kennerly has a full life, but she's always regretted giving her daughter up fo adoption and losing her first love, Reid. Now her grown daughter has found her— her own baby girl in tow!—and Nina may finally have a second chance at the fam she always should have had.

#1365 FAMILY AT STAKE • Molly O'Keefe
Single Father
Widower Mac Edwards's twelve-year-old daughter has spun out of control. Now he's in danger of losing custody of her. The one person who can help keep his fa together is Rachel Filmore—the woman he once loved…and the woman who bro his heart.

#1366 A MAN OF HONOR • Linda Barrett
Count on a Cop
Heather's father was a bad cop, which is why she'll never depend on a cop again. Out on the streets, helping runaways, she's forced to accept Officer Dave McCoy' protection, but she'll never trust him. Not until he proves where his loyalty truly l

#1367 REMEMBER TEXAS • Eve Gaddy
When marine biologist Ava Vincent accepts a job in Aransas City she has no idea her estranged brothers live there, too. Ava ran away as a kid and carries a secret s shameful she believes no one can ever forgive her. Yet when she meets Jack Willi a widower with a troubled son, she discovers she wants to have a future with him. Still, she can't believe anyone can accept her past, much less Jack.